"Don't."

Her word plunged between them without conviction. Her breath caught in her chest as if there were no air left in the world. She couldn't tear her eyes from his—his face was rigid, unmoving, but she saw a myriad of emotions pass over it, each in turn.

Then, suddenly, involuntarily, she was twisting from his grip, panicked. But just as abruptly her quest for freedom was denied when she was spun back around into his steely embrace.

His lips descended to her protesting mouth and before she could catch her breath, Branch's mouth crushed hers in a brutal kiss.

Dear Reader,

We, the editors of Tapestry Romances, are committed to bringing you two outstanding original romantic historical novels each and every month.

From Kentucky in the 1850s to the court of Louis XIII, from the deck of a pirate ship within sight of Gibraltar to a mining camp high in the Sierra Nevadas, our heroines experience life and love, romance and adventure.

Our aim is to give you the kind of historical romances that you want to read. We would enjoy hearing your thoughts about this book and all future Tapestry Romances. Please write to us at the address below.

The Editors
Tapestry Romances
POCKET BOOKS
1230 Avenue of the Americas
Box TAP
New York, N.Y. 10020

High Country Pride

Lynn Erickson

A TAPESTRY BOOK
PUBLISHED BY POCKET BOOKS NEW YORK

Dedicated to:
the children,
Megan, Erika and Lucas

This novel is a work of historical fiction. Names, characters, places and incidents relating to non-historical figures are either the product of the author's imagination or are used fictitiously. Any resemblance of such non-historical incidents, places or figures to actual events or locales or persons, living or dead, is entirely coincidental.

An *Original* publication of TAPESTRY BOOKS

 A Tapestry Book published by
POCKET BOOKS, a Simon & Schuster division of
GULF & WESTERN CORPORATION
1230 Avenue of the Americas, New York, N.Y. 10020

ISBN: 0-671-46137-0

First Tapestry Books printing December, 1982

10 9 8 7 6 5 4 3 2 1

POCKET and colophon are registered trademarks
of Simon & Schuster.

TAPESTRY is a trademark of Simon & Schuster.

Printed in the U.S.A.

Author's Note

In writing this story, I have used the modern name, Colorado River Valley, so as not to confuse those familiar with the area, but it was actually dubbed the Grande River Valley by the earliest settlers.

Zimmerman's Drug Store, Collin's Livery Barn, Doc Tichenor's Surgery, and *The Rifle Reveille* did indeed exist; and Abram Maxfield's cattle did graze on his farm, which later became the town of Rifle.

Ninety years ago, Rifle appeared on the map due to the coming of the railroad and the subsequent building of the largest stockyards in the United States. Today, Rifle appears again as the center of the booming oil shale industry.

Lynn Erickson

Prologue

The Rifle Valley, Colorado
Spring 1870

THE OLD ABANDONED LINE SHACK, MADE HAPHAZARDLY of logs and sod, nestled against the wall of Hubbard Mesa near a small stream. Harriet Tate, her long skirts and petticoats bunched up around her rounded thighs, urged the chestnut mare into a canter toward it and felt her wavy honey-colored hair stream out behind her on the warm, dry wind.

Would he be there yet?

She couldn't bear to wait. She had such wonderful news to tell Joe!

She pulled the mare up sharply in front of the tiny cabin and slid down off the horse's back, landing as

1

lightly as a butterfly. Her large green eyes searched the familiar area quickly.

"Joe?"

His horse wasn't in the stand of cottonwoods. He wasn't there yet. Impatience began to gnaw at her.

She couldn't wait to tell him, to see his deep blue eyes light up with joy, to feel his strong arms around her, to feel his lips on her own. She knew she was completely unreasonable in her love for handsome, blond Joe Taggart, but she didn't care. She was so in love that she felt her very bones melt at the thought of him; he was the center of her existence and had been ever since the day, six months ago, when he and his two half-grown sons had homesteaded the section just north of the Tates' land. She smiled, remembering the first time she'd seen him—so tall and strong and hopeful. He'd confidently named his place Wolf Butte Ranch, after the wind-twisted red butte that rose up from the river valley right above his new cabin. It wasn't really a ranch, at least not yet, but he was working so hard, just as hard as her own father, to make the rich land produce. Joe had dreams—big dreams—for Wolf Butte Ranch. And he had the money to make those dreams come true.

Harriet's straight, fair brows drew together in a frown. Joe Taggart's money came from his wife's family. Joe hadn't lied to her—he'd told her right from the beginning about his wife, Tanya. She'd been very ill ever since the birth of their third son and had stayed behind in Virginia with the baby to recover. So nobody in the Rifle Valley had seen Tanya Taggart yet. She was a wraith, a name, an empty image. And Harriet hadn't cared as long as she could have Joe. . . .

She tossed her head, shaking smooth, honey-colored

curls. Joe loved *her*. Hadn't he told her so a thousand times? He'd do something so that they could be together, surely he would. And Tanya was obviously a sickly thing. Maybe she'd never recover, or if she ever came west, maybe the Indians would attack her wagon or bandits would attack her train. Maybe she'd never arrive. Maybe . . .

Harriet was appalled at her own thoughts. To wish for the death of someone else was totally foreign to her nature. Quickly, she submerged the traitorous thoughts.

The sound of hoofbeats abruptly caught her attention. Joe! Breathlessly she ran to meet him, saw him pull his horse up so that it slid on its haunches, leap off, run toward her.

"Darling! I'm sorry I'm late," he said, drawing her into his arms. She could feel the corded muscles of his thighs, the iron-banded strength of his arms. She couldn't wait to tell him now.

He pushed her away from him, held her at arm's length; she could feel his fingers dig into her shoulders. Strangely, his blue eyes were tense and clouded under the shade of his wide-brimmed hat.

Her heart froze with fear. "What is it, Joe?"

His eyes slid away from hers. She could see the muscles of his throat work as he swallowed. He met her worried gaze, imprisoned her in his arms again.

"Tanya's coming in a few days. I just got a letter . . ." His voice was raw, etched with regret and something else. Self-loathing?

Harriet's heart gave a sickening lurch, then began to beat slowly, heavily. The happy words died on her lips. "Oh," was all she could force out.

He pressed her to him and she could smell his

3

scent—leather, man sweat, dust, sagebrush. She drew the aroma in, savoring it, placing the smell and feel of him in her memory.

"I'm so sorry. I never should have . . ." He couldn't finish; his voice was ragged.

"Never mind, my love. We've had our times, haven't we? We knew . . ."

He looked at her, love and misery written equally on his face. "You're so young, so beautiful, so pure. It's my fault. I never should have let it happen . . ."

Harriet laid a slim white finger against his lips. "Shhh. No regrets. I wanted it as much as you."

His look was tormented. "She's my *wife.*"

"I know, my love." And then Harriet Tate knew how much she loved this man. She would never tell him about the new life growing within her, never burden him with the knowledge. It was the last thing she would give him from the boundless wellspring of her love—peace of mind. No, she'd never tell him now. The decision made her feel better—almost peaceful.

Her fingers stroked the back of his neck, roaming among the golden blond hairs that grew there. She loved the feel of him so. Could she live the rest of her life with only memories of him?

"Darling, what are we going to do? I can't bear doing this to you," he was saying.

"We will act like people have since time began—we'll do the best we can. We'll manage." She gave a little laugh. "Life goes on."

He groaned, buried his face in her burnished gold curls. "There's now, anyway. We have now . . . to remember."

"Yes . . . to remember," she whispered against his

4

chest, feeling his work-roughened hands glide over her back, her shoulders.

She would love him once more, then let him go . . . back to his wife and three sons. She'd have to live her life without him. Her heart contracted in anguish. But she would possess a part of him forever. The thought buoyed her spirits, gave her something to hang on to among the towering swells of grief and loss that buffeted her.

And when she bid him good-bye today, she would turn her face toward home and never look back. She would look forward, to her own future and that of her child, on the homestead that her father had cleared and slaved over with the help of Frank Clayton, the Indian-dark, intense young drifter who had turned up, half frozen, in a January blizzard and had somehow never left.

Frank Clayton—whose black eyes never stopped following Harriet's golden beauty as she did her chores around the cabin, whose soft drawl was gentle in her presence, whose love for the land that had nurtured his forefathers was equaled only by his love for the beautiful young girl.

Chapter One

March 1891

EDNA LANGTREE'S HIGH-PITCHED VOICE CHIRPED UNEND-
ingly above the clatter of the train as the young raven-
haired girl smiled mechanically across at her. It had been
a long train ride from St. Louis to the Colorado Rockies
and Lara stifled a yawn with a slim hand, trying not to be
rude as she did so.

"I just don't know," Edna was saying, "how I'll
manage out here in the wilds. Chicago, you understand,
my dear, is *so* civilized. I simply don't know." She shook
her graying head ruefully.

Lara Clayton shifted her weight uncomfortably in the
seat and wondered how to comfort the Eastern woman;
Mrs. Langtree was most likely correct—she wouldn't
manage well at all on the Western Slope of Colorado. In
Denver City, perhaps, but not in the rustic mountain
community of Glenwood Springs. Edna Langtree obviously wasn't bred to be a frontier woman.

Now Lara, on the other hand, was. At the moment, dressed smartly in a beige wool traveling outfit and her fashionable red fox hat and muff, she hardly looked like a country girl, one who only two years before had donned blue jeans and ridden the vast, high rangeland with her father. And she had always done so before the long trip to St. Louis; even while other girls played at their mother's feet with soft rag dolls, Lara was out on the range, sitting astride her father's saddle, her chubby fingers clutching the horn. This elegantly attired woman sitting quietly on the train was not, she had come to learn, really her.

She raised tilted, bright green eyes up to Edna's frowning face. "I'm sure once you see Glenwood Springs all your fears will disappear, Mrs. Langtree. It's really a charming town. I'm certain your husband must have written about the wonderful hot springs there . . ."

"Those!" Edna screwed up her nose. "That sulfur! Why, the whole town must smell dreadfully."

End of that subject, thought Lara uncomfortably. "Won't it be lovely to see your husband again?"

"My dear, I'm fifty-two years old. Married since I was nineteen and raised four children. When Oscar decided to move from Chicago, seek a new life out West"—she grimaced distastefully—"I told him to go on, leave me, do whatever he felt he must. But as for me? Well. It's been eighteen months since I last saw Oscar. I've gotten four letters. That's all. And in those very few letters all Oscar can talk about is his new dry goods store and how much I'll love it." She sighed in exasperation. "Love it indeed!"

"It sounds very nice, Mrs. Langtree," Lara offered, then turned her eyes away and looked out the window of the brand-new passenger train. Poor woman, she

7

thought, traveling to a strange town high up in the heart of the Rockies to join a husband who sounded as if he were more interested in his store than his marriage. Why would a man leave his wife in Chicago and venture so far from his roots? Surely a man would want to share the adventure with his loved one. She glanced back at Edna Langtree, who had all but pressed her nose against the cool glass.

"Only a mountain goat or a fool would live here!" she gasped.

Lara stifled a laugh. Glenwood Canyon, through which the train was now passing, was terribly awesome. Split and gouged deeply by the mighty Colorado River, the striped canyon rose hundreds of feet in perpendicular walls to pierce the azure sky. The gorge itself was narrow and laying the railroad tracks had been an engineering feat of great magnitude. Of course, laying track anywhere in the Rockies was a feat, but this particular stretch had been one of the most challenging.

"How can you bear to live here?" asked Edna unthinkingly.

Lara's hackles rose. "I love it here, Mrs. Langtree. This is my home. And besides"—she turned her slanted eyes and looked absently out the window—"Rifle is not like this at all. In fact, the terrain in the mountains can change dramatically in as little as a few miles. Rifle is in a more gentle part of the Colorado River valley. It's wide open and spacious. It's . . . well, it's just beautiful."

"I see." Edna dabbed at her nose with a white, lace-trimmed hanky. "And I take it, Lara, that you prefer the so-called Wild West to the drawing rooms of Saint Louis?"

When Lara had first taken her seat on the train from

Denver City and met Mrs. Langtree, she had told her about the past two years spent at Mrs. Bryant's School for Young Ladies in St. Louis—the finishing school from which she was now returning.

"Yes," replied Lara thoughtfully, "I much prefer the mountains." She could have gone on to tell her that she disliked St. Louis, the social teas and the dances, the too polite, too ridiculous conversations she was forced to endure. If her mother, Harriet, had not insisted, then Lara never would have gone. It was just that her older sister, Jennifer, had attended the school and returned to Rifle a charming, well-rounded, happy young woman. Harriet Clayton was so pleased that arrangements for Lara to leave for St. Louis had been made immediately. And much against Lara's will. Even her father, Frank, had argued in favor of Lara's position, but pretty Harriet, with her soft voice and honey-silk curls, had prevailed. She almost always did win out where Frank Clayton was concerned.

But, Lara remembered unhappily, Frank was gone now. Two months ago, in the midst of winter, he had succumbed to influenza and died in his sleep. Upon hearing the terrible news, Lara had written back immediately, insisting that she come home at once, but she couldn't make it in time for the funeral, and two weeks ago the letter had arrived from Harriet, agreeing, admitting that she and Jennifer needed Lara now. Although greatly saddened that her father's death had spurred Harriet to summon her home, she was immensely pleased to be returning. She wondered suddenly if they'd heard from Craig . . .

"Frankly," Edna was clipping on, "I should think this sort of life—ranching, I believe you mentioned—would

9

age a woman dreadfully. Why, you're so lovely. A young lady belongs in a gentler setting, my dear—a nice city where she has the opportunity to meet a proper young man."

"There are *proper* men"—Lara emphasized the word carefully—"in Rifle, Mrs. Langtree, I assure you." She knew then, by her cool, arrogant tone, that she had upset the woman, and what was worse, Lara realized, was that her own assertion about "proper" men was not quite true. Rifle did have its share of men, more so now that the town had boomed overnight because of the arrival of the railroad, but the eligible, suitable men were, for the most part, already married or engaged. At least, Jennifer had written to Lara often enough of that fact. The other men, as Lara already knew too well, were mostly drifters or ranch hands—crude, uneducated, perhaps pleasant to know, but not the marrying kind. It was quite possible that Edna Langtree, this stranger sitting across from her, was absolutely correct—there wasn't a decent man for her among them.

A strained silence fell between the older woman and the nineteen-year-old girl as the train rambled and wound along the narrow strip of track leading out of the canyon and on into Glenwood Springs, where the land once again opened up into a wide, fertile valley blessed with two rivers, the Roaring Fork flowing down from Aspen and the wider, thundering Colorado.

As the woman would be leaving the train shortly and chances were that Lara would see her at some future time in Glenwood Springs, she wished she could find words to soothe Mrs. Langtree's ruffled feelings. But, as Lara had painfully learned, finding the right thing to say was not her forté. Hardly that. In fact, when confronted by strangers, Lara was extremely tense and ill-at-ease. She had been only vaguely aware of this social shortcoming as a child on the ranch, but living in St. Louis had brought to the fore this uncomfortable knowledge; she was an utter failure in social situations—tongue-tied, weak kneed, and awkward.

How Jenn will laugh when she finds out, thought Lara, knowing what a social butterfly her sister was. And how very opposite the two sisters were: one like the mother, fair-headed and shapely, while the other, herself, resembled the father with ebony hair, skin tinted an autumn wheat shade, and eyes that tilted up at the corners, green like her mother's, but hinting at her father's ancestry even though he had been only one-fourth Indian. Perhaps, she thought, that was where her quietness, her shyness around strangers had been born. And perhaps, too, where her love for the untamed, open rangeland had originated—from the prideful Indians.

Well, she thought with a flash of inner knowledge, if I'm a failure in the drawing room and diminished by it, then I'll gather my strength from the land and there I'll make my life and I'll thrive.

"So this is Glenwood Springs," said Edna, compelling Lara out of her musings.

"Oh. Yes. We're here." Lara remained seated until the train came to a jerking halt in front of the brick platform and tidy wooden station that sat across the river from the hot springs and did, she had to admit, smell faintly of sulfur.

Lara escorted the woman down the steps and onto the platform. "Is Mr. Langtree going to meet you?" she asked, then realized that if he wasn't, the question was quite embarrassing. But thankfully, before her cheeks burned scarlet, a tall, gray-bearded man approached them, then took Edna into his arms, welcoming her warmly.

Introductions were made briefly and Lara promised to make the thirty-mile train ride from Rifle to Glenwood Springs and pay their store a visit as soon as summer arrived.

"And you must promise to pay Bitter Creek—our ranch, that is—a visit too. You'll love it there, Mrs. Langtree, and my mother would be very glad for the company, I'm sure."

"No doubt," replied Edna. "Thank you for the invitation. I'll promise a visit if I'm still here." She glanced in a martyrlike fashion up at her husband, but Lara missed his look when the "all aboard" call came from down the platform.

"Good-bye," she said quickly, glad to turn away and head toward the train again. The conductor took her arm at the elbow and began helping her up the step.

"Looks like bad weather ahead," he said, nodding to the west.

Lara peeked around the corner of the car and saw that he was indeed correct; the sky toward Rifle was dark and menacing. A sudden gust of cold wind whipped her skirt around her ankles. A March storm was in the offing. That could be bad. Spring storms were often the worst in the mountains, striking suddenly from a cloudless warm sky and often dumping two feet of snow in the valleys. Would Harriet and Jennifer have trouble getting from the ranch into Rifle to meet her train? She hoped not. But if so, then she would simply have to spend the night in Rifle—perhaps at the new hotel they'd written her about.

As the train lumbered west, Lara began to grow more

excited with each familiar passing landmark. Even as the wind began to whip through the valley and snowflakes splattered the windowpane her spirits remained undaunted. In a few more minutes she would be home.

The notion fortified her. Would her mother and sister have changed? Had *she* changed? And the ranch. Was their foreman, Shad Harper, still the same old big-bellied, gruff, fun-loving soul? She hoped so. It would be strange, though, not to have her father there anymore—not to rise with the sun and ride the awakening range together. It would be very sad, and take a lot of getting used to. But if Harriet, as she had written, had accepted his passing gracefully, then she, too, would have to do the same. And besides, she reminded herself, her father had always told her that she was the strong one, the only child to really care about Bitter Creek—the land, the cattle, the traditions. Even her older brother, Craig, hadn't loved the land the way she did. And now that Craig and her father were gone, her mother and sister needed her. Well, she was ready to face the challenge.

The mountain terrain outside the window now was white, covered with snow. Occasionally Lara could see a timid rabbit dart through the brush-spangled hills and there were deer, too, standing motionless, their ears perked toward the steel monster, watchful, as if sensing encroaching civilization.

The new train followed the winding path of the Colorado River on its south bank, through narrow hilly passages, then into widening terrain until the valley expanded again and Lara knew Rifle was only a few more miles. The minutes ticked by unendingly. She reminded herself not to be terribly disappointed if the storm had delayed her family—the train could press on through all weather while the road leading from Rifle north toward Bitter Creek Ranch might be impassable by now. Why did it have to storm today?

She craned her neck to see ahead through the driving snow; the storm hid the summits of familiar, low mountains from her view, but she recognized a ranch house or two nestled in the tall, bare cottonwood trees along the river; they were almost there. Even though the sudden spring storm had put a damper on her homecoming, Lara was still so excited that her heart pounded in anticipation and her weariness from traveling disappeared altogether.

It was hard to see the contours of the land, but new buildings began to come into view, silhouetted darkly against the white backdrop—so many new structures that Lara could hardly believe her eyes. Jennifer had written of the tremendous growth, of the new stockyard that was rapidly becoming the largest in Colorado, but actually seeing Rifle now with her own eyes snatched Lara's breath away. And it was all due to the recent arrival of the railroad—first the cumbersome stock cars and then, only several months ago, the coming to Rifle of the first passenger train. Civilization had arrived; it was thrilling, but also a little frightening.

The clattering of the train wheels slowed, then jolted, shrieking, to a stop. Lara grabbed her reticule, rose, and went to the door. Before she was even down the steps and onto the platform she could see her mother and Jennifer, huddled together beneath their wool capes, standing under the eave of the new station house.

She dashed across the slippery platform, half-losing her footing in her buttoned leather boots, and flew into their embrace.

"Oh, Mother!" She kissed Harriet, throwing both arms

around her, then turned to Jennifer. "It's so good to be home! You look wonderful, Jennifer!"

Jennifer giggled, kissing Lara back. "And *you*, my little sister, have turned into a butterfly!" Then Jennifer disengaged herself, stood back assessingly. "My Lord, Lara. You really *do* look beautiful. Doesn't she, Mama?"

"Oh, yes," cried Harriet, tears springing to her eyes. And then they were all three crying, embracing, joyous.

Finally Harriet found a young boy bundled in a too-large overcoat to help with Lara's bags. The trunk was coming later.

"I left Shad at the ranch to watch things," Harriet explained, "and Jennifer and I drove the buckboard into town. We were going to have lunch then meet your train. It was warm and sunny this morning and I thought the three of us could manage."

"Where's the buckboard now?" asked Lara, glancing around.

"At Collin's Livery Barn. Jennifer and I engaged two rooms at the Winchester Hotel for the night. We'll never be able to drive home in this storm, dear. Are you too disappointed?"

"Oh, no," Lara laughed, feeling the raw wind drive through her beige wool jacket. "But let's get inside. I'm not at all used to this weather! Two years away from Colorado winters is a long time!"

The three women put their heads down against the horizontal, slashing snow and began trudging toward the spanking new hotel with the boy on their heels. The streets were muddy, the ruts filling with snow rapidly, and there were only a couple of hastily erected wooden sidewalks, so by the time they reached the Winchester their boots and long skirt hems were drenched in mud. Still, Lara adored it. She was home, and home had changed so; from Abram Maxfield's ranch house and post office Rifle had grown overnight into a real town with a hotel, a livery, a pharmacy, a large feed store—everything. And people—lots of people bundled against the storm.

At the hotel desk the manager produced their room keys, clucked his tongue, and said briskly, "You realize how lucky you are that we have rooms left. The hotel is brimming over already. Why people would ride into town on a day like this is beyond me. Now they're all stuck here!"

Lara giggled. The man must be new to the mountains or he would know that these spring storms could whip across the desert and strike the mountains without giving a moment's notice.

Harriet took the room keys, straightened her back, and told the manager as much.

The sisters shared a comfortable room done in greens. The furniture, a mahogany dresser and mirror, an over-stuffed chair, and a double brass bed were very nice indeed, imported from Chicago. The carpet was green flowered and soft. The room smelled fresh, new.

Lara relaxed back on the bed, the pillows propped behind her, her muddy boots tossed near the iron potbellied stove in the corner. She and Jennifer, who sat primping herself before the mirror, chatted like school-girls while Harriet napped across the hall in her own room.

There was an instant of silence. Lara took the opportunity to ask a question that had been in her thoughts for hours. "Have you heard from Craig?" she asked quietly.

Jennifer shot her a sharp glance. "No. And Mama is so upset. He doesn't even know his own father is dead."

"Where do you suppose he is?" sighed Lara.

"I don't know. Nobody knows. It almost killed Mama when he left like that."

"I sort of understand. I was only fifteen then, but when Missy died and old Sam Fuller was running around saying Craig did it . . ."

"He was a fool. He was too young to go and marry the girl like that!" said Jennifer.

"But they were so in love . . ."

"Love! See what it came to!"

"I suppose so," replied Lara thoughtfully.

The subject died, but the sad memories lingered on, coloring the atmosphere.

Then they talked about Mrs. Bryant's finishing school and Lara confessed her unease around strangers and crowds.

"You'll get used to it," said Jennifer, dabbing color to her already rosy cheeks. "And besides, if you want to meet a nice man, you'll have to. Although God knows how you and I will ever meet anyone while we're stuck out on the ranch!"

Lara frowned, studying her sister. "You'll do all right, Jenn," she said. "You always have."

"For pity's sake, Lara! I'm almost twenty already. Oh, sure, I have callers, but two of them are old widowers . . ."

"Old?"

"Well. One's in his forties already. . . . And besides, the men here are new in town, struggling at new businesses. I want a wealthy man, Lara, not some pauper that's going to keep me working all day then flat on my back all night!"

"Jennifer!"

17

"Well. It's true. Maybe crude, but true. All a man wants is a housekeeper and his private plaything at night." Jennifer turned in the chair and caught Lara's eye. "Although, I must confess, the plaything part is sort of appealing . . ."

Lara gasped. "Jennifer! You . . . you haven't . . . I mean . . ."

"Oh! Good Lord, no! I'm not *that* stupid. I'm saving it all for a handsome, rich man. One I can snag."

"Then how, I mean, well, how can you know that doing, you know, doing *that* with a man will be appealing?"

"Oh, Lara," muttered Jennifer in exasperation, "don't be so naive! Haven't you ever been kissed? You know. Your stomach gets all funny and your knees feel like buckling. I just know I'll love it!"

Lara grew pensive, her dark, winglike brows knitted together in a frown. Should she tell Jennifer? Why not. They were, after all, sisters. "Do you ever have strange dreams? I mean, while you're still awake at night?" Jennifer smiled, nodding. "I do too. Ever since I went to Saint Louis, that is. At a party I once saw this very handsome man and for weeks all I could do was dream about him—you know, things like over a candlelit table, his hand on mine, and then later, when he would drive me home"—Lara blushed suddenly—"well, he would kiss me."

"And then?"

Lara laughed. "Then he'd kiss me harder . . . holding me tightly . . ."

An abrupt knock on the door startled the two girls; they jumped, frightened suddenly, as if caught with their hands in the cookie jar.

"Are you two awake?" came Harriet's voice through the wooden door.

Jennifer rose and scurried over to let her mother in. "We were just talking." She turned back into the room and winked conspiratorially at Lara.

"Are you ready for dinner?" asked Harriet.

Jennifer, who had been fussing at the mirror, claimed she was starved.

"You two go on down," said Lara. "I need to change and redo my hair—I'm a sight."

"We'll get a table then," replied Harriet. "Now don't be too long, dear." She stepped over before leaving and placed a warm kiss on Lara's brow.

When they were gone, Lara rose from the bed, stretched, then went to the washstand, where she scrubbed the travel dirt from her hands and face. She then stripped down to her chemise and petticoat, rummaged through her large bag, and selected a high-necked, warm burgundy dress with off-white lace at the collar and cuffs, tiny pearl buttons down the tight bodice, and a small bustle at the back. The dress flattered her dark coloring and accentuated her firm, high bustline and slender waist. Her figure, compared to Jennifer's soft roundness, was more angular, thinner, almost boyish, save for the curve of her hips and breasts, which, although not large, were firm and pert. She guessed her bosom was one of her best assets since she had noticed the tendency for some girls' bigger breasts to sag at a very young age. At least hers still rode high and round.

Once dressed, she pulled the pins from her hair and hung her head down to brush out the long, straight thickness until it shone like an ebony mane.

She had just tossed her head back, scooped the mass

19

into her hands to form a pompadour, when she became aware of a loud noise through the wall, apparently in the room next door. It had sounded as if someone, or something, had hit the wall behind the dresser mirror.

She froze, hearing muffled voices then—men, perhaps two of them. Was there an argument going on? And then more gruff, muffled voices—the same two sounds. Definitely there was a loud argument going on next door.

She hurried to finish dressing her hair. For some unknown reason she didn't want to hear the terrible noises. It was as if she were eavesdropping; it made her skin tingle uncomfortably. If only, she thought, she had gone straight to dinner with her family!

More loud voices. Her stomach knotted. And then she could make out a few words—several crude swear words and then—she couldn't miss it—the name Taggart.

It rang in her head. *Taggart*. And with the single word came a flood of memories.

Her fingers began to shake slightly as she placed the last pin into the pompadour and she could see two stains of color rise on her cheeks in the mirror. *Taggart*. Why did she have to be reminded of them now, on her homecoming? Was one of the men in the room next door a Taggart?

The mighty Taggarts—their neighbors from Wolf Butte Ranch. Lara had been raised with the feud. It had been going on since her mother's marriage to Frank Clayton. It must have been when they were both new here that the feud started, Lara thought, because no one ever mentioned a time when the two ranchers had been friendly. Her father had always refused to talk about the origins of the feud, only muttering angrily that the Taggarts were too high and mighty for their own good—or anyone else's. And her mother seemed to get flustered whenever

Lara asked *her*—and told her daughter that they'd just never gotten along.

But it was more than that, Lara knew. It was a deep-seated hate and distrust between the two neighboring families and she couldn't remember a time her father hadn't hated the Taggarts—especially Joe. The reasons didn't even matter anymore; the battle lines were drawn, the sides chosen, and it would always be that way.

And it hadn't helped matters any when Craig Clayton, at seventeen, had upped and run away with Missy Fuller and got himself married to her. Missy's father, Sam, was the Taggarts' foreman and had been ever since 1887. His small homestead had been ruined in the fierce blizzards of '86 and '87. Then, when Missy had sickened and died of some terrible fever that same year, Sam Fuller had nearly gone crazy and had run around blaming Craig for Missy's death. And *that* had made things much worse between the two ranches.

Then Craig had left the valley. It was about then, too, that the whole situation began to get worse. Disdaining little irritations, the Taggarts began really showing their feelings: fences were ripped down deliberately, tough Texas longhorns were driven into Clayton's range to spread disease and destruction among their tamer Shorthorns and Herefords; water holes were poisoned with alkali salts; cattle disappeared.

And all these years the Taggarts kept denying they'd done any of those things.

The Taggarts.

Lara thought of the name and how she'd listened to her father curse it all her life. But what, really, did she know of the Taggarts? She knew that Joe's wife had died many years ago and that he had three sons, grown now, that Lara hadn't seen in years. She doubted she'd even recognize them. And she certainly hoped she'd never run into any of them.

A dark cloud settled over Lara as she opened the door to leave; she wished she had never heard their name, least of all tonight. The voices were still loud next door—even louder now that her door was open.

And then she heard it—a gunshot—and she froze with her hand on the knob.

Lara had no idea how long she stood there, motionless, her heart thudding madly, threatening to burst. It seemed like hours.

The hall was so quiet, so dimly lit, and when no one came rushing to help, Lara thought she must have imagined the whole thing—the fierce argument and then the shot. But then suddenly she heard a sound at the other door and, as if it were happening in slow motion, the door opened and a tall, lanky man wearing a Stetson, his face hidden from view in the shadows, walked out of the door, went swiftly down the hall, and disappeared around the corner. For a moment in the slow vision, she thought the man had turned his head toward her, stared at her, but then maybe she had imagined that, too.

Why didn't someone come to help? And what about the shot? Was the other man inside the room injured? What if he were . . . ?

Slowly, agonizingly, she began to move toward the half-opened door. What if he were bleeding? Maybe she should get help first.

And then she was standing on the threshold, her eyes fixed on a still figure lying in the middle of the carpet, a dark pool spreading beneath his body even as she stood transfixed to the spot. Somewhere in the recesses of her mind she registered that the growing stain on the green carpet was blood.

She took a hesitant step—later she would wonder if she had been advancing or retreating—and bumped straight into a moving object.

She screamed.

"It's all right, miss. Please . . . just step aside," came a man's voice.

Then there were others, lots of them, shouldering past her and into the room.

She guessed afterward that she must have run then because suddenly she was in Harriet's arms at the base of the steps in the lobby, crying out her shock in a torrent of unintelligible words.

In quiet, soothing tones Harriet consoled her and led her to an overstuffed couch, where she finally began to regain a semblance of reality. Jennifer was there, too, she registered, offering her a lacy hanky. And then there was another presence.

"Excuse me, ma'am," said the strange man, "but I understand you were witness to the . . . to the shooting."

With hot tears burning behind her eyelids, Lara tried to focus on the owner of the voice. He was graying, nicely built, his brown eyes seeming kind, concerned. She tried her voice. "I . . . I really didn't . . ."

And then Harriet stroked her brow carefully. "Lara, dear, this is our deputy sheriff, Ned Lawson. If you could try to help . . ."

"But I can't help!" she cried finally. "I didn't see anything!" Her mind raced suddenly. Hadn't she heard an argument, then the shot, and then seen that man, the tall man in the Stetson?

She tried her voice again; this time it shook only slightly. "I did hear an argument, but that was all. There was a man, though, but I honestly couldn't see his face or anything. Truly. The hall was so dark."

"A man?" asked Ned Lawson. "Surely, you saw something. Was he fat, thin, tall, or . . ."

"He was tall. Yes. And quite thin, I think. Lanky, you'd say."

"Is that all? Was he young . . . old?"

Lara strained her memory. "I just don't know. It was so dark."

"All right then, Miss Clayton, what happened next?"

She thought back on the incident with great effort, her fingers twisting the hanky nervously. "I guess I went to the door then. I saw that poor man on the floor and there was so much . . . blood . . ." Lara turned her green eyes up to the deputy's face. "Is he . . . is he dead?"

"'Fraid so, ma'am. You sure you didn't hear or see anything else?"

"No . . . I'm sure," she answered truthfully.

"Well, thank you, ma'am. But you'll get in touch if you remember anything else, won't you?"

"Yes," Lara murmured, and then watched him retrace his path up the stairs.

"Mother?" asked Jennifer. "Don't you think Lara could use a brandy or a sherry—anything? Perhaps we all should go into the dining room."

"Yes. We should. Do you feel up to it, Lara?"

"Yes. And I'd like a sherry if I may." Or two, thought Lara, feeling every nerve in her body tingle miserably.

As it turned out, one sherry did the trick, and no one seemed to object to the beautiful, dark-haired girl's action as she downed the sherry in a few short minutes.

"Lara Clayton deserved it," the voices whispered. "The poor young girl. Terrible thing to witness."

It was nearly an hour before the gossip about the incident died down enough for business to resume as usual in the dining room.

Although Lara had lost her appetite completely, she ordered along with her family. She did, however, feel much better as both Harriet and Jennifer tried to cheer and soothe her. Listening to Jennifer's idle gossip about their neighbors almost brought a smile to her lips several times.

"And remember little Suzy Felton? You know, the carrot top with the funny nose?" Jennifer screwed up her pretty face, imitating Suzy Felton. Lara giggled abruptly. "Well, anyway," Jennifer went on, "she's a good eight months along. Every hand on her father's ranch has . . . well, you understand. And she's still claiming to be a virgin!"

"Jennifer!" gasped Harriet in a hushed voice.

"Well, so what, Mama? It is true and everyone knows it."

And so the conversation went on through the soup course and half of dinner. All the while Lara's spirits were lifting anew; it was good to be back home, to hear the familiar voices, to engage in the female chitchat. It was warm and safe company and Lara began to gossip also, holding her own. The memory of the shooting faded until she actually felt her appetite return.

It was while their plates were being cleared away and dessert was being ordered that Lara had the odd but distinct feeling that she was being observed; someone's eyes were on her, she sensed, even though she hadn't noticed anyone staring.

Very slowly, she drew her attention away from the two

women and casually let her eyes roam the crowded dining room. The lamps were low, the din loud, and at first she could see or hear nothing out of the ordinary. It wasn't until she began searching the tables farther away, near the far wall, all the while sensing someone staring at her, that Lara finally found the source of her unease.

It was a man. And an extremely attractive one at that. She snatched her eyes away.

And yet the image of his face remained. Yes, he was very handsome, but there was something else there too—something in his intense gaze that eluded her and made her want to look at him, to study his face.

Trying to keep track of Jennifer's prattle, she felt goose bumps rise on her flesh. She knew the stranger must still be watching her.

But in spite of her discomfort, strangely, her eyes were drawn back to the man who studied her so brazenly. Curiosity began to win out over her embarrassment and, unable to stop herself, she braved another look at him. Perhaps he hadn't realized she had noticed him.

But he had. When she raised her eyes again he was watching her openly. With a sense of shock, she saw a faint smile upturn the corner of his thin lips. Their gazes locked.

His eyes were blue—such a brilliant, clear blue that she could not mistake the color even from across the room. He tipped his head at her, the smile never leaving his lips, as if she were an old acquaintance. Either that or . . . another kind of girl.

The very nerve of the man! How rude! She pushed her chin high in the air, as Mrs. Bryant had taught her, and carefully placed her glance back on her dessert plate.

In her discomfort, feeling spots of red stain her cheeks, Lara barely noticed Jennifer leaning close to her. "So you finally noticed him," observed Jennifer, smiling conspiratorially.

"Noticed who?" Lara placed a spoonful of vanilla ice cream in her mouth, savoring it slowly, pretending unconcern.

"Don't be coy with me, sis. You know who I mean. *The* high-and-mighty Branch Taggart!"

Lara choked on the cold ice cream. "Who?" she gulped in shock.

"Branch Taggart, you ninny. Joe's oldest son. Don't you know him?"

"No, I don't . . ." Lara whispered.

"Well, everyone in Rifle knows Branch. He's going to inherit Wolf Butte Ranch when old Joe dies. Branch runs the place now. Don't you just think he's the most divine . . . ?"

"Stop it, Jennifer!" she snapped curtly, recovering. "The man is a Taggart and it upsets me to even think about . . ." But whatever more Lara was going to say froze on her lips.

That was it. That was what she hadn't been able to remember from the incident upstairs. It had been the word *Taggart* that she had heard through the wall. Could it have been Branch in that room?

As the garbled facts sifted through her thoughts, Lara's first instinct was to go find Ned Lawson and turn this Branch Taggart in to the law. But how absurd, she realized slowly. Ned Lawson would laugh in her face, for as Jennifer had put it so well, the Taggarts were high and mighty, powerful. And besides, what proof did she have? A single name heard through a wall? If only, she thought now, she had gotten a better look at the man in the hall.

For a moment she tried to conjure up Branch Taggart's image in her mind—he hadn't appeared to be lanky, but he was sitting. How could she tell? And how tall was he? Did he really resemble the figure of the man she had seen?

Well, she told herself, she would just have to sort the thing out in her mind when she was calmer, less confused. Right now she felt tired, too exhausted from the journey and then seeing that poor soul lying on the floor like that. Tomorrow, when she was rested, she could always go to Ned Lawson with her story. If only Branch Taggart would stand up and she could get a better view of his stature.

"What's the matter with you anyway?" asked Jennifer. "The most attractive man in the valley pays you attention and you look as if you'd seen a ghost! Really Lara! I'd give my right arm if Branch would just once notice me!"

Lara turned abruptly toward her sister, her green eyes flashing angrily. "That's a ridiculous thing to say, Jennifer! How could you after the way Father felt about *them!*" She hissed the word vehemently.

But Jennifer was not to be put off. "Oh, Dad was always a fool where the Taggarts are concerned. They're the nicest men around. And I'll tell you something else, Miss Stuck-up, if I want to associate with them, I will!"

"That's enough," said Harriet finally, her green eyes studying the two girls pensively. "You will not argue and especially not in public. Is that quite clear?"

The girls, if a little grudgingly, did nod their heads in obedience.

Still, Lara was upset by her sister's attitude and even more rattled that Branch Taggart was still watching her. Why wouldn't he stop?

And then a thought struck her like an electric shock coursing through her limbs: if he had been the man in the hall, could he have recognized her? And if so, then was that why he was studying her? Was he wondering if she had seen him?

Unthinking, she turned her head and met his gaze once more; she saw only his cool eyes, felt them touch her, searching, as a tremor shook her body. His expression gave away nothing; there was no hint of a smile this time. His eyes, although she felt they mocked her, were unreadable.

Chapter Two

THE CROWD IN THE DINING ROOM HAD THINNED AND IT WAS all Lara could do to keep from falling asleep at the table. It was typical of Harriet, she recalled, to dine for hours. "One does not gulp down one's food," she had said so often. "One dines, my dear."

Well, tonight her mother was dining and socializing. Several friends who were also stranded in Rifle because of the storm had stopped by the table to chat with Harriet Clayton and her two lovely, if very different, daughters. Of course, they all knew that Lara had been away at finishing school and wanted to hear about her experiences in St. Louis. It was a rare thing for a ranch girl to attend such a chic school, and Lara felt, by their questions, that she had become something of an enigma. It made her terribly uncomfortable. Didn't they know how much she had disliked St. Louis—the parties, the social niceties—and that she was still at heart just Lara, a country girl?

If only she could leave and go up to bed! But hadn't Mrs. Bryant said a thousand times over, "Miss Lara Clayton, you will remain here until the other guests retire. How could you think of being so impolite! And for heaven's sake, *talk* to people—don't be so tongue-tied, my dear. You look like a frightened rabbit!"

And so Lara remained seated in the Winchester Hotel dining room, stifling her yawns.

She had managed, during the last few minutes, to put Branch Taggart out of her mind—let him stare rudely at her; she'd pretend not to notice. And somehow she did forget him, thinking only about putting her head down on the soft pillow in her room. She certainly hoped Jenn didn't want to stay up and chat! Not tonight.

"Why, Mr. Ackroyd," Harriet was saying to someone over Lara's shoulder, "how very nice to see you again. And, Branch, how are you?"

Branch? Lara's heart jolted.

Quickly she turned in her seat, looked up, met his cool, appraising glance. Her breath snatched in her throat.

"I'm just fine, Mrs. Clayton," he was replying, "except for this storm. I reckon you're stuck in town for the night also?"

"Why, yes, I'm afraid so. Oh, how rude of me!" gasped Harriet. "Lara"—she glanced at her daughter, smiling proudly—"this is Mr. Branch Taggart. I'm not sure you've ever been introduced. And Mr. Noah Ackroyd, our new editor at the *Rifle Reveille.*"

Jennifer batted demure lashes at the two men. "Nice to see you again." She smiled coyly.

"Mr. Ackroyd," said Lara then, trying desperately to control the quaver in her voice. "Welcome to Rifle." She ignored Branch completely, the open snub obvious to the entire group.

Harriet cleared her throat, attempting to hide her mortification. "Won't you join us for coffee?" she asked politely, pinioning Lara with a hard glance.

Branch said nothing; Lara could feel his presence above her left shoulder as if he were touching her—her skin burned and she had to keep herself from shrinking away from him.

"Why, thank you, Mrs. Clayton," replied Noah Ackroyd. "That would be pleasant."

Lara couldn't believe it. Surely Branch Taggart wasn't going to sit down with the Claytons! But she could see the two men, out of the corner of her eye, draw two empty chairs up to the table. Jennifer scooted hers over to make room as Noah Ackroyd placed a chair between Lara and Jennifer and Branch placed his next to Jennifer's other side.

Thank God he hadn't sat next to her!

"Mrs. Clayton told me last week about your staying in St. Louis." Noah directed his conversation to Lara. "You must tell us all the news there. Did you enjoy finishing school?"

Lara felt like there was cotton wadded in her throat; she tried to direct her attention to Noah and his question, but all her senses were tuned to the other man quietly evaluating her. "I, well, yes, I suppose I liked school," she lied with difficulty. "I mean, I did learn a lot there and St. Louis is a lovely city."

"And Mrs. Bryant? Why, all the way back in New York we've heard that she's become quite famous for her success with . . ." He hesitated. "That is, she has seen many a girl make an excellent match. The finishing schools on the East Coast have their competition now, I understand."

Lara's green eyes rested on the sandy-haired newspaperman; he was nice-looking and tall, thin, thirtyish, and wore round silver-rimmed spectacles. She sensed that she would like him. On the other side of Jennifer, however, sat a man she had been bred to distrust. Still, if Noah was nice-looking in a refined, bookish way, Branch Taggart's virility, his masculine good looks were overpowering. He, like Noah, had blue eyes, but where Noah's were a pale, unexciting hue, Branch's were crystal, piercing blue—like a brilliant summer sky. She had never seen eyes that color before! His hair was worn medium long; it was a light golden shade that curled, thick and crisp, over his collar. It was hard to tell if he was truly blond or just out in the sun a lot. His skin was tanned deeply; crinkle lines appeared around his eyes. He must be over thirty, maybe even older, she guessed. And then she noticed the wide breadth of his shoulders— hardly what one would consider to be "lanky." She felt an uncomfortable twinge of guilt.

Lara managed to answer Noah's many questions about St. Louis as best she could, and where she grew tongue-tied, Jennifer, who had also spent time in St. Louis, supplied the answers—always with a flashing smile, always captivating the attention of everyone. That was Jennifer: the perfect hostess. A charmer.

"And so, Miss Clayton"—Noah was speaking—"I wonder if I might print a small column on your experiences in St. Louis and perhaps your view of Rifle's enormous growth since your absence?"

"Oh," she replied, disconcerted, "I can't imagine why anyone would want to read about my opinion . . ."

"Of course they would. Trust my judgment, Miss Clayton."

"Well, then . . ."

"Of course you'll help Mr. Ackroyd, dear," interrupted Harriet firmly.

"If you really want my opinions, I'd be happy to."

"Perhaps," said Noah, "when you're resettled at Bitter Creek, I might call on you?"

Lara felt herself blush hotly. He had just asked for permission to call on her, and by the look on his candid features he meant more than just a visit to do an article for the *Rifle Reveille*. She had no idea how to reply, and what was worse, all eyes were on her now.

"Lara would enjoy that, I'm sure," coaxed Harriet, saving the moment. "Wouldn't you, dear?"

"Why, yes. Certainly," she whispered, casting her green eyes demurely downward.

If only, she thought, Branch Taggart weren't here, it would be so much easier to talk to Noah Ackroyd. How could Harriet have invited *him* to sit with them?

She glanced up; Jennifer was engaging Branch in conversation and, of all things, about ranching! She could just throttle that sister of hers! And imagine Jennifer talking about the ranch, as if she knew one single thing about it! Why, Jennifer didn't really know the difference between a fenced-in ranch such as theirs and the open-range grazing ranches like the Taggarts'! Her sister didn't have the slightest notion what she was talking about! Lord, thought Lara hotly, a range war could break out at the drop of a hat, considering the fact that the Claytons had justifiably fenced off one of the Taggarts' watering holes not so long ago and the Taggarts were still furious about it.

She listened in disbelief to their conversation while Jennifer prattled on about roundup and the Cattlemen's

Association and things in which she couldn't have been less interested. Jenn was an incorrigible flirt and would no doubt start chattering away about water rights and really open up a can of worms if she didn't watch herself.

Nevertheless, Lara noticed, Branch seemed to take Jenn's words with a grain of salt. In fact, he seemed mildly amused rather than angered.

Only Jennifer could pull off a conversation such as this!

Noah, Lara observed, was deciding with Harriet on a convenient date for his visit and this gave her the opportunity to study the group in silence for a few minutes. There was her mother—so sweet, so self-assured, and lovely for her forty years. And Jennifer—a younger replica of Harriet, if a little more buxom and rounded than her mother. Both were lovely women, secure in their femininity, easy with strangers. What was wrong with her? Perhaps she had not only inherited her father's complexion but his reserve, too.

And then there was Branch. His head was turned toward Harriet at last and Lara could clearly see the straight, hard line of his jaw and the slightly curved, generous nose that was enticingly masculine, fitting perfectly his other strong features. His eyes, at the corners, were drawn very slightly downward, lending him a pensive, closed look—almost brooding, she thought. He was, she hated to admit, extremely handsome with his broad shoulders, his tall, well-muscled frame, and the light, crisp-looking hairs curling on his chest above the buttons on his shirt.

Suddenly she caught herself in midthought: she was actually staring at him openly, her breathing quite uneven, her eyes devouring his virility. Had she completely lost her mind? And what was far worse, he had turned his head and seen her ogling him like—like a brazen street woman! And his lips were upturned now, his slight smile sardonic.

Oh, God! He knew. Branch Taggart knew she found him attractive!

Her heart skipped several beats and the blood rushed up her neck, reaching her cheeks. She tore her eyes away from his face and desperately sought Noah's attention. "What day will you be visiting, Mr. Ackroyd?" she asked, breathless, praying it wasn't the wrong thing to have asked.

"Why, Mrs. Clayton asked me on Wednesday, for supper, if that's suitable?"

"Perfect." Lara forced herself to smile brightly, as if in anticipation, then lowered her lashes coyly, like Jennifer would have done. Let Branch Taggart think she was interested in Noah—anything to save face.

They chatted for a while longer, the hour growing late. Lara could see that her mother and Jennifer could go on all night in the company of two handsome men. But as for herself, the minutes were ticking by like hours, awkward and unending.

Finally it was Branch who pushed himself away from the table, rising. "If you'll excuse me, ladies, Noah, I think I'm going to retire. I've got to get back to Wolf Butte early if this storm breaks tonight."

"I'm afraid," said Harriet, "that we must also retire. I'm certain Lara must be exhausted." She smiled at her daughter affectionately.

The women rose, following Noah, who led the way through the dining room into the lobby.

"Well, I'll be leaving you then," said Noah. "Luckily my place is in town. So nice to meet you, Miss Lara. Until next Wednesday?"

Lara smiled, returning his warmth. "I'll look forward to it," she replied, then watched him leave, flipping his coat collar up in the face of the storm.

She was turning back to her family, standing at the base of the stairs, when she saw Branch stride from the dining room, carrying a hat—a Stetson—in his hand. It must have been on the hat rack near the door, she registered, and then simultaneously realized there was something about a Stetson . . .

Then it came to her. The image of the man, the killer, upstairs, wearing a similar hat flooded her vision.

She drew in her breath.

"Lara?" said her mother, "are you coming?"

At first she couldn't answer; she was speechless, frozen, her eyes fixed on Branch, who was standing next to them now with an arched brow, seeming to be waiting for them to lead the way upstairs.

"Come on," said Jennifer, taking her hand. "Let's go to bed. You're tired."

"Yes . . . tired," whispered Lara, still staring at Branch, the Stetson in his capable-looking hand.

They walked up the stairs to the second floor, where their rooms were located. Branch, mercifully, seemed to be headed to the opposite end of the long hall. For an instant, at the head of the stairs, while Harriet bade him a good night, Lara was seized with the impression that his presence filled the hallway threateningly. She hadn't noticed just how tall he was before. And the killer—he had been quite tall too. Could it possibly have been him? Certainly the Taggarts were ruthless: they cut fences, poisoned watering holes, their ranch hands had even engaged in barroom shoot-outs. Was Branch Taggart a murderer? He looked as if he had the strength. And there was that closed look in his brilliant blue eyes . . .

"Good night," he was saying to Harriet, who then headed toward her room with Jennifer following.

Somehow, though, Lara wasn't able to move, and it seemed as if suddenly she was alone with Branch in the dim hallway. Later she would imagine that it was the flash from the match he struck on his boot sole and put to his cigarette that drew her attention—the sudden flare of the match must have startled her, holding her mesmerized, rooted to the spot. All that she knew at the moment was that her stare was fixed on the shadowed lines of his jaw, the thin downward curl of his lips—an almost cruel curve—as he lit the cigarette. It was a long moment before she realized that she was openly staring at this man, and now she was quite alone with him in the narrow hallway.

Lara felt her cheeks flush scarlet, but before she could force her feet forward, he spoke, his voice a low, lazy drawl. "Aren't you going to retire?" he asked easily, and she realized that was the first time he had spoken directly to her.

She searched desperately for the sharp-witted proper retort he deserved. How dare he insinuate she would deliberately stand alone in the hall with him! "Of course I'm going to retire, Mr. Taggart," she countered. "You don't think I relish standing here talking to an utter stranger!" Quickly she picked up her skirts and began to spin away.

Then, shockingly, Branch shot out a steady hand and took hold of her arm, forcing her back around to face him. "Are you so very sure of that, Lara Clayton?"

She snatched her arm away from his grasp. "How dare you!" she whispered. Then: "You're no gentleman, sir!"

She fled down the hall, but before she could follow Jennifer into their room, she heard his low, infuriating chuckle reach out to her through the darkness, and she could almost picture the lean curl to those cool lips. The arrogant bully! She slammed her door behind her, not caring who she awakened with the loud noise.

Jennifer stood near the dresser, ready to speak, but Lara cut her off. "I'm furious with you!" she half cried. "How could you and Mother invite *him* to sit with us! How could you!"

"For heaven's sake, Lara, calm down," Jennifer replied, undaunted by the tirade. "There's nothing wrong with talking to him. In fact, isn't he the most handsome thing you've *ever* seen?"

"Oooh!"

"Come on now, admit it. I saw you staring at him— interested, I'd say."

"Jennifer! No. You're wrong!"

"Say what you like, little sister, but I saw it that way." Lara met her glance with icy silence.

"And besides," Jennifer continued, "I happen to like the Taggart men. If you'd give them half a chance, you'd find them very nice. Why, you should see his younger brothers, Robert and Guy. They're so divine!"

"Every male," retorted Lara, "is *divine* to you!"

"So what?"

"Have you forgotten the feud? The way Dad hated them? And for good reason. How can you forget?" Exasperated, Lara tried to reason with her sister. "Jenn, there're range wars going on all the time between ranches like theirs and ours . . ."

"Over fences, I know," replied Jennifer calmly. "Who cares? It's so silly anyway."

"But to sit and discuss ranching with a Taggart? Jenn, they're diehard open-range ranchers. Why . . . why, you might have started God knows what with your prattle!"

Jennifer giggled. "You ninny! Do you think Branch Taggart gave a hoot what I was talking about? Why, I'm sure he thinks women are a bunch of empty-headed females! He's just like all men, Lara—you can say anything you want and it goes in one ear and out the other! Someday they'll learn better . . ."

"It's just fortunate for you that he wasn't listening then. He might have remembered that there's a feud going on between our families!"

"It wasn't my feud . . . or Mama's, Lara. Let it drop. It's time."

"I don't see how."

"All right then, don't. But you can't stop me from talking to them or liking them."

"You're a fool then, Jennifer. In fact"—Lara placed her hands on her hips, loosing her final arrow—"I think *your* Branch may have shot that man next door." She was gratified to see Jennifer's eyes widen in shock.

"How can you . . . ? Did you . . . see him?"

Lara thought better of her statement. "No, I didn't actually see him. But I still have my reasons."

Jennifer let out her breath. "I'm sure you're wrong." She resumed, matter-of-factly, brushing out her long, honey-colored hair.

And really Lara had to agree with her sister. The man in the dimly lit hallway hadn't actually resembled Branch —he had been too thin, too lanky. Still, it had been awfully dark . . .

She began unbuttoning her dress, letting her hair fall thickly down her back, and was finally ready to drop into bed, exhausted. Jennifer joined her shortly, turning the lamp down. For a while both were silent, lost in their own thought, half sleeping.

"Lara?" came Jennifer's whisper. "Are you still awake?"

"Umm."

"I'm sorry we argued."

"That's all right, Jennifer. Really."

"Can I tell you something without starting up again?"

"Yes."

"Promise?"

"Yes, Jennifer."

"If you knew what Branch Taggart has been through the last several years, you'd most likely see him in a different light."

Except for Lara's promise, she would have stopped Jennifer right there; instead, she listened, hating to be reminded of him but grudgingly curious.

"It must have been around the time you left for St. Louis," continued Jennifer into the darkness. "Branch was married, you know . . ."

Lara felt an odd, involuntary lurch in her breast.

". . . to a pretty blond girl named Jewel from back east somewhere. It's said she hated Rifle, really hated the boredom at the ranch. I guess this Jewel was a real city girl. Anyway, several months after they were married she took up with a drifter, a ranch hand named Jeff, who was reported to be quite a good-looker. Jewel then disappeared with him somewhere, and Branch, as the gossip around town has it, practically became a hermit."

"But where is she now?" Lara couldn't keep from asking.

"Dead."

Lara gasped. Had Branch found the lovers . . . ?

"I understand Jewel came home after a time. She was

41

pregnant, that much was for sure. Now the story gets tricky, though. No one knew if it was Jeff's child or Branch's. Only Jewel, I suppose, knew that. Anyway, Jewel evidently didn't want the child; she left again, and the next thing anyone heard she was dead. It's said she tried to . . . you know . . . get rid of it in Denver City and died from it. . . . Who knows?"

"How horrible!"

"Yes. It must have been. Poor, stupid girl. And frankly, I feel sorry for Branch—no matter what, I shouldn't think he deserved that."

Lara tried to assimilate the information; it was a dreadful story and she wouldn't wish that on anyone—not even a Taggart. Perhaps Jewel was the source of that brooding, hidden look in his eyes. Perhaps . . .

A short while later, when Lara should have been the one to sleep, it was actually Jennifer who drifted off.

The hotel was quiet, the only sounds the wind howling around the brick corners and faint footsteps coming from outside, from the veranda that ran all the way around the second story of the hotel.

As Lara listened, half dreaming, to the night sounds, it occurred to her that the person walking on the veranda in the storm must be terribly restless.

And then she wondered, could it be Branch out there? Were the sleepless footfalls his?

For a long time she lay awake listening, questioning, the vision of blue-blue eyes tormenting her thoughts.

Chapter Three

"WELL, GIRLS, WHAT DO YOU THINK?" ASKED HARRIET, pulling aside the heavy velvet drapes and looking down onto the street. "Do we try it or not?"

Lara and Jennifer crowded up to the window behind her. The street was rutted and muddy, but the spring sun had already melted most of the snow. It still lay in untidy brown piles on the shadowed side of the street.

"Oh, please, let's go home," pleaded Lara. "I'm so anxious."

Harriet sighed. "I knew you'd say that. Jennifer, what do you think?"

"Well, I'd love to stay another day even though I know Lara wants to get home. And if the buckboard gets stuck and we have to push it, I'll ruin my new shoes and my coat. Let's wait till this afternoon at least."

"No! What on earth will I do all day? I want to get home," cried Lara. "Can't we go now?"

"Girls, calm down. Let's compromise. We'll leave after breakfast, and surely then there will be enough people along the road to help us out if we get stuck," suggested Harriet. "How's that?"

"Fine," said Lara, breaking into a sunny smile.

She finished dressing in front of the mirror. She'd wear one more of her new city outfits and then, when she got home, it would be plain skirts and blouses, and jeans for riding. She chose a green wool skirt, pulled back into a small bustle, and a fitted matching coat with leg-o'-mutton sleeves and black Persian lamb trim down the front, on the turned-back cuffs, and around the high collar. The green fabric made her eyes even more emerald and flattered her golden skin. Jennifer watched enviously, straightening her own blue velvet suit as best she could.

Breakfast was quite good: freshly baked rolls and butter, strong coffee, bacon, eggs, steak if you wanted it. Lara could hardly believe that she was sitting in a hotel dining room eating breakfast on fine china where she had once, not so long ago, galloped her pony after Mr. Maxfield's stray cows. She really couldn't fit her mind around the enormity of the changes that had taken place.

"Excuse me a moment, girls," said Harriet, rising, "I'll just ask the clerk to send to the livery stable for the wagon. Then we'll save ourselves one trip in the mud."

When she returned, they went back up to their rooms and Lara finished packing her last few things. Jennifer lounged on the bed and complained that she had to wear the same outfit she'd worn to town yesterday, not knowing she'd be staying the night. "If I'd known," she reflected, "I would have brought along my new red dress. It's beautiful! Darn! It would have been perfect for dinner

44

last night. Where am I going to wear it to now? To milk old Samantha or throw Paiute some hay?"

"How is old Paiute?" asked Lara eagerly, referring to her father's blooded pinto stallion.

"Same as ever—crotchety, nasty, hungry," shrugged Jennifer.

"You just don't understand him—you never did. He never gave me any trouble."

"Good. You take care of him then. Everyone's afraid to ride him now—even Shad."

"I certainly will," said Lara, her small chin rising, her slanted green eyes flashing.

"You always were crazy about him and about the whole ranch. Haven't you changed? Didn't you see anything better in two years at school?" asked Jennifer wonderingly.

"Better!" Lara whirled on Jennifer, her hands on her slim hips. "It was awful! I don't like the city and the parties and the silly, blabbering people! This is home! I feel better now than I have in two years!"

"You are crazy," said Jennifer slowly. "Now I know it."

There was a knock on the door then, forestalling a continuation of Jennifer's view of ranch life.

"Girls! The wagon's here. Let's go."

Lara gathered up two bags and her reticule. She eyed the one bulging carpet bag that was left.

"Oh, all right," said Jennifer, picking it up. "Lord! What's in here—rocks?"

"No, just some books and a few things for you and Mama."

Jennifer's face lit up. "Presents? Oh, goody. I can't wait!"

They descended the stairs to the lobby, still chatting.

Today the place looked more cheerful, lighter, the sun streaming through the tall windows to lay down bright stripes on the carpeted floor. The noise of the traffic from outside entered the hotel: jingling harnesses, squeaking wheels, the suck of horses' hooves in mud, the muted bellowing of countless cattle in the stockyard down by the railroad line.

Lara strode across the lobby, leaving Jennifer and Harriet behind, wanting to get out into the bright March day, feel the warm Colorado sun on her back, see the utter clarity of the sky again. Lugging the two bags, she had to turn sideways to pass through the crowded lobby in places. Her arms were beginning to ache.

"May I help, ma'am?" She heard a drawling masculine voice next to her ear.

She turned, wondering if the man was asking her the question, or if it were meant for Jennifer—a much more likely possibility.

Her glance met a pair of ice-blue eyes that were suddenly horribly familiar, and a smile that, for all its polite appearance, she knew was presumptuous and mocking.

"Well, may I?" he asked again, grinning at her, his head slightly tilted, his hat held politely in his hand.

She couldn't catch her breath. It was as if someone had punched her in the stomach. But neither could she make a fool of herself—not in front of him!

Mrs. Bryant's words came back to her, the repeated lessons etched in her brain: "How to turn down a gentleman's proposal if it seems dubious." Thankfully, she needed no conscious thought to straighten her back and mouth the words: "Thank you, but I can manage myself." And her little pointed chin tipped up resolutely, her shoulders squared, and she brushed past him coolly while her stomach churned and her heart beat furiously.

She nearly ran outside, bursting into the fresh air as if she were suffocating. The livery man stood holding the team of horses, behind which Lara recognized the familiar old buckboard. With great effort she hoisted her bags into the back and stood on the wooden sidewalk, waiting impatiently for her mother and sister to catch up with her.

As it turned out, she waited a full ten minutes, irritated, but determined not to go back inside for fear of running into Branch Taggart again. What on earth was keeping them? Her small foot in the high-buttoned black leather boot tapped the wide boards impatiently.

Finally Jennifer came out into the sunlight, blinking her big round blue eyes, looking as pleased as a cat with a dish of cream. Behind her came Harriet, and just after Harriet strode Branch Taggart, carrying the bulging carpetbag.

How could they? Just because her father was dead, these two heedless women were becoming *friends* with the Taggarts? Lara's loyalties were tighter structured, more rigid than that! Her father's death only made it more important for the Claytons to stand up for their beliefs. Hadn't the Taggarts tried to drive them out time after time? Hadn't the Taggarts rustled their cattle, cut off their water, brought suits against them in court, harassed them ceaselessly for years? How could Harriet smile like that, speak so politely to him, nod her head so calmly at his words? It was disgraceful! She felt her body stiffen all over, her stomach knot, her tongue turn to wood in her mouth.

"Lara, dear, Branch has so kindly offered to drive us home in case we have any trouble. Isn't that nice?"

Harriet asked helplessly, looking at her younger daughter with hopeful eyes.

Jennifer smirked.

"Mother . . ." choked Lara. "I think . . ."

"I reckon I just couldn't let three such pretty ladies drive home all that distance with the roads like they are and your place right on the way," said Branch, coming to Harriet's aid. "Dad would have my hide."

"Mr. Taggart," said Lara tightly, her lips frozen into a stiff line, "thank you so much, but really, we can manage ourselves."

"I insist," he countered, turning the full power of his masculine strength toward her. His eyes held utter determination in their depths and a kind of sparking humor too. "I'd never rest easy lettin' you ladies go on alone, and especially, Miss Lara, on your first day home."

She could do nothing short of making a terrible scene, which she couldn't quite bring herself to do. "Mother?" she whispered.

"Lara, I do think it would be better to have a man along . . . today," said Harriet.

"Oh, yes, in case we get stuck," chimed in Jennifer. "How kind of you, Mr. Taggart." Her voice was silk and velvet.

"Call me Branch, please," he said then, but Lara had the distinct feeling that his blue eyes were still watching her, that his words were all for her ears alone, that his undertone of mockery was fathomed only by her. What did the man want?

"I'd rather not," she said then unreasonably.

"Not what?" asked Harriet.

"Not ride with . . . *Mr.* Taggart," she replied coldly.

"Goodness, Lara, don't be so rude. Where *are* your manners?" asked Jennifer.

Lara couldn't answer her. The whole scene was becoming ridiculous. Branch stood there, easy, infuriatingly relaxed; Harriet was embarrassed, Jennifer was furious. It was like some awful play in which the characters had forgotten their lines and the audience was waiting with dreadful anticipation to see what came next, but no one knew—they were all frozen in their stances, horribly self-conscious, lost.

Except Branch. He laughed, an easy, indulgent laugh. "Come on, everybody, let's get going. Perhaps Miss Lara will feel better about it when she sees how bad the roads are."

Just like that. As if her desires were no more important than a snap of his finger. Then she felt his hard, strong hand on her sleeve and she was propelled, as if she were no more than a feather, onto the hard-sprung back seat. Jennifer followed, then Harriet on the front seat next to Branch.

Expertly, he clucked to the horses, slapped the long reins, and then headed north out of Rifle on the Government Road.

Lara could still feel the place on her arm where he had touched her; it burned as if his fingers had been red hot, branding her. She sat in the back of the wagon staring at his broad, straight back that stretched the leather of his sheepskin jacket tight as he drove the team. And beneath his Stetson, which he wore tilted forward, she could see his hair where it touched the shirt collar, curling slightly, light where the sun struck it. She felt utterly helpless, overwhelmed by Branch's strength and confidence.

He was chatting easily with Harriet, saying that Sam Fuller, his foreman, had already left town earlier on their buckboard loaded with supplies and that he'd take it kindly if they'd lend him one of their horses to get from their place. He'd be sure and return it right away. "That is, if you don't mind, ma'am?"

"Of course you can borrow a horse," Harriet replied. "We have very little use for our riding horses these days, I'm afraid. Maybe now that Lara's home . . ."

And so it went on as they drove north up the familiar road toward Bitter Creek. Lara fumed silently in the back seat, not saying a word the whole way. Harriet and Jennifer carried the conversation easily, ignoring her only too obvious rudeness.

The road was rutted and muddy, just as bad as they'd expected. They did have some trouble at one point when their heavy, iron-rimmed wheels sank into the soft shoulder as they passed another rig headed into town. Their pair of horses couldn't even pull the rig free until Branch got down, cut some dried sagebrush, and laid it under the wheels. Then, with his expert handling, the two broad-chested geldings gave a mighty heave, laying into the traces, and the wagon lurched free with a sucking sound.

"Everyone all right?" asked Branch, turning on the seat.

"Oh, yes," trilled Jennifer. "What would we have done without you, Branch?"

Lara sat rigid on the jouncing seat, clenching her teeth to keep from saying something outrageous. She could just as well have gotten the wagon out. They didn't need *him!*

It was only a few more miles before the turnoff to Bitter Creek Ranch. The land became achingly familiar to her, filling her with gladness in spite of Branch's unwelcome presence. The red twisted humps of rock snaked along next to the road on the right, cut by dry gullies and deep ravines; on the left, sloping, dry rangeland stretched away, dotted by white-faced cattle, and as they got closer to Bitter Creek, Hubbard Mesa loomed against the sky. It was bright and sunny, but with a slight chill to the air, and a westerly wind bent the brown grass and sagebrush as if a hand pressed lightly, briefly on the land, then passed on. Snow still lay on shadowed north faces of the gullies, rocks, and clumps of grass.

Then they were turning off Government Road onto the long driveway that led up to the ranch itself, and the ranch house was there, on a small knoll, surrounded by aspen trees that Frank had planted years before: a whitewashed plank house, sprawling, with the original log cabin still a part of it. And over to the right, the corrals and barn, and beyond that the fields stretched away to the base of the red mesa, dotted with cattle and horses.

Home.

Lara felt the tight knots of tension ease. She even forgot Branch for a moment. Her lips parted in an unconscious smile, her green eyes shone with near rapture and filled with a glistening film of joy. She was home at last.

Lightly, she jumped off the wagon almost before it had stopped and, lifting her elegant skirts, she ran across the muddy yard to the barn, stopped in the middle of it, drew in the familiar odors: hay, horseflesh, leather, saddle soap.

A horse nickered in a stall, the dairy cows shifted their weight in the rustling straw, swept-wing swallows dove overhead in the dust-filled beams of sunlight that shot through the upper windows.

She was home.

Lara ran out of the barn, ignoring the mud that

dragged at her hem and skimmed over to the house. She entered it slowly, almost reverently.

It was all the same—the wide-planked kitchen floor, the old scarred kitchen table, the cupboards and pantry that Frank had built, the parlor with its maroon horsehair sofa and chairs, its silver and china—and clean, smelling sweetly of soap and beeswax and woodsmoke.

"Lara!" she heard from the front door. "Where are you?"

"Here, Mama," she called, "in the parlor."

Harriet appeared at the parlor door, Jennifer behind her. "My, you left us quickly."

"I had to see everything! It's been so long . . ." Lara walked slowly around the room, touching the familiar objects lightly—photographs, bric-a-brac, doilies, cut-glass lamps with crystal fringe dangling around their globes.

"Where do you want the bags, ma'am?" The masculine voice intruded on her reverie. She stiffened. That a Taggart should set foot in this house! Her father would have had the shotgun out by now, trained right on Branch Taggart's middle!

"Oh," said Harriet, "put them anywhere. Thank you so much."

Lara watched him through the parlor door. He put the bags down, tipped his hat politely to the ladies. "Now, if you'll just show me where the horses are, and the tack, I'll be on my way." He smiled, showing even white teeth. He filled the house with a masculine presence that was totally unfamiliar.

"Oh, I'll show you," offered Jennifer quickly. "They're just out by the barn."

Lara deliberately turned her back on them both, glad

he was leaving. Inadvertently, her eyes rested on a photograph taken perhaps ten years ago. It was of her father and Craig, standing each with one foot on the carcass of a huge buck they had shot that fall. They both looked proud, happy. Tears started to her eyes, hot and burning. She remembered the occasion well. Craig had been around eleven or twelve. It was his first buck. He had been thrilled beyond belief because Frank had complimented him on his shooting. Frank and Craig had rarely been on such good terms as this, Lara remembered. Normally they were at odds. No matter how hard Craig had tried, he never could please Frank. He was always doing something wrong, it seemed. Frank had been hard on him, much harder than on the girls, but perhaps that was because Craig was a boy and men always expected more of their sons.

She looked again at the photograph, studying it, as if she could find some small portion of comfort in it: Frank, his dark eyes hooded, his thin lips pulled into a rare smile, his straight black hair mostly hidden under his hat; Craig, his face half boy, half man, much fuller than Frank's, blonder, blue eyed, much more like his mother. They didn't even look as if they were related in the photograph, Lara mused. She was really the only one to take after Frank's spare, dark appearance.

Her resolve suddenly hardened. She strode into the kitchen, where Harriet had tied on an apron and was starting a fire in the big wood stove, puttering around.

"Lara," she said over her shoulder, "do you want to start a fire in the parlor?"

"Mama, that can wait. I want to talk to you."

"What is it, dear?" Harriet struck a match, fanned the fire.

"Mama, sit down. We have to talk . . . seriously."

"Goodness, you sound peeved. What is it?" asked Harriet, sinking into one of the wooden chairs, leaning her elbows on the table.

"Mother, it's about the Taggarts. How could you . . . let that Branch . . . how could you even . . . *talk* to him? They were Dad's enemies . . . for years. How could you . . . ?"

"Lara." Harriet's green eyes were suddenly almost sad. "Your father is gone. We all loved him and respected his wishes, but now we have to get along without him. It was his fight. Jennifer and I . . . well, we really don't feel the same way. It seems silly now . . ."

"It was our fight, too," said Lara tightly. "How can you forget what they've done? All the awful things . . ."

"They've always denied doing them. You know that. And I for one believe them."

"You know Dad always said it was lies."

"Lara, they've had things happen to them, too. Things they say we did. Stolen cattle, poisoned water holes. Everyone does."

Lara felt the heat of her anger stain her cheeks. "We never did those things! Why, you know they just said it to make us look bad. Dad was right about them!"

Harriet sighed. "It's been hard all these years. If they want to make peace, I say let's do it. After all, we're three women alone out here. What can we do?"

"We can make this the best ranch around here. We can raise our cattle, sell them. Now that the railroad is here we're going to do even better. Even our horses will have a good market."

"Lara, we can't run this ranch. Why, even Shad admits that. We need a man. Now that Dad's gone . . ."

"Why not?" asked Lara. "I know as much about running this ranch as anybody. I can do it!"

"Two years at Mrs. Bryant's didn't change you any, did it? I thought you'd learn a little . . ."

"Mother." Lara put a gentle hand on her mother's sleeve. "I did learn one very important thing at Mrs. Bryant's. I learned that I belong *here*, at Bitter Creek, not in a city somewhere playing social games."

"Oh, Lara, I only wanted you to be happy. I thought . . . you were such a tomboy. A lady has to find her happiness in other ways—in her family, her children, her home. It's the way we're made."

"Not me," reflected Lara grimly. "Dad taught me to ranch and that's what I'm good at, that's what I *know*."

"Oh, Lara . . ." Harriet eyed her youngest child, so like Frank that it was agonizing to see her: the straight, heavy black hair and high cheekbones, the almost bony, Indian-like molding of the face, the quiet but implacable Indian stubbornness, the inborn love of the land. It always surprised her to see her own green eyes looking back at her out of that face. "A girl can't run a ranch. It isn't done. Why, it'd be a disgrace."

Lara leaned across the table, her expression almost pleading. "Mama, I can do it. You know I can. I can't let the ranch go to seed. We can't just roll over and say die. We have to show the Taggarts!"

"*You* may have to show them. I don't."

"It's more than just the fact that Frank Clayton and Joe Taggart hated each other. Don't you see? It's the difference between our way of life and theirs. We have to prove our way works, that Dad's way was right. He worked so hard! Why, those Taggarts would love to let their herd run wild from Rifle up to Meeker! They'd let them run over the poor homesteaders' crops, everything. They don't care! They're old-fashioned, irresponsible. Their cattle aren't worth half what ours are!"

"You certainly sound like your Dad," reflected Harriet drily.

"He was right. The open range is gone and they're too stubborn to admit it. They'll lose in the end. They don't even winter-feed their cattle. Half of them die in the bad storms and they don't care. Dad wanted more than anything else to show them they were wrong. It's what he lived for. Mama, you know that. You can't turn around and be their *friends.*"

Harriet faced her daughter across the table. Lara was so young, so full of ideals. "Lara, dear, when you get older you'll see that everything isn't always so black and white. It's the difficult shades of gray in between that we have to learn to live with. Yes, your father was right, but he's gone, and keeping the Taggarts as enemies won't bring him back or make us any more right than we are. Isn't it enough that we're successful now?"

"No. We have to be the best. It's what Dad wanted. He taught me how and I want to do it. Oh, Mother . . ."

"Isn't he just the nicest . . . ?" interrupted Jennifer, coming into the kitchen. "Isn't he just . . ."

"No, he isn't," said Lara coldly. "He's a Taggart."

"Oh, Lara." Jennifer grimaced distastefully.

"Why don't you go on up to your room and get settled in?" said Harriet gently. "Everything's been cleaned and aired for you. You're home now, Lara. Please, can't you enjoy your homecoming?"

"Oh, Mama, I'm sorry. It's just that . . . Dad . . . everything's changed . . ."

"I know," said Harriet softly. "But we're still here. We're your family. We'll manage."

Lara rose and kissed her mother's upturned cheek. "Yes, we will, won't we? And I really am glad to be home. You'll never know how glad . . ."

Harriet sat at the kitchen table, staring into the middle distance, thinking. The room was beginning to warm as the fire caught and crackled cheerfully in the old wood stove. The chores could wait a little while . . .

How could she ever get through Lara's stubbornness? Her daughter was so like Frank it was absolutely eerie. She had made Jennifer promise not to tell Lara of the visits Joe Taggart had paid her since Frank had died. After all these years, Joe had come to see her. His wife had been dead for years; now Frank was dead too. But what had been white-hot passion between them once had been eroded by the years of hard work, worry, children, and changed into simple friendship. She quaked to think of Lara's reaction if she knew.

As for Harriet herself, she only wanted a secure, peaceful life. She would really like to sell the ranch and live in Denver City, surrounded by civilized comforts—plays, concerts, eligible young men for Jennifer and Lara. Perhaps a nice new house, a bit of style, shops and paved streets and people. She didn't have the mental energy to run the ranch, nor any desire to do so. Joe had offered her excellent money for the land; she could accept his offer and move to Denver City. Joe was making it easy for her. Yet, in a way, his thoughtfulness made her situation impossible. How could she sell the ranch that Frank had slaved over for so many years to his deadly enemy?

After those first few difficult years with Frank, she had never asked him how he felt. She knew. It was in his expression every time he looked at the child that wasn't his. He tried. He was kind, understanding—he loved her.

But the wound to his pride never quite healed. He didn't take it out on the child—not exactly—but he hated Joe Taggart with every bit of energy he possessed. All in all, they'd had a happy life; she never once regretted marrying Frank. He worked hard, he made the ranch successful after her father died, he raised the children well and fairly. He was one of the first men in the valley to import Hereford cattle from the East and to breed a better beef cow. He searched for and finally found his half-thoroughbred pinto stallion that many of the valley's ranchers had put their mares to. He was a good man, a good father, a good husband.

And now he was gone and Harriet had to deal with these problems alone.

She couldn't bear to tear Lara from the home she loved—not when she'd just returned. She hated to keep Jennifer here, frustrated, wanting the bright city lights, parties, a husband. She had to be fair to both of them.

And what of Craig? What if he ever returned and wanted the ranch? Maybe it was better he was gone. He'd always hated ranching, preferred his time in the little schoolhouse, preferred hanging around Doc Tichenor's surgery in town when he'd moved there.

Her motherly heart ached for Craig—so unhappy, so ill-fitted to the life Frank had cut out for him. She prayed he'd found happiness wherever he was; she prayed he'd forgotten his ill-fated marriage, the poor girl's death, the whole nightmarish episode. Yes, he was better off somewhere else, far from this valley, far from the twisted seeds of fate that he had never planted but that he had reaped. Life had a way of making the innocent suffer, Harriet mused sadly. She wondered, as she had for twenty-one years now, if Joe knew. He had to know; it was so obvious. Maybe someday, when they were both so old they were beyond earthly cares, she would ask him. . . .

The girls were coming back downstairs. Harriet roused herself and began to think about dinner. She'd have to put the roast in soon or it would never be done in time. And there was the bread to bake. . . .

Chapter Four

LARA PULLED ASIDE THE LACE-EDGED CURTAIN OF HER
bedroom window and grinned inadvertently to herself at
the bright blue morning sky. It was spring.

She could see the barn and corral from her window,
the breakfast smoke rising from the bunkhouse chimney,
the silvery green tips of sagebrush that dotted the land
rising gently toward the foothills to the west. It was the
same scene she'd viewed from her window for all of her
life, except for the last two years at Mrs. Bryant's, and
it was overwhelmingly familiar, achingly sweet to her
eyes.

She dropped the curtain, hugged herself, and danced
a few light steps around the room, her straight black hair
swinging heavily against her back. "Home! I'm really
home," she whispered to herself.

Quickly, decisively, she opened her wardrobe, pushed
aside all the new "city" clothes she'd brought home from

St. Louis and dug in the back of the closet for a moment. Yes, it was still there, the bundle of Craig's old clothes that she'd "borrowed" once and never returned. She shook out the faded plaid shirt, the worn blue denims and eyed them critically. They'd do.

She pulled on the shirt and buttoned it, surprised at how it pulled so tautly across her bust. But, after all, it had been two years. Then the pants. They felt strange after so long in skirts, but she knew they were the only practical thing to wear for the day's work ahead of her. The trousers fitted snugly on her hips, tighter than they'd been before she left for St. Louis. Funny, she hadn't seen the change in her own body, but she guessed it had happened too gradually for her to notice.

She turned her back to the mirror over her bureau and craned her neck to see how the pants looked from the rear. Well, they'd do, but she certainly didn't look like a cowboy. She curved too much, for one thing, and stuck out in back a bit too much, for another. It irritated her vaguely. What she really wanted was to look like one of the ranch hands, to fit right in, to be the young, carefree girl who'd ridden the acres of Bitter Creek with her father all those years. She pulled the tails of the plaid shirt out of the waistband and let them hang down to her hips. There, that was better; her curves were hidden. The men would never notice. Quickly, she twisted her heavy black hair into a coil and pinned it up, pushing her wide-brimmed hat down to cover it all.

"Lara?" She heard a tap on her door.

"Come in, Jennifer," she called.

The door opened. Jennifer stuck her head in. "You up . . . ?" she began. Then she gave a gasp. "You're not going to . . . You're not!" she wailed.

"Not what? Quit screeching," laughed Lara.

"Wear that, that . . . outfit!" cried Jennifer. "It's disgraceful. Mother will have fits."

"Mother *never* has fits, Jenn, you know that. And if I'm going out with Shad today, well, you know it's the only practical thing to wear." She paused, then narrowed amused eyes at her sister. "I suppose *you'd* wear a velvet riding habit and feathers and go sidesaddle!"

"Well, at least a skirt . . ."

"Pish tosh! Ridiculous. If I'm going to be a cowboy, I better dress like one."

"Who says you're going to be a *cowboy?*" asked Jennifer disdainfully.

"I do."

"You can't. It's shameful. Whoever heard of a lady cowboy? You'll be the laughing stock of Rifle. People will *talk!*"

"Let them." Lara tossed her head carelessly. "Someone has to keep an eye on things around here."

"Shad does that."

"Well, Shad can't do everything. Daddy worked hard and now he's gone, so I'll have to. Mama's busy and you prefer the household chores."

"Of course I do, Lara. It's not my place to go out riding like a man!"

"Well, it is *my* place."

"Ooh, you're so stubborn!"

"I think the word Daddy used was *determined,*" laughed Lara over her shoulder, going down the stairs to the kitchen.

"Mama! Good morning. Oh, it's so good to be home! Those biscuits smell wonderful. I'm famished!"

Harriet pulled a pan of golden brown biscuits out of the oven, popped them in a basket, and turned around to face her younger daughter.

Her full lips pursed, her straight brows drew together. "Lara . . ."

"Mama, don't start on me. Jenn's already read me the riot act."

"And so she should have."

"I promise I'll only dress like this here, on the ranch. No one will ever know. The men are used to it. They don't care."

"Lara, you're a lady now. They'll notice. Some of the hands are new . . ."

"Then . . . I'll stay clear of them. Besides, everyone looks the same on a horse. Please don't scold."

"Well . . . I never could make you listen to reason if you had your mind made up. Your father spoiled you." Suddenly Harriet's voice went very soft. She turned and busied herself at the stove.

"Mama. He didn't spoil me. He taught me to be a rancher, to take care of the land and the cattle and horses. It's important and I want to do it. It's *worthwhile.*"

Harriet turned again and faced her intense dark-haired daughter. "I know." She smiled gently. "You do what you must. It'll work out. We'll try it for a while and see."

"Thanks, Mama. I knew you'd understand." Lara grabbed some biscuits and took a bite out of one. "I'm going over to the bunkhouse to see Shad. Wouldn't want to miss him!" And with a mischievous twinkle in her eye, she was gone, banging the door behind her exactly like she had when she was ten years old.

Harriet sighed and turned back to the stove, a small furrow of worry between her straight, golden brows.

* * *

The afternoon sun threw the long shadow of the barn across the dirt-packed, muddy ground where the hitching posts stood. The ranch hands dragged heavy saddles off their horses' sweaty backs and let them slide to the ground with the slap of well-worn leather fittings. Each mount seemed to give a sigh of relief and some shook themselves like dogs, jingling their bridles. One by one, they were led to the gate and slapped off into the field to graze and roll in the soft, soothing mud.

"There, Miss Lara," said Shad Harper, hooking the gate behind the last horse. "Better git on up to the house. Your Mama'll be wondering what took you so darn long."

"Well, she'll have to get used to it. I'm going to ride out with you whenever there's work to be done, Shad."

"Can't say's we don't need help, miss, but I ain't atall sure you're the right *kind*, if you get my drift." A crooked smile appeared on the old foreman's weathered face, softening his words and showing his real affection for Lara.

"Shad Harper," replied Lara quickly, "the day I can't do a good lick of work and keep up with any of you, you let me know and I'll quit."

"Now, Miss Lara, you know 'taint that. Yer Dad sure taught you good. But the men ain't use to it, y'unnerstan'."

"No, I don't understand. But they'll get used to it," she replied. "They'll have to."

"Sure, Miss Lara, I guess so. These here men'll git used to almost anything, I reckon, 'long as the grub's good and their wages come on time. *And* they git Saturday nights in Rifle." He cocked his head and grinned at her, showing long yellow teeth, then pulled a little sack of tobacco from his shirt pocket and began rolling a cigarette automatically, hardly watching his fingers. "Anyhow, it's sure good to have you back, miss."

"It's good to be back, Shad. I'll never leave again."

"Ha! Aincha gittin' hitched ever? Yer husband'll want you to leave here. Ever thought on that?" Shad lit a wooden match, striking it on the sole of his boot. His gnarled, work-roughened hands cupped the flame as he held it to his cigarette.

"Not much, really. There's no one here I'm interested in. I may never get married," Lara replied thoughtfully.

"Fat chance, Miss Lara. You'll get hitched someday, and not so far off either. Mark my words."

"Oh, Shad!" Lara felt strangely embarrassed talking about marriage with the old foreman. "You're silly."

He winked at her with amusement, then said, "Come on in the barn fer a minute. There's somethin' I want to show ya." He led the way.

Inside the barn, in a stall, was one of the Claytons' chestnut mares, Goldy.

"Oh, Shad!" Lara cried with delight. "She's so close."

The mare was quite obviously ready to give birth any day. "Yeah. I was 'fraid of another spring storm so I put her in here this morning. I'd be 'bilidged if you'd stay close by tomorrow 'cause I got some heavy fence fixin' up on the north hundred. Me an' the boys won't be back till late."

"I'd be glad to," replied Lara honestly. There was nothing quite so wonderful as a birth.

Shad left for the bunkhouse then while Lara stood patting Goldy's brown nose and talking gently to her. It had been a hard day riding the land, checking the cattle and fences. Lara felt the hours in the saddle, absently rubbed at a sore spot on her bottom. Soon she'd be used to it again, though, and it made her heart swell with pride to know she was able to do a good day's work alongside the men.

She walked back across the yard toward the ranch house, her eyes scanning the buildings and the rangeland beyond. Bitter Creek was a ranch to be proud of—it was everything she had ever wanted and it was a marvelous feeling to have returned home and to know where she belonged.

Smiling to herself, she glanced up and saw smoke from the chimney, smelled freshly baked bread filling the air with its secure aroma. Yes—it was good to be home. . . .

It was late by the time the dishes were washed and dried and put away. The kerosene lamp flung streams of yellow flickering light over the table, glinting off the surface of the dark coffee still warm in the three cups.

Lara sighed and pushed her chair away from the table. "Mama, that was good."

"Thanks, dear." Harriet caught Jennifer's pointed look and nodded imperceptibly. "Lara, dear, there's something we want to discuss with you . . ."

"Oh, no, not my pants again," laughed Lara. "I'm too tired to argue."

"No, dear, not that."

"What is it, Mama?"

"Well . . ." The pause stretched out too long. Harriet plunged in. "We've had a very generous offer for Bitter Creek."

"What?" Lara's head snapped up, her green eyes turned dark, hooded.

"Someone wants to buy the ranch. He's offered a very fair price. We . . . I'm seriously considering it."

"You can't mean it!"

"I knew you'd feel that way, Lara, but the fact remains that three women without a husband or brother among them cannot run a huge ranch like this."

"I *can,* Mother, I *can.* Why don't you trust me? Let me try before you throw it all away!"

"I would hardly be 'throwing it all away,' Lara. I could go to Denver City and live well the rest of my life, have a nice house, entertain, let you girls meet the right kind of people . . ."

"The right kind of people for me are here on this ranch, Mother," said Lara tightly, "not in Denver City. I just got home. Do you mean to drag me away again? Well, I won't go!"

Lara stood, scraping her chair legs harshly on the wooden floor. "And just who wants to buy the ranch? Some Eastern dude or English gentleman who wants to play at being a cattle baron?" she asked bitterly.

"No, dear. Joseph Taggart wants to buy it," said Harriet softly, staring her angry daughter right in the eye.

"Taggart? Joseph Taggart?" Lara's face went as pallid as a daytime moon. "You couldn't," she whispered. "You're joking, Mama."

"No, I most certainly am not. And neither is Joe Taggart."

"Joe. I see. Now that Daddy's dead, it's *Joe* Taggart. Oh, my." She fought the threat of tears.

"Lara." Harriet rose and reached a hand out to stroke her daughter's dark head. "We have time to decide about this. It's a big move for us all. I just wanted you to know."

"Thanks so much. My homecoming is now complete," said Lara tearfully.

"I'm sorry you feel that way. For Jennifer and me it was a huge relief."

"Well, I hope I have time to convince you how wrong it

is, and that's what I'll try to do. Meanwhile, please refrain from mentioning the Taggart name in this house. You'll have Daddy turning over in his grave!" Lara delivered her speech in a high, thin voice that nearly broke at the end. She turned then and flung her way out of the kitchen and they could hear her run upstairs to her room.

"I told you, Mother," sighed Jennifer. "She's as stubborn as Daddy."

Dust motes stood out distinctly in the shaft of light that reached across the box stall as Lara leaned back on her heels and wiped her brow with her forearm. The mare, Goldy, had been in labor all night, apparently, and all morning, and there was something wrong. The foal was not crowning yet and poor Goldy was exhausted. Lara fought down a surge of panic and patted the mare's sweaty flank reassuringly. She could see Goldy's swollen belly strain to expel the foal and she could hear the mare's laboring breath. She felt so helpless.

"It must be breech," Lara whispered to herself.

She strained to remember what her father had told her about difficult births. She remembered a pulley and ropes and some complicated equipment from an occasion when Frank had delivered a breech calf.

"I'll be right back, Goldy," she said soothingly, then darted out of the stall to the tack room. Yes, there was the pulley with a hook to attach it to the wall and a tangle of ropes with looped ends to drag the reluctant foal into the world. Lara's heart beat furiously. She'd never done this by herself. Could she do it? She'd likely lose her prize mare and the foal if she couldn't.

Darn that Shad Harper! He'd gone off to mend some fences one of the boys had reported broken and wouldn't be back until late. There was no one to help her.

When she'd asked her sister, Jennifer had only made a face and smoothed her cornflower blue dress over her hips. And Harriet was busy, as usual, in the house.

She set up the pulley, stretched the rope across the stall, and took a deep breath. "I've gotta do it, Goldy. Hope I don't hurt you."

Steeling herself, she reached into the mare and felt for the tiny hoofs. Yes, there they were! She slipped the loops around the foal's legs and tightened them. She ran back to the pulley and began to pull on the rope until the ropes were straining, until her back was nearly broken trying to drag the foal into the light of day. But still Goldy lay gasping on the straw and the foal didn't budge.

Finally, exhausted and breathless, Lara sank onto the straw and gave a sob of frustration. She needed help. She couldn't do it herself. Oh, where was Shad or one of the hands? Why didn't they get back?

Then she heard hoofbeats outside and her heart gave a glad leap. Someone was riding up to the barn! One of the boys must have returned early! Thank God.

She rushed out just in time to hear Jennifer's voice call out from across the yard to the rider, "Why, hello! I didn't expect to see you so soon again." There was a tone to her voice that Lara found vaguely disconcerting. Who was it? She rounded the corner of the barn. Her heart froze.

Leading the Clayton's mount he had borrowed, Branch Taggart was reining his own horse up to where Jennifer stood. He was leaning forward casually over the pommel of the saddle, saying something to her.

Seeing his easy manner, Lara's stomach rolled over with anger. He came riding in here so cool and casual, just as if he owned the place already! He wouldn't have dared when Frank Clayton was alive!

She wasn't sure how long she stood there in the gilded afternoon sun eyeing Jennifer and Branch, but it was some time before he seemed to sense another presence in the yard and turned slowly toward Lara.

Standing her ground, she met his easy gaze coolly. The moment stretched out and Lara had the odd sensation that they were the only two people in the world.

The sun suddenly seemed terribly warm as tiny beads of perspiration formed on her brow; she felt slightly dizzy, queasy.

And then finally Branch moved, raising his free arm to tip his hat politely. As he did so, his cool blue eyes traveled leisurely from her face downward and then back slowly again. "Afternoon, Miss Lara," he drawled smoothly. "Brought your horse back."

Still feeling the effect of his eyes measuring her, as if he had stripped off her clothes, Lara refused to even give him the benefit of an answer. Straight backed, she turned on her heel and disappeared back into the barn.

"Your sister seems a little out of sorts, doesn't she?" Branch turned his gaze back to Jennifer.

"Oh, please excuse Lara's behavior. Sometimes she's so rude. Would you like to come in for a cup of coffee? And I think Mama baked this morning . . ." Jennifer's round blue eyes gazed up at him admiringly. Her honey-blond curls were arranged perfectly, her dress flattered her neat figure.

Branch smiled winningly, dismounted, and began tying the horses to the rail. A cup of coffee sounded just fine and Jennifer Clayton's invitation was plainly genuine. But Lara Clayton? That was another matter altogether. Perhaps he should go . . .

But, on the other hand, Branch reasoned, why should he leave just because that little raven-headed chit disliked him? In fact, he recalled quickly, she had always been tight-lipped and unsmiling whenever he'd seen her around Rifle before her schooling. Seems she hadn't changed then.

He patted the mounts on their rumps, loosened their girths. He glanced toward the barn. No, he realized abruptly, he was wrong on one account—Lara had changed. From a scrawny young girl, her figure had rounded, turning her into a woman now—still thin, but there was no mistaking the swell of her hips nor the firm high breasts that rose and fell so noticeably when she was irritated. Perhaps, he mused lightly, he should go rile her some more . . .

Branch turned back to Jennifer. "Your sister always dress that way?" he asked casually.

"Oh, never mind Lara. She'd like to think she's a ranch hand. One of the mares is in there about to foal. Why don't you come into the house, though, and have a little something?"

"Maybe I'd better go see if she needs any help," he said, his blue eyes drifting toward the barn again. "I'll stop in a little later for that coffee, though, Miss Jennifer."

Lara pulled again on the rope, bracing her feet against the wall, heaving until she thought her arms would break. Nothing.

She squatted back on her heels to catch her breath. Suddenly she had an odd sensation as if someone had walked on her grave. Goose bumps rose on her flesh. With a gaze, she turned quickly on her heels to find Branch Taggart standing behind her, a casual shoulder resting against the open door of the stall, his hair golden where a sun shaft fell across it.

71

The sight of him standing there, so tall, seeming to fill the open space, snatched the breath from her throat.

What did he want? Words failed her utterly. She swallowed hard.

"Sorry I startled you," he offered in that deep, lazy tone. And those ice-blue eyes, lit now by the golden light streaming in from above, gave little away. He seemed to be at one instant measuring her, the next, mocking her, her attire, her position next to the struggling mare. And then she saw another look flash briefly in his eyes: could it have been admiration?

Unspeaking, Lara dropped her gaze back onto the mare.

"Looks like you need some help, Miss Lara," came his voice from above. "I have a little experience . . ."

She wanted desperately to turn him down, but she *did* need help, and the mare—Lara couldn't bear her suffering anymore. She was at the end of her resources. But without waiting for her reply, there was Branch, already rolling up his sleeves, entering the stall.

Silently he took over, as if he did this sort of thing every day, and then his clipped orders left her no room for argument. Finally Branch kneeled down by the mare and maneuvered something—she couldn't see what—then said, "Pull." Lara pulled on the rope, but this time she felt it give a little. Goldy's stomach heaved.

Branch's blond head was bent over; Lara could only see his broad back, the muscles under his shirt cording as he maneuvered the foal. "Again," he ordered, and Lara pulled.

The pulley creaked. There was a slippery sound, the mare blew, and Lara nearly sat down as the foal slid out, releasing the tension on the ropes.

"Got it!" said Branch. "Nice little filly." His voice was calm, pleased.

Lara knelt down by the newborn foal in the straw. It was a brown and white pinto, a beauty. Its thin, ribby chest heaved with life. Tears of joy came to her eyes.

Branch was rubbing the foal's wet sides with a gunny sack, pulling the baby onto its spindly legs. Goldy looked around, nickered, then accepted Branch's presence as if he weren't a stranger at all.

"There," said Branch finally, pushing the foal toward its first meal. He turned and grinned disarmingly at Lara. "Not a bad job at all. Could have been very messy."

Lara stood stroking the still-wet neck of the baby as it nursed. The miracle of the foal's birth filled her with a kind of peace. She turned large, shining eyes to Branch, forgetting, for a moment, who he was. "Isn't she a beauty? Just like her daddy."

"Sure is," agreed Branch. "That old pinto of yours—the stud?"

"Yes."

"He's something to be proud of."

They stood then side by side in the stall, watching the foal nurse. A feeling of accomplishment filled Lara, a companionship with this person who had helped her bring the foal into the world, a marvelous simplicity.

"Thank you," she said softly, not daring to look up at him.

"Glad I came along," was his quiet reply. Then: "Come on. Let's go get that coffee your sister offered. I bet we could both use some."

He put an easy hand on the small of her back as they moved out of the stall. She felt a sudden weakness in the pit of her stomach at his touch, a coiling sensation that was alien to her. Inadvertently she looked up at Branch and her heart began an odd slow pounding at the sight of his strong profile. Her skin crawled strangely all over as he turned his head and glanced down at her, smiling.

Again, somewhere in her consciousness, Lara registered that he was the most totally virile man she had ever seen. And it was so much more than his handsome features, his powerful-looking frame, his lithe carriage—it was an all-encompassing strength and self-confidence.

At the door of the barn he removed his hand to swing open the door. Lara felt an odd loss, then just as quickly put it from her mind.

"I suppose," she found herself saying, "that we do at least owe you a cup of coffee . . . something . . ." Oh, Lord, she realized, she hadn't meant it to come out that way.

Branch shot her a bemused look for a long moment. "I think I'll pass on it, but thanks."

"Well, then . . ." The words fumbled on her lips. "I suppose I should go on in . . . change clothes . . ." That was worse! Now *he* knew that she was conscious of her unfeminine attire. Oh, blast, she thought, frowning, what did she give a hoot what he thought anyway!

She began crossing the wide yard separating the house and barn. He could find his own way over to his horse. She had already thanked him—for a Taggart, that was enough!

Suddenly, however, she heard him speak her name. "Lara," came a soft, easy drawl.

She turned slowly back to face him. He was striding toward her. Again she felt the power of his presence. "Yes?" she managed to reply.

He stood over her; a brow quirked. "I'm sure it's been

difficult at Bitter Creek since your father died," he stated flatly. "Ranching is not for women."

Lara's eyes snapped up to meet his appraising gaze. "I . . . I could have pulled the foal free. I was getting tired, that's all." He met her stumbling explanation with cool silence. "Ranching is really quite simple," she went on uneasily. "I've been doing it all my life. I can ride a horse better than most men, too," she finished while tilting her small chin up.

"Is that a fact?"

"Yes."

His glance fell to the opening in her shirt—the V formed above the top button—then back to meet her eyes. "You're an attractive woman, Lara." A smile curved his lips—a smile that never reached his eyes. "Has your mother mentioned our offer?"

So that was it! Lara's green eyes flashed brilliantly. Her breast rose and fell with sudden anger. "Yes," she whispered—almost a hiss. "Mother mentioned it."

"And don't you think it's a reasonable solution to your problems?"

"I certainly do not!" Her voice rose. "I can run this ranch just as well as my father did and we sure don't need any help from you Taggarts!"

A low, inadvertent chuckle escaped him. "Sorry if I've upset you . . ."

"I'm not upset!" How dare he laugh at her! "Now, I think you just better leave, *Mr.* Taggart." Her cheeks were flushed red with anger, her hands clenched into fists at her sides.

Branch hesitated as if there was something more he wanted to say, but then he seemed to change his mind, a slight smile still etched on his lips.

"Yes, ma'am," he said mildly, tipping his hat politely, then he turned his broad muscular back on her and strode to his horse, swinging himself effortlessly into the saddle and reining his mount away.

"Where's he going?" cried Jennifer from the porch, startling Lara. "I had plum cake and coffee all ready for him."

"He's going home," Lara gritted out.

"Oh, you fool!" wailed Jennifer.

Lara still stood in the yard staring after Branch, staring at the slight trail of dust his horse had left hanging in puffs above the road. Suddenly she felt deflated, exhausted. She wondered if she weren't, indeed, just that—a fool.

Chapter Five

IT MIGHT HAVE BEEN A DREAM: RAISED VOICES AND MEN shouting against a strange roar reached deep into Lara's mind and reluctantly roused her from sleep.

It seemed more like a nightmare.

She opened her eyes. Again the voices—rushed, clearly panicked—reached her ears.

"Get the buckets!" came a cry knifing through a momentary still.

"Jesus . . . it's too late!" That was Shad's voice—she recognized the gruff tone.

And then, almost simultaneously, the distinct, sharp odor of burning wood and hay reached her nostrils. She rushed from her bed to the window.

Her heart clutched sickeningly—the barn was ablaze! Towering flames leaped into the awakening sky. Huge black billows of smoke were silhouetted against the soft oyster pearl of dawn.

Unthinking of her fine white linen nightgown, she raced from her room, barely stopping to bang on her mother and sister's doors, and was in the yard finding a spot in the hastily gathered bucket line.

Shad Harper was next to her in a moment. "Got most of the horses out," he shouted over the deafening roar of the fire. "All of 'em, in fact, Miss Lara, 'cept . . ."

And she knew. "The stud!" came a cry of anguish torn from her throat. "Oh, my God . . ." Her stricken green eyes turned up to his wizened face, then back to the burning barn. "Old Paiute . . ."

Shad shook his head. "I'm real sorry, miss, real sorry," he called painfully over the fire's thunder while taking another heavy bucket from her hands.

The poor beast. Lara felt sweat suddenly drip from her brow into her eyes; the orange mass of flame became an indistinct blur of undulating color; the heat from the blaze seared her skin, making the flesh on her face and arms feel as if it were curling up like burning paper.

Buckets of water, dozens of them, passed through her hands and on down the line while images of their pinto stud flashed through her mind.

Perhaps, she kept praying, Shad was wrong—maybe the horse escaped. And then, unbidden, she almost imagined she could hear his frantic cries, see the fear in those wild white eyes. Dear Lord, how he must have suffered—how horrible a death. Lara's arm began to shake involuntarily between buckets; her muscles spasmed from the labor. It seemed to be getting even hotter. If only, she thought, the sweat would stop—the salt seemed to make the burning far worse. And the never-ending roar from the blaze—it was deafening, horrible, sounding as if a tornado were caught in a tunnel.

Still the fire blazed uncontrollably—twisted spirals of orange flame piercing the sky. It was hopeless. They all knew it, but futilely continued to draw water from the well until heat from the morning sun mingled on their faces with that of the smoking rubble—the mass of embers and smoldering planks that had been the barn.

Harsh smoke filled her lungs, her face was oily and soot smeared, her hair, her nightgown were coal black, but Lara never once gave her appearance a thought. What filled her mind and sat oppressively in her stomach was a sense of loss, of terrible waste.

The barn, of course, at much expense, could be rebuilt, the other horses and the new foal were saved. It was the loss of Old Paiute, her father's pinto stallion, that caused hot tears of anguish to burn paths down her sooty cheeks. She would never be able to replace the stallion.

Slowly, while her family and the ranch hands watched helplessly, Lara walked nearer to the fire site, to the blackened ash and hot glowing embers that once stood so proudly.

Why? her mind cried. Why?

"Lara"—Harriet placed a consoling hand on her daughter's shoulder—"it's time to come into the house. There's nothing left to be done here now—we've done all we can."

Lara turned her head and looked into Harriet's eyes. Yes, her mother suffered the loss as deeply as she. "But the stud . . ."

"I know, dear, I know . . ."

They embraced each other then; the inevitable sobs came; their slender frames rocked gently while silence hung around them as if all the air had suddenly been swept from the valley.

* * *

Harriet silently prepared breakfast for them and seated herself, along with Jennifer, to try to put some nourishment in their stomachs; there would be a lot of work to be done as soon as the embers died. They would clear away the rubble and begin anew. Life went on—there was the bad and there was the good.

Only Lara remained standing, dressed and washed now, eyeing the scene from the kitchen. Tight white lines creased her brow; her hands hung at her sides in fists. "Shad," she said clearly, her voice controlled, "how do you figure it started?"

Shad placed his fork down slowly; the clink it made against the plate shook the air, causing heads to lower. "I figger a kerosene lamp musta been knocked over— somethin' like that. Maybe . . ."

"A lamp left burning all night?" Her words fell on the group like pebbles. "I doubt it seriously." Lara's fists clenched more whitely. "Who was the last to check the barn last night?"

"I was." Shad's gaze met her steadily.

"Then you left a lamp burning?"

"No."

He needn't have answered. She knew already that Shad would never, *never* have made such a grave mistake.

"That leaves only two other possibilities," whispered Lara vehemently. "One is that there was a storm and a bolt of lightning hit the barn, which, of course,"—she walked toward Shad now—"would have woken us all up. . . . And I think we all know the other possibility, don't we?"

A pregnant silence filled the room.

Harriet rose abruptly from her place next to Shad.

"No," she whispered, "no. What you're concluding is wrong, Lara—all wrong."

"I think not, Mother. I think you know it, too, and for some unfathomable reason you choose to hide the truth from yourself." Suddenly Lara spun away from the table, the skirt of her cotton print dress rustling as she went to the window, her eyes resting on the still smoking ruins. "I'm going to change clothes and ride into Rifle."

"But why? . . . Lara, no, please . . ." Desperation filled Harriet's voice.

"To see the deputy, Ned Lawson. And he *damned* well better do something about it this time!"

"Lara!" Harriet was shocked by her daughter's language.

"I don't care," cried Lara earnestly as she left the kitchen. "I really don't. I just want to see them pay!"

Clad in a yellow print cotton blouse and a leather skirt she had split and sewn to form full pant legs, Lara rode into Rifle astride her horse like a man. That eyebrows raised with indignation on the town streets at her attire mattered nothing whatsoever to her; she was too consumed with wrath to have taken the time for a ladylike buggy ride. The Taggarts would pay.

Dismounting in front of the deputy's office—the nearest sheriff was in Glenwood Springs—Lara strode in purposefully, not even bothering to close the door behind her.

Ned Lawson looked up from his desk; his dark eyes took in her riding skirt, her whole appearance, then quickly shrank away to a spot over her shoulder. "Yes? Miss Clayton, isn't it? What can I do . . . ?"

"You can arrest those Taggarts!" Her rage surfaced,

boiling over like hot lava onto a suddenly bewildered Ned Lawson. "They're criminals!"

"What?" Taken aback, he rose quickly to his feet. "Now listen, miss—you can't just come in here like this and accuse someone of that. And besides . . . what did they do?" A bushy brow rose.

"They set our barn on fire . . . around dawn. Our stallion was killed. . . . He was priceless!" Tossing her hair like a smooth ebony mane over her shoulder, Lara half spat, "I want them charged with arson! And I want our stallion replaced before they go to jail!" And then she ached to tell Lawson about hearing their name through the wall the night of the murder at the Winchester Hotel—tell him about the man in the Stetson and that Branch had been wearing one, too. But she couldn't— Ned Lawson would ask her why she hadn't come forward sooner and she'd have to tell him how flimsy her suspicions were.

Instead, she cried, "I want them arrested!"

"Now look here, Miss Clayton—you can't come in my office like this and demand I arrest one of the pillars of our community. Just who do you think you are?"

A small gasp escaped her lips. "Don't you believe me? Do you want to ride out to Bitter Creek and see what's left of our barn for yourself?" Challenge sparked like sunlit emeralds from her eyes. "I want them arrested!"

With a deep breath Lawson came from around his desk to stand over Lara. "I'm not sayin' your barn *didn't* burn—not at all—but to accuse someone of arson is a grave matter, miss. You got proof of this accusation?" Now Lawson's eyes challenged her.

Lara was speechless. Proof? What proof did she need? Who else would have done it? "You know they did it . . . everyone knows it! It's just that no one around these parts has the guts to stand up to Joe Taggart and his empire. Well, I do," she finished defiantly.

Ned Lawson's back stiffened perceptibly. "Now you get this through that pretty little head of yours, miss. What everyone around here *does* know is that your father and Taggart were feuding for years, far back as anyone can recall. But Frank's gone now and it's all over . . . buried. Taggart's got no reason to burn your barn and that's the truth of it. Feud was between Frank and Joe. Let it go, girl, it's over . . ."

"It's not over, Mr. Lawson. Far from it. Taggart wants our land. He needs that water hole that's on our property. Everyone knows that. Ever since my dad put up fences, he's been cut off from it and it's hurting his profits. He's been trying to buy us out and now he's trying to burn us out!"

"I'd be guessin', miss, that after your pa died Joe Taggart did the neighborly thing by making your ma a fair offer. Joe Taggart, whether or not you believe it, is a good, decent man. He's as honest as they come 'round here."

Lara could not believe her ears—was *everyone* in this valley ignorant of the facts? A decent man? An honest man? Good Lord!

Exasperated, furious beyond control, she strode to the open door. "Pardon me for saying so, Mr. Lawson, but you're blind. . . . You're all blind if you can't see him for the thieving crook he is!" And with that off her chest, she rushed out, red splotches of fury staining her cheeks while she remounted, jerked the reins roughly, and gave her horse a good solid kick.

Her mother, Jennifer, and now the deputy—they all

treated her like a spoiled little child! But she wasn't. She knew the rules of life, knew them as well as her father had. If Frank Clayton were still alive, folks would stand up and listen when he spoke.

But not her. They all treated her like an inconsequential adolescent, telling her things like, "You'll understand when you're older." How absurd! Oh, perhaps she wasn't as worldly as some her age, but when it came to the reality of the ranch, she did not delude herself.

Returning to Bitter Creek, Lara's fury abated momentarily at seeing the hands already clearing away the smoking rubble with their shovels. Hopefully by summer there would be a new barn. They would survive, she knew, and at least it wasn't the house that had burned.

Avoiding the ranch hands, she entered the house. The last thing she wanted was to admit her defeat with Ned Lawson; it would undermine her already precarious position with the men here.

She walked up the stairs to the landing. What would her father have done?

"You're back!" Jennifer came from her own room, placing an arm around Lara's waist. "What happened? Is Lawson going to arrest Joe Taggart?"

They walked to Lara's bedroom. "No. Like everyone else around here"—she cast Jennifer a quick sidelong glance—"he thinks Taggart is just wonderful . . . 'a pillar of the community,' he even said." Frustrated, she plumped herself on the bed.

"It seems to me that just yesterday you yourself were enjoying a Taggart's company." Jennifer sat at the dressing table, keeping her gaze on Lara. "Well? Admit it."

Oh, God, Jennifer was right. For all of Lara's faults, dishonesty with herself was not one of them. It was true, she had for a few moments enjoyed the nearness to

Branch, and, she admitted with great self-loathing, there had even been something more than enjoyment.

The deputy's words came back to her: ". . . did the neighborly thing." Hadn't Branch just yesterday rolled up his sleeves and helped bring the struggling foal into this world? Why? And then to burn down the barn! Perhaps he knew nothing about it. Perhaps it was just his father alone whose hatred would not die. Branch's image suddenly filled her mind—crystal blue eyes, sharp and intelligent, yet seeming to hold some part of himself back, something he kept hidden from the world. And there was a powerful aura always surrounding him—a physical strength, yes, but more, much more. It was total, undeniable virility.

Still musing silently, unaware of Jennifer's interest, Lara felt a slight tremor seize her stomach while Branch Taggart's image drifted in and out of her consciousness. It was funny how you recalled little things about a person— things you hadn't actually paid any mind to at the time: a muscle working in a jaw, the way a person's hair fell naturally at the collar, the firm look of a thigh beneath jeans. Was it the small things that brought an image to mind?

Lara's stomach tingled again. She had felt these strange tremors before, but only at night in the privacy of her room at Mrs. Bryant's and only when her thoughts drifted unbidden into a fantasy: Lara would be seated in a carriage, a terribly strong, handsome man next to her, no escort. He would slip an arm around her waist, draw her closer; his lips would begin to descend. . . .

The fantasy touched her mind now, then fled. It was true; the make-believe man *did* somewhat resemble Branch Taggart, but there the likeness ended. *Her* man was kind and soft-spoken, strong and protective yet wonderfully gentle. There was no hunger for power, no arrogance. Still, Branch did fit a lot of the bill—everything but what the Taggart power had bred into him: total lack of humility and respect for his fellowman.

"He does have a lot in his favor," mused Lara aloud.

"He certainly does." Jennifer's face lit up.

Suddenly Lara was embarrassed. "I only meant, Jenn, that he's becoming just as powerful and arrogant as his father."

"I know what you meant." Jennifer twisted on the chair and began toying with a honey-colored ringlet of hair. "He is . . . well, he's so well proportioned, so handsome that . . ."

"I don't care to talk about Branch Taggart, Jennifer!" she interrupted harshly, anger again boiling in her veins. "Don't you realize that they burned our barn? Destroyed our stud? And I don't care if Branch was involved or not. He's a Taggart and he'll always be one."

Jennifer rose, unperturbed. "You're so blind, Lara. He's obviously interested in you, and if it were me . . ."

"I want to be alone," Lara countered quickly, closing the conversation, which was leading into disquieting territory.

"All right." Jennifer went to the door. "And, Lara . . . Mother and I are both just as upset over the barn and Dad's stallion. You're not the only one who cares about Bitter Creek."

Once she was gone, Jennifer's words hung oppressively in the still air. It was true, they did care about the land, but not for the same reason as Lara did; she had an inborn passion for the richness of her life on the range whereas her mother and Jennifer saw the ranch only as a tool to fulfill their dream: to sell the land at a profit and move to the city. Yet she honestly couldn't blame them. Life here was lonely and raw if you cared for social niceties, and Jennifer did deserve more; she was a lovely woman and men would no doubt flock around her in a big city. But not here. There were too few unattached or suitable men. And Harriet? She was still young and attractive—perhaps she would someday remarry if given the chance to meet someone. Funny, she hadn't thought of those things before.

Walking to her window, Lara looked down over the yard to where the barn had stood. Was she wrong to want to keep the ranch? Was it fair to her family? Yet the fact remained that someone—most definitely Joe Taggart —was trying to force them to sell. And *that* was unjust!

If Lara were experiencing a twinge of guilt over her staunch love for the land only moments before, it was replaced abruptly by a surge of anger welling up once again in her breast. They must be forced to pay. If only she had the nerve to confront them, to let them know that she had matches, too. If it was a fight they wanted . . .

But how could she confront them? She was furious enough to ride over there this minute and have it out, but surely words would fail her. Could she face that shame? If only, she thought for the hundredth time, she were more like Jennifer: if only the precise thing to say would come to her at the right time.

And then the question brushed her mind again: what would her father have done, what words would he have used on Joe Taggart to bring the man to his knees?

She simply had to put aside this futile anger and gather her wits about her. She could do it; she was Frank Clayton's daughter: proud, intelligent, strong. Yes, all she had to do was form the words of confrontation in her thoughts now, practice them, and she'd do just fine.

Slowly, like tiny seeds shedding their cumbersome casings, the words began to grow in her mind until Lara could clearly envision herself standing in front of old Joe Taggart, holding her own, telling him precisely what was on her mind.

Chapter Six

THE ROAD THAT LED FROM BITTER CREEK TO THE
Taggart place was straight as a shot along the river valley
through the sere, ocher landscape until it reached the
snow-dusted foothills. Lara rode along it, alternately
seething inside and terrified at her own audacity. Was she
really going to confront the Taggarts in their own staunch
fortress of a house? Did she really have the nerve?
Forcing her fears back into their secret, dark places, she
practiced her speech over and over until it came easily to
memory. She told herself that she could do it. Joe
Taggart, even if he despised her, would have to have
respect for his new adversary. The thought buoyed her.

The sun was beginning its downward curve into the
earth's sphere of influence; long, thin layers of afternoon
clouds rested on the horizon ready to be tinged by the
solar halo, and for a moment Lara forgot her own

emotional turmoil and watched the clouds turn pale pink, then magenta, then darker golden and lavender, splashed with deep red. It never failed to touch her—the sparse glory of the land. Somehow the beauty and wonder-filled familiarity of the scene sustained her in her intention. There was no one else to do it, to stand up for her mother and sister, to see that justice was done.

A cold black shadow suddenly slid swiftly across her path as she rode and it stole her breath. She gave a short laugh then; it was only Wolf Butte, throwing its long shadow toward her from the entrance to the Taggarts' ranch. She'd forgotten where she was for a second. But there ahead of her was the rough, precisely delineated land she knew so well and the clear, darkening mauve and gray sky silhouetting the strangely shaped red rock escarpment the Indians had called Wolf Butte.

Wolf Butte Ranch—officially named after the old Indian landmark, but always called the "Taggart Ranch," as if insinuating that the family who lived there were so powerful that the land could never be identified with anything but their name, the name that bespoke power, riches, cattle.

Fear burst in her heart again as she thought of really facing them. Would she see only the father, white-haired, aristocratic Joe, or would his sons be there too? Would Branch laugh at her again? He wouldn't dare!

Still, this had to be done. She couldn't let them get away with this latest atrocity.

As she recognized the entrance to the Taggart Ranch, the high, square gateway with the silhouette of Wolf Butte up at the top of the crossbar, she tried once again to pull her thoughts together, but her heart beat furiously and her hands were slippery wet on the reins.

The clear evening light was dimming, sending long

shadows out to reach for her. A sudden movement out of the corner of her eye made her give a sharp gasp, but then she realized it was only a clump of tumbleweed, a round bundle of dead sagebrush, rolling across the road in the evening breeze. She laughed to herself weakly, relieved.

What did I expect? she wondered. A guard with a gun? The wolf of the old Indian legend? The Taggart foreman, Sam Fuller, shaking his fist at me?

Her horse trotted down the wagon road that was lined with rows of newly planted cottonwood trees, a rare luxury in this brush-covered landscape. Lara thought of the water it must take to irrigate them and couldn't quite imagine it. It was one more nail in the elaborate structure of their great vision.

Her heart was a drumbeat in her ears, her stomach churned with nausea, but she was so close now, nearly there—she would not, *could* not turn back. She hadn't the courage to face herself if she turned around now and backed out. If they were to respect her, then first she had to respect herself.

The avenue of cottonwoods ended abruptly and then the unusual Southwestern-style house filled the scene. It was a long, low hacienda built of thick timber and stucco walls to withstand the hot destruction of the sun and the bitter slashing winter winds. The walls were white, shadowed now by the evening light, the roof aged pink tile; the windows, deeply recessed, were gleaming with candlelight like many-paned eyes, secretive, as if promising glories inside beyond ordinary human perception.

Lara dismounted and flung the reins casually over a hitching post with a great deal more confidence than she was feeling. She drew a deep, shuddering breath. It didn't help in the least. Suddenly she had no idea what she was going to say—not a clue. She'd go in there and make an utter fool of herself, mumbling and stammering. Well, too bad. She was here now and she'd have to go through with it. The words would come back.

She smoothed her heavy dark hair back to where the ribbon held it away from her face and tucked her yellow print shirt into the waistband of her leather skirt. It didn't matter what she looked like after all. She wasn't here to impress anyone; she was here to confront them and to warn them of her knowledge, to let them know that, no matter their influence, they couldn't get away with what they'd done.

She walked to the massive oak double front door, raised the heavy wrought-iron knocker and let it fall. The sound echoed in her ears like a death knell—final, irrevocable. She waited, standing as erect as she could, but all hollow fear inside.

But when the door opened, she was ready to do battle. All her fighting instincts had become aroused as she stood waiting, but it was only Concepción, the Taggarts' housekeeper, who stood there looking calm and unruffled into Lara's flushed face.

"Hello," Lara said.

"Can I help you?" The Mexican woman looked as if a ghost had ridden from the range.

"I'd like to see Mr. Taggart. Could you tell him, please? I'm Lara Clayton." She hoped her voice sounded strong and confident.

"The family's at dinner, Señorita Clayton. Are you . . . expected?"

"No. But I must speak to Mr. Taggart. It's quite . . . important," she ended lamely.

"Well." Clearly Concepción was in a quandary. "They're entertaining guests."

"Tell them I'm here," demanded Lara, her voice becoming louder than she wanted, beginning to sound shrill. To be held up at the door like a common drifter—this was too much!

"Just a minute," said Concepción, embarrassed.

"No, I won't wait." Lara pushed the doors open and walked into the flagstone-floored vestibule. "I think they'll talk to me."

"Señorita," whispered the housekeeper, scandalized.

And then a voice reached them from inside the house. "Concepción! What's going on? Is someone there?"

"Oh, Señor Taggart, it's only . . ."

"It's me, Mr. Taggart, Lara Clayton," she interrupted, sounding much more forceful than she'd expected, and to her own surprise, she strode past Concepción and followed the sounds of voices, clinking silverware, and the ring of fine crystal.

Lara was aware of Concepción following her, worried, trotting along next to her longer strides, afraid to try to stop her, clucking a string of Mexican phrases like a mother hen whose chicks are straying into danger.

Lara came to the end of the echoing hall. A large semicircular archway stood in front of her, the stone floor ended, and a bright Indian-patterned rug covered the floor. She raised her eyes and stepped into the room beyond the archway.

At first the candlelight from the wrought-iron chandelier blinded Lara and she had to blink her eyes until they adjusted to the light. Then she saw the table that almost filled the room and the remains of a sumptuous dinner on the heavy white linen tablecloth. The pale ovals of the faces that lined the table seemed to reflect back at her, wavering and uncertain in the light at first. Then her focus cleared and she saw them distinctly, each one of them.

And their politely shocked, surprised faces gave her a small unbidden surge of satisfaction.

At the head of the table sat Joe Taggart—much older-looking than she recalled—white haired, bushy browed, his deep-set blue eyes seeming to threaten her. Then there was Sam Fuller, her brother's father-in-law, glaring fiercely. There were several people she recognized faintly—the mayor of Rifle, the local doctor, and then two fair-headed young men—Robert and Guy Taggart, no doubt. Right of Joe was an unfamiliar face—a young woman, in her twenties perhaps. She was beautifully dressed; her hair struck Lara as too perfectly coiffed, each wave set in to make the best effect. Diamonds glinted in her ears and around her throat.

And next to her sat Branch Taggart.

Lara's eyes took the details in, registering each on her mind as if in a photograph that records everything unthinkingly, without judgment, until it is glanced at again some time in the future—the silver trays and candles, the gold-edged porcelain dishes, the snifters of brandy, coffee cups, stained and crumpled napkins.

And Branch Taggart's face, the only one that showed amusement, a slight smile on his lean lips, a teasing crinkle to his blue eyes. His look galled her, made her flush hotly up the back of her neck, and she glared coldly at him as if daring him to keep looking at her in that insolent way.

And then a strange thing happened. The scene around her faded to insignificance—the candle flames diffused, the faces melted into a pallid blur, the corners of the room dissolved in silence. It was as if she were looking through a tunnel at him: the sun-kissed, crisp blond hair, high, tanned forehead, the straight nose with slightly flared nostrils, the cruel, curved lips, the square, slightly heavy, but graceful line of his jaw and chin, but most of all his cool, ice-blue eyes, which met hers in a kind of merciless merriment, mocking her yet egging her on at the same time.

She suddenly felt gooseflesh rise on her body as if a cool breeze of premonition swept her. Quickly she wrenched her eyes from Branch's unflinching perusal and forced her gaze toward his father.

"Mr. Taggart," she breathed, finally breaking the spell of the silent, stop-motion scene, and suddenly she heard the rustle of clothing, the creaking of chairs, and the tinkle of silverware again.

"Why, Lara Clayton," said Joe, "I believe it's been years since I've seen you . . ."

"Father, I rather doubt that Miss Clayton came all the way out here to trade civilities," Branch cut in drily, his voice deep and lazy as he leaned back in his chair without taking his eyes off Lara.

"Just what is it you wanted to speak to us about, my dear?" asked Joe Taggart, still eyeing her steadily.

Lara drew a deep breath, only too aware of her dusty, wrinkled clothes in the face of these people's careless but impeccable elegance. None of that mattered, she reminded herself, clenching her hands into fists, trying again to stand straight and unflinching before the faces turned toward her. "Perhaps you'd prefer to speak to me in private, Mr. Taggart," she said, her voice sounding small and insignificant to her own ears. The big, high-ceilinged room seemed to make her voice echo.

"I can't imagine why," replied Joe Taggart. "I have no secrets from these people." And his large gnarled hand swept the air in an imperious gesture.

Well, then, thought Lara to herself, if you want it right out in front of the mayor and your family, you'll get it.

She felt the anger and misery of the terrible day fill her to overflowing, welling up from her very core.

"Mr. Taggart." Her voice was low and filled with emotion and she could feel the atmosphere in the room tense up instantly. "As you very well know, our barn burned to the ground early this morning . . . our prize stallion was killed . . ." She had to stop, finding it more difficult than she thought to remember the practiced words, but she cleared her throat and went on. "Ned Lawson thinks it was an accident . . . but I know better. It wasn't an accident. That barn was set on fire on purpose!" She heard a gasp of surprise and the beautiful girl sitting next to Branch turned to him with a frown on her brow, but he was still staring unblinkingly at Lara and didn't seem to notice the girl's look.

"Now, Miss Clayton, what on earth makes you think that? I've never heard of anything so . . ."

"Ridiculous, Mr. Taggart? Not at all. We both know, don't we, that you've always wanted to get rid of us Claytons? You've been trying to get hold of that water hole ever since we fenced it in. But you couldn't do it, could you? It's ours legally—an oversight on your part. And then there was no other way but to . . . burn us out!"

A louder gasp this time; the strange girl put her slim, ring-laden hand on Branch's arm and old Joe Taggart half rose from his seat. "You've come unhinged, girl," he growled, settling heavily back into his chair.

A gruff voice broke the awkward silence. "Mr. Taggart, you want me to show her out?"

Lara's eyes snapped around to the author of the voice. It was Sam Fuller, his old hatred of her family evident in his threatening expression.

She shifted a nervous glance back to Joe Taggart, wondering, but he only shook his head negatively.

"No, Sam, let her speak her piece. She'll be done soon." And old Joe settled back and folded his gnarled hands across his stomach, waiting.

The candles on the table seemed to flicker, casting eerie shadows on the wall, and Lara could hear her breath whistling painfully in her throat. But the heat of battle gripped her—she hadn't finished yet.

"Yes, you did it, or one of your hirelings, and you think you've won because no one will dare fight you, you're so influential!" She spat out the words and found herself walking up to the table, leaning over it on her arms, thrusting herself into the middle of the dinner party. She never even gave a thought to the embarrassment she must be causing the other guests—she just didn't care anymore. "But I'm not through. I may be the only Clayton left with the guts to fight you, but you'll find that I'm not so helpless as you think!"

She stopped for a moment to catch her breath, and then she heard a low, drawling voice coming from the table to her right.

She whirled to face it and found herself staring directly into Branch Taggart's keen, level blue eyes again.

"Miss Clayton, I'm afraid you're overwrought, and really, there's no need for all this."

"No need?" She felt her breast heaving with anger, her cheeks burn with indignation.

"I sympathize fully with your loss, Miss Lara, but this is not the place . . ." His low indolent voice filled her with fury.

"Then where is the place?" she asked, trying to keep her voice from breaking.

Branch turned to Joe. "Dad, reckon I'll handle this. If you'll excuse me, everyone?" He rose, pushing his chair back, and came around the table; as he strode toward her he seemed to grow taller and taller with each stride, and bigger, too, until Lara thought his frame would blot out the whole scene and take everything over, and suddenly she felt like shrinking back from the over-whelming sense of power that surrounded him.

He put his hand on her arm and she felt a shock of fear and loathing and something else, too, where he touched her. "Please come this way, Lara," he said and some-how, against her will, her feet carried her out of the room and down the hall to where he led her, but she could still feel the place on her arm where he'd touched her burning and throbbing.

Then he opened an iron-studded, thick-planked door and ushered her in, turning up the lamp. "There," he said. "This will be a little . . . cozier."

"I didn't come here to be cozy," snapped Lara, standing nervously in the middle of the room, which was obviously a study, full of books and containing a big, dark desk piled with papers and several large overstuffed chairs. Above the hearth was the head of a bull elk—tremendous—and Lara knew somehow it was the largest trophy taken in the area.

"Please sit down, Lara," offered Branch, and he still had the almost lazy, taunting grin on his gracefully curved lips.

"I'd rather not." She poised herself as if for flight.

"Okay. Never mind. What exactly did you come here for, if you don't mind my askin'?" he drawled, leaning his tall, wide-shouldered frame against the desk, folding his arms across his chest.

And then Lara didn't know what words to use—how to

make him see. He was being so eminently reasonable, so sane, that her accusations seemed suddenly feeble and unfounded.

"I came to . . . to . . . to let you and your family know that they can't get away with . . . with arson—that I'll find proof somehow that you did it."

"Lara." For the first time his voice took on a serious tone, and a frown line appeared on his brow. "You can't seriously believe that one of us set fire to your barn . . . destroyed a valuable stallion. That's just not our style."

"You did!" she cried, feeling more and more helpless and bewildered. "You did, because just yesterday I told you we wouldn't sell out . . ."

"It's simply not true. It was an accident, that's all. I know how you must feel, and I want you to know you have all our sympathy, but to try to find a scapegoat for an accident . . . Why, it's just not true." His voice became low, intimate, and for a second she felt herself sliding into acquiescence with his calm, compassionate words, but she steeled herself against him, sensing that he only wanted to disarm her.

"You have no idea how I feel," she cried, "and don't try that Taggart charm on me. You've always hated us Claytons and I know it!"

"Lara, that's ridiculous. So our fathers had their feud going. It kept them both busy, gave them an excuse to blame someone for hard times or just plain accidents. And your water hole—sure we could use it, but it's not all that serious. None of it is."

"That's where you're wrong, Mr. Branch Taggart. It is serious! How can you possibly think otherwise or call cutting fences and stolen cattle accidents?" Fortified by her anger, Lara ranted on. "And now you want those watering rights back and you think you can buy us out!

Well, you'll find out differently. You'll never get Bitter Creek—never, never!" And then to her deep shame and total surprise, Lara burst into tears over which she seemed to have no control whatsoever. Her body was wracked by sobs and she couldn't talk or catch her breath. She sank down into one of the chairs and buried her face in her hands, so ashamed, yet so torn by overwhelming misery that she wasn't even able to rise, to leave the room, to run away and hide from Branch's mocking gaze.

Then she felt a hand on her shoulder, gentle and strong, and she knew it was Branch's hand, but she hadn't the energy to do anything.

"Lara," he said, his low drawl becoming softer and slightly rough, as if he were not used to using this tone of voice, "I'm so sorry. Please believe me, I'm so very sorry."

"No, you aren't!" she cried, gathering all her strength abruptly to rise and face him, to brush off his hand and his false words. But when she stood, too quickly, all the blood left her head and she couldn't catch her breath, and everything dipped and swung around her while a cold, sick sweat stood out suddenly from every pore. She felt herself fading, too weak to push his hands away, much too weak to do anything at all, and then she was sitting on the chair, her head pushed down to her knees, and his voice was calling her name from a distance while she gasped for breath.

After what seemed an eternity, she felt a small measure of strength flow back into her body and, as she sat up with his strong, warm hands helping her, a flood of dreadful shame swept her. "I'm . . . I'm all right now," she said, trying to sound calm, keeping her eyes down.

Branch's face hung closely over her; she felt his

nearness acutely but was too embarrassed to meet his eyes.

"I'd like to go now," she mumbled, watching her hand settle in her lap, the fingers trailing like an averted glance.

"Are you all right now? It's getting quite late. I don't think it's wise for you to ride back alone . . ."

"I'm fine," she said, and then she finally had the courage to meet his gaze. His eyes were so blue, and, surprisingly, so worried-looking, so concerned, that she was puzzled for a second. Why should he care?

"I think you better sit here for a few minutes to make sure you *are* all right," he said, turning his broad back to her, walking to a sideboard, and pouring an amber liquid from a faceted decanter into a glass. "Here, have some of this."

"No, really, I'm fine," she protested, trying to rise. But he was next to her in an instant, his strong hand pressing her back into the chair.

"Not yet. Please, have some brandy, then I'll let you go," he said, smiling at her, his blue eyes crinkling in laugh lines at the corners. It gave his face a whole different look, his smile, and she could hardly believe that he was the same man who'd sat at the opulent table with a sardonic grin on his handsome face.

She took the tiny glass and sipped at it. The brandy made her throat burn and her stomach began to feel warm and glowing. She was too ashamed to protest, to refuse him or make a fuss. She'd made a fool of herself already; now all she could do was get away from there as quietly as possible, get far away and try to forget the whole sordid scene.

She turned the glass in her hands, keeping her eyes on it all the time, watching the amber liquid sparkle brightly, as if it were vitally important to study its every detail, but she was only too aware of Branch standing very close to her, reaching for a pouch of tobacco in his vest pocket. She tried desperately to recover her senses while Branch busied himself rolling a cigarette, wetting the paper then striking a match on his boot heel.

The match flared, then lingered in the air for a moment. "Mind if I smoke?"

Lara nodded her assent woodenly, watched him draw in the smoke, then became aware of the all-encompassing male aroma surrounding him. She could almost feel the heat of his body. She had to do something—anything—to break the frightful tension.

"I don't usually do things like that. I mean . . . getting faint. It's just that I didn't eat anything today and the fire . . . It's been such a horrible day," she said, looking up weakly at him.

"Yes, I guess it has," he said, measuring her with his look. "Promise me you'll take better care of yourself from now on."

"I hardly think it's your problem," she cut in primly, wondering at his seeming concern, almost possessive in quality.

"Well, it is if you're going to come to *my* house to faint," he said, grinning slightly.

"I didn't mean to!" she cried. "It just . . . happened."

"Now don't get angry again. I didn't mean anything by it."

"I'll go now," she said, standing, trying to pull herself together. She still felt shaky and weak, but she wouldn't let him see it. She was aware of how she must look: red puffy eyes, mussed-up old clothes, probably pale as a ghost. "I'm sorry to have caused you any trouble, but everything I said still stands."

His face suddenly darkened, the scowl on it altering his

appearance—he was no longer the easy host but a menacing stranger with a cruel line to his mouth. "You're not going to start that again! Be reasonable. Any sane person would realize that we would have nothing to gain by doing such a thing. That water hole is not worth burning a barn."

"I guess I'm not what you call sane then," said Lara, meeting his gaze directly. She knew then that she had to get out of the room that was suddenly close, suffocating her.

Branch was trying to convince her of something, but she couldn't spare the energy to concentrate on his words. She turned quickly, shouldering her way past him, afraid he would try to stop her, afraid that at any moment his hand would touch her arm and she would be powerless to resist him. She kept walking down the hall, hearing her footfalls echo too loudly on the flagstones, and then she was outside, gulping in the cool night air.

It was only when she was riding back along the dark road to Bitter Creek that her body began to tremble uncontrollably and the tears began to slide down her cheeks, unchecked, tasting salty when they wet her lips. And as the sobs tore at her chest, the road wavering and swaying in front of her eyes like a ribbon that someone was shaking, the coolly blond good looks of Branch Taggart rose unbidden in her mind's eye and she could still not fathom the genuine concern that she was sure she'd seen in his eyes.

It was all that Branch could do to keep from detaining her by force. He had insisted on riding back to Bitter Creek with her to see her safely home, but she had thrown the offer in his face.

Still, he knew somehow that no matter the danger out

there, Lara Clayton would ride out alone. Thank God it was only a few miles . . .

Branch stood in the shadowy doorway and watched her leave; grim admiration tugged at his mouth while the image of Lara, her black hair catching the moonlight as she rode off, filled his mind. The girl-woman was truly an enigma.

"Oh, Branch? Here you are!" Stephanie came up behind him, startling him out of his reverie.

He turned and smiled down at his distant cousin from Denver. "Yes. I was just watchin' our unexpected guest leave."

Stephanie lowered long, dark lashes over clear blue eyes. "Miss Lara Clayton is certainly something, isn't she?" A flush glowed on her cheeks. "And those clothes of hers! Why, it was positively shocking. I nearly swooned when she came in and began accusing your father . . ."

"Lara Clayton," interrupted Branch tightly, "has had a hard day of it. She was just upset. That's all. And as for her clothes . . ."

"Yes?" There was an edge of annoyance to Stephanie's tone.

"Well, I guess she dresses that way because it's necessary when you're running a ranch."

"She's . . . what?" A slim white hand came to the swell of her breast, ostensibly to quiet the flutter of her heart.

"Running Bitter Creek Ranch. Her father just died and her brother is God knows where."

"It's just *too* shocking!"

Branch thought for a long moment. It was a crime to see a woman work herself to death out here on the raw land. Women belonged in a quieter setting, with nice, soft things surrounding them.

Abruptly a bitter taste rose to his mouth. This land could too easily destroy a woman—far too easily. Hadn't he learned that lesson the hard way? His own wife had been a perfect example: married hastily, brought out here to the lonely life of ranch wife. And then she'd changed—the soft white skin had hardened, her eyes, he recalled painfully, had taken on a faraway look. And then came Jeff—the hired ranch hand, the drifter. Oddly, Branch never blamed Jewel—or Jeff, for that matter. Even after she'd gotten herself pregnant by Jeff and disappeared, Branch blamed himself for bringing the gently bred girl to the West. He blamed himself for her death, too.

"Oh, Branch?" Stephanie placed a warm hand on his.

"Umm?" Jewel was in the past. The future was what counted, the land. If he had to go it alone, then he would—it beat the hell out of seeing another human being wither and die out here.

"It's getting chilly." Stephanie smiled brilliantly. "Denver never seems to get this cold in spring." She shivered lightly.

Branch turned and began leading his lovely cousin back inside; her diamond earrings caught the light from the hall lamps and sparkled; her lips glowed rosy pink, warm and inviting. Up until this minute he had practically ignored Stephanie's latest visit—she came for a couple months every summer—but suddenly he saw her, realized she was attracted to him, realized, alarmingly, that he found her attractive also.

Quickly, Branch steeled himself, wondering how his life had so suddenly become entangled with females again and just as suddenly vowing to put a stop to it at once.

Chapter Seven

BY WEDNESDAY MORNING, THE WRETCHEDNESS THAT HAD colored her spirit had faded. It had been two nights since her ride out to Wolf Butte Ranch and two full days of self-loathing over her performance at the Taggarts'. Nothing had come out right; none of her practiced words had come forth as planned. Harriet and Jennifer, sensing Lara's futile mission, had carefully avoided upsetting her. It was as if everyone, Shad Harper included, were walking on eggshells when Lara was around.

And now, just when the humiliation was beginning to fade with time's kindness, when she was able to face herself in the mirror again, Lara was confronted with a new problem: Noah Ackroyd of the *Rifle Reveille* was coming for that interview and dinner.

Lara hardly felt like entertaining but knew that to say so would greatly upset her mother. Resigned, she made preparations for his visit; she decided to wear one of her best day dresses, one purchased in St. Louis. The cherry red cotton print sported a small bustle at the back, a high lacy collar set into a lace insert over the bosom. The long full sleeves were also tripped in creamy lace. It was not the most sophisticated dress, but springlike and sunny, and the trim waistline enhanced her slim figure to its best advantage. It was suitable, Lara thought, for the casual dinner.

Having decided not to ride out with Shad for the afternoon, she took a leisurely bath. Noah would arrive around four. She lathered and soaked for a full hour, then vigorously rubbed her hair dry with a soft linen towel. It was wonderful to spend time primping herself, a luxury she had not had time to indulge in since her arrival back.

Pulling the corset strings tight, slipping on her best chemise, which tied with a blue silk ribbon, her petticoat, and finally the dress, Lara swept her hair up into a simple pompadour and secured it with long hairpins. A few dark tendrils escaped down her neck leaving a natural, fresh look—not too contrived.

She surveyed the result in the mirror; the girl who peered back at her almost seemed a stranger. How long had it been since she had taken a moment to really *look* at herself?

There were vague, tired circles under her eyes, but they hardly showed beneath the golden tan of her skin. How Mrs. Bryant would scold! A proper woman shielded her delicate skin from the sun, but Lara had clearly been spending hours out-of-doors unprotected. Yet the glow to her skin seemed clean and fresh, enhancing the clear green of her eyes. She saw the trace of Indian ancestry in the spare, sculpted grace of her high cheekbones. Her mouth was distinctive—Jennifer said it was her best feature next to her eyes—the upper lip curved in a thin, aesthetic line, the lower lip fuller, almost pouting.

"Men love a mysterious mouth," Jenn had told her once.

She studied herself closely. Would a worldly man like Noah Ackroyd find her attractive?

Noah arrived by buggy precisely on time and Lara found herself studying him closely during the interview. Over the rim of her teacup she saw quite a handsome man dressed in a lightweight linen suit and vest that had not begun to wilt yet. He was tall and lanky and looked like a man who did his homework. He seemed intense—perhaps a little bookish with those spectacles—but attractive nonetheless. His straight sandy hair kept dipping into one eye and he had a nervous habit of tossing his head, squinting, then readjusting his round, silver-rimmed glasses with an index finger. His mouth was thin and wide, friendly. His eyes were pleasant, comprehending, and his voice emerged even and smooth. He made Lara feel at ease even though she found it quite difficult to express her impressions of Rifle's extraordinary growth.

"I've only been home a week, Mr. Ackroyd," she explained, "and I'm afraid it's all so new, I hardly know what to say."

But Noah seemed not to mind; he closed his note pad, absentmindedly dropping it into his coat pocket, and smiled warmly at her. Jennifer winked at Lara, as if to say, "He's not here for an interview anyway. He's here to call on you."

Lara dropped her gaze awkwardly. Jennifer had a single-track mind.

Dinner—a chuck roast, potatoes, carrots, and hot

biscuits—was excellent and Noah a charming conversationalist; he regaled the three women with tales of New York and his adjustment to life in western Colorado. He made himself sound like a bungling flatlander and the women giggled behind their napkins. Lara found herself relaxing completely and was thoroughly enchanted when he removed his linen jacket, rolled up his white shirt sleeves, and insisted on helping with the dishes.

After much arguing on Harriet's part, Noah did have his way, carefully wiping dry the good bone china plates and stacking them in the corner cupboard.

Dark clouds rolled angrily across the valley before sunset, dropping precious moisture on the sere land. It was a sudden spring shower and passed as quickly over the land as it had come. Gilded rays of sun fanned over the house and yard from the west, tinting the brush-spangled hills in a soft, golden glow.

"The storm's past," observed Harriet over coffee. "Why don't you show Mr. Ackroyd the new calves, Lara?"

"Oh, Mother . . . I'm sure he's not interested . . ."

"But I am," countered Noah. "Really. Us city folk can use all the education we can get out here."

And so Lara, feeling a little silly, walked across the wide yard to the corral with Noah's hand supporting her elbow. If only Noah Ackroyd could see her on a busy workday—her shirttail hanging out, the wide-brimmed hat pulled down over her head, and, of course, Craig's old jeans!

She pointed out the most basic facts of ranching to Noah, who seemed genuinely interested. "Our ranch is fenced in." She pointed to the high country above and to the west of the ranch house.

"You have fences all the way up in the timber?" He seemed taken aback.

Lara laughed. "Of course . . . miles of them. It's the best grazing land in the summer and in the winter we bring the cattle lower into the valley, where they can survive."

"Do you lose a lot of them?"

"Only in a severe winter and only if we can't get out to them with hay."

"So you don't believe in open grazing then?"

"Hardly!" She laughed tightly, thinking of the Taggarts. "The days of open range ranching are numbered. It just doesn't make good sense anymore to let your cattle roam free. Why half of them would end up in Wyoming, the other half in Utah! Roundup would take forever! And homesteaders would most likely fence off the best watering holes for your cattle. It just isn't practical anymore."

"But the government still allows free grazing on public domain," he observed.

"Oh, yes. And they may always."

Lara then pointed out the piles of new lumber stacked in the yard. "As you can see"—she nodded toward the new barn site—"we're rebuilding our barn. It was quite a loss . . ."

"I heard." Noah leaned his forearms onto the top rail of the corral. The sun dipped over the hills; the light in the yard turned pink, soft and fresh after the rain. "I also heard about your visit to Ned Lawson that day." His eyes rested on the nursing calves; he cleared his throat almost as if he were embarrassed by his statement.

Lara felt the new tension between them. Was *that* what he really wanted to talk about? Was he looking for a scoop or was he simply making conversation? Carefully, she answered, "Yes. I rode into Rifle and . . . made an accusation. However, he didn't take me seriously."

Noah shifted his stance, facing her. "Do you want to talk about this?" His clear eyes held hers.

Lara shrugged mentally. Why not? "It's not news," she began. "The feud between the Taggarts and Claytons is as old as Rifle . . . older."

"So I've been given to understand."

So he knew; of course, everyone here did. "I'm certain they set fire to the barn but I can't prove it. Plain and simple"—involuntarily, her voice rose—"the Taggarts are thought to be above reproach. That's just the way it is."

"Nobody, Lara, is above reproach." Noah laid a hand over hers on the rail. It never occurred to Lara to move hers away—the gesture felt oddly natural, a safe luxury.

"They are," she replied bluntly.

"Might just make an interesting article. Airing both sides, of course, but at least you could tell your story."

"To what end?" Although her voice emerged dully, Lara slowly began to ask herself if perhaps Noah wouldn't make a strong ally. Still, what good would it do? "I don't know . . ."

"It's news, Lara. And if you're correct about them setting the fire, well, then, perhaps an article in the *Reveille* would deter them from trying anything else. Who knows?"

Lara smiled up at him. "That's very kind of you, Noah . . ." His given name came easily to her tongue. ". . . but I'm afraid that they're determined to buy us out. Nothing will stop them now that Dad is gone."

There was a long moment of silence. Noah fixed his gaze on the tiny calves; a muscle worked in his cheek.

111

Finally, he turned back to face Lara, his hands coming to rest on her shoulders. "You should have a man out here, Lara. It's not right for three women . . . alone and all that. It's too hard, too dangerous."

Somehow, when her mother or Shad brought up the same subject, Lara's back would stiffen, but Noah sounded so sincere, his voice so full of concern, that she just couldn't fault him. Not this kind, well-meaning man. "We're doing all right," she replied quietly.

"I'd like to . . ." His voice trailed away.

Lara looked up into his eyes questioningly. What was he trying to say that was so difficult? There was something in his gaze that she could not put her finger on for a moment. And then she knew. She read it in his eyes and knew instinctively that Noah was interested in *her,* that his words were more than mere passing concern.

Slowly, Noah bent his sandy head. His hands encompassed her shoulders more firmly.

Her eyes closed. That he was going to kiss her registered somewhere in her mind and that she would welcome his kiss registered also, surprising her.

Their lips touched lightly. She felt a small flutter in her stomach.

"You're lovely, Lara," Noah whispered. "You take a man's breath away . . ." Again his lips brushed hers carefully, as if she might break. "You'd set them back on their heels in New York."

The experience was rather pleasant, she thought absently, but somehow not as thrilling as she might have imagined.

The light in the yard grew dull; shadows crept out like tiny creatures from behind the rocks and around the house. It grew difficult for Lara to read the expression on

112

Noah's face as he stood now gazing out over the endless range, his back resting on the rail.

When again his voice reached across to her, it was strangely tinted with pain. "I care for you, Lara . . ."

"Noah." She was suddenly afraid; she willed him desperately to say no more. "Please . . ."

"Let me go on," he urged in a strange, thick tone. "I felt something for you from the very first moment I saw you in Rifle . . ."

"Please . . ."

"But I can't, Lara!" He sounded alarmingly like a penitent confessing to his priest. Lara's bewilderment turned to embarrassment. She wished a hole would open in the earth and swallow her. "I'm engaged. She lives in New York . . ."

"Don't, Noah . . . please, don't say anymore!"

". . . She doesn't want to come out west . . . I don't know quite what to do." His hands gripped her above the elbows; his touch had lost all its gentleness.

"I'm sorry," Lara fumbled, unable to say anymore.

"And then I met you. I don't even know if I want her to come west. It's been like torture this past week."

"You shouldn't . . . you can't say these things to me, Noah. You're just lonely. You're engaged."

"I know," he groaned.

She saw his head descend again toward hers, but this time Lara pulled back. "Don't!" she whispered vehemently. "You've no right!"

He dropped his hands away abruptly. "God! I'm so sorry. Of course I have no right. I've insulted you . . ."

"No, you haven't, Noah. But we mustn't let this happen again . . ."

"I won't. I promise, Lara. It's just that you're the most

lovely woman I think I've ever seen." Lara's heart gave a squeeze; was he insane? "Every man for a hundred miles around must want you, Lara . . . I can't help myself."

She was horribly flustered. Even in Mrs. Bryant's drawing room she had never come up against a situation that disconcerted her so. Here was a man, very nearly a stranger, for whom she felt a mere friendship, but who was telling her these awful things—intimacies in which she had no wish to share. She hadn't the faintest idea how to react. Should she get angry? Should she laugh it off? Heavens! The first would upset everyone, the second would shame poor Noah.

If only she had the presence of mind to say the right thing. But, searching her brain, she couldn't think of the right thing to say; not a word came to her.

She must have been looking at him with a horrified expression because suddenly Noah's face creased into a smile. "Lara," he said quietly, "I'm scaring you to death, aren't I?"

"Yes," she whispered frankly.

"Please forgive me. You're so vulnerable. I forget . . . coming from New York. Women here are different. At least, *you're* different." He took her hand between his, but in a companionable way that didn't frighten her. "Let's not play games, you and I, all right? Can we be friends and always tell each other the way we truly feel?"

"I'd like that," she said shyly. "I don't have any men friends. And now my Dad and my brother are both gone . . ."

"Well, consider me a substitute for both. What do you say?"

Lara felt quite relieved. He really meant it. "I say yes." She smiled shyly up at him. "Now tell me about your fiancée." Anything to lead him onto another track.

Noah laughed. "I'd feel like the worst cad discussing Katie with you."

"Why?"

"Well, it's hardly the thing to do—discuss one girl with another."

"Out here we don't stand much on 'the thing to do,'" said Lara quietly.

Noah smiled wryly. "So I've been learning. No need to remind me so nicely. A sharp word or two will do."

"Oh, but I couldn't . . ."

"Never mind. It's just my keen East Coast wit. Pay no attention." Noah's face was only a pale oval in the dark, his spectacle frames glinting where the lights from the house hit them. He pushed the glasses up on his nose in a now familiar gesture.

"It's so different out here, you know," he began. "Your lives are based on a totally different set of values. The land." He gestured to the darkening rangeland beyond the barn. "I'm trying to understand. I believe it's part of my education."

"Why did you decide to come out here?" asked Lara.

"Curiosity. The urge to see something new and different and romantic . . ."

"Romantic!" laughed Lara.

"Yes, romantic," said Noah gravely. "I'm an incurable romantic. Don't you realize how us Easterners view you people out here? The cowboys, the Indians, the wild horses, the huge, open land that anyone can own if he works hard enough?"

"To me it just seems ordinary. It's how I was raised . . ."

"It would, I guess. But try to see it all objectively. There's never been another country like it. Never, anywhere. There are untold riches in this land. And the people. Well, it takes a certain breed. As for me, I'm only an onlooker. You know what I'd really like to do?"

"What?"

"I want to write a book about the West. One that really explains it all to the rest of the world. I'm not sure I can do it." He pushed his glasses up again. "But I'd like to try."

"A book," mused Lara. "I think that's wonderful of you."

"Oh, I'm just a scribbler. I don't know . . ."

"You can. My Dad said you could do whatever you wanted if you tried hard enough."

"Katie said that, too," replied Noah, very quietly.

"Well, there, you see. And she's right."

"I've certainly talked enough about myself, haven't I? Come on. You must be getting chilly. I'd better say good night to your mother and sister before they wonder what I'm doing to you out here."

"Noah!"

"Don't worry. I won't start again. But you are extraordinarily lovely, Lara. A man can't help but notice . . ."

And then he turned toward the house and said nothing more that was not polite or respectable. Only Lara's slight flush and averted glances gave away her agitated sensibilities and only her sister noticed.

Jennifer sat at Lara's dresser later, combing her hair. "Of course he's infatuated with you, ninny. You *are* the prettiest girl around."

"Jenn!" Lara stood motionless.

"Well . . . I've always told you that. You're just so blind when it comes to yourself."

"But I'm not really . . ."

"Oh, yes you are. Think about it." Jennifer rose. "I'm going to bed. But you just think about what I said. It's true. You're wasting your life out on this ranch."

116

It was so terribly vain, but she couldn't stop herself from thinking about Noah's revelation and then Jennifer's words too. And she had to admit that she did have certain desirable attributes: her eyes, her slim figure, a shapely bustline. But the prettiest? Even prettier than Jenn? And as for wasting her life out here . . .

Unwillingly, she recalled the feel of Noah's hands on her shoulders, the sweet brush of his lips. A yearning gnawed at her stomach. Was Jenn right? A sudden loneliness swept her. Would she be able to live alone . . . forever? And what about the feel of a man's lips, which promised so much more, her hidden, repressed desires? Could she always deny this yearning?

Chapter Eight

LARA FOLLOWED THE RUTTED TRACK ALONG THE FENCE that bordered the northern reaches of Bitter Creek Ranch. It was a job she loved doing: checking the fences, riding easily, totally relaxed in the warm May sun, idly, automatically checking on the well-being of all the white-faced cattle and sleek horses that grazed so peacefully on the land.

On the other side of the barbed-wire fence lay Wolf Butte Ranch, but she paid it no heed. The size of the neighboring spread was so large that this corner was far removed from the ranch buildings—miles in fact.

It made her heart swell with pride and contentment to see the sleek mares, the cows and their calves, the well-fed, healthy yearlings, the mild-eyed steers. It would be a good year, especially with the price of beef sky high back East and the closeness of the Rifle stockyards, which facilitated shipping Western Slope beef to the best markets.

Prairie dogs scuttled from under her bay gelding's feet, causing him to flick his ears in annoyance. A hawk circled high up on an ascending current of air, lazily, gracefully. Insects clicked and buzzed in the tall grass.

Lara was daydreaming, totally lulled by the mellow afternoon, when she slowly became aware of a muted bellow coming from up ahead of her. She kicked the bay into a lope and followed the sound over the next rise. It was a calf caught in a tangle of barbed wire, mooing disconsolately for his mother, who stood helplessly several yards away.

Lara pulled up at some distance from the calf, dismounted carefully, keeping a wary eye on the cow—a nervous mother could suddenly become vicious—and walked slowly toward the struggling calf. The mother cow eyed her whitely, switching her tail, blowing.

Lara reached the calf, laid calming gloved hands on it, leaned down, and carefully slid the tangle of wire off the small hoof. The calf cried, then galloped toward its mother, its little tail straight up in the air like a flag. Lara smiled to watch it go.

But her smile slowly turned to a puzzled frown as she began to examine the tangle of wire. The top strand was broken, the bottom one sagging down nearly to the ground so that cattle could cross easily from Clayton land to Taggart and vice versa. She looked closer; the top strand had coiled back upon itself into the tangle that had trapped the calf. She found the end of the wire and drew in a quick breath. The wire had been cut—the shiny, diagonally sliced end was proof. The wire had been deliberately *cut*. Her full lips tightened. There was no question as to who had done it—the Taggarts again.

Then she noticed horse's tracks in the damp earth where the lower wire sagged to the ground—a tangle of several horses' hoof prints. She wondered abruptly if some of Bitter Creek's horses had been rustled. She knelt down to examine them more carefully—one set was that of an unshod horse, a wild one. How odd. The mustangs rarely came down from the higher country, at least in the summer. They were much too human shy.

Curiosity besting her, Lara led her bay over the wire, remounted and set off to follow the tracks. Certainly it would be all right to cross Taggart land this far out; she had the best excuse of any—missing horses.

Loping easily along the path made by the horses, Lara's imagination began to work. A wild horse excited everyone's fancy. Why, her father used to tell tales of the "ghost horse," the pure white stud that galloped over the range and that no one could ever catch. And then every rancher had lost a horse or two to the wild hills. Maybe she could recover some.

She topped a small rise, heading up toward the foothills, when she saw the puff of dust not a quarter of a mile ahead. Quickly she urged her gelding into a ground-eating lope. She could see the dust cloud get bigger, closer. Good, the horse wasn't in a hurry; but she knew it would sense her soon and be off like a shot. She loosened the rope that hung neatly coiled from her saddle. Her bay was strong and range wise, but not very fast. Still, she could try . . .

Then she saw him: ears perked forward, thick black neck arched, crimson-lined nostrils flaring as he faced her square in the center of the track as if in warning.

He squealed, whirled, his black spotted haunches working powerfully under silky hide, and disappeared into a stand of filmy cottonwoods. Lara rode on, mindless now of anything but following the horse, excited, amazed. The stud—for it could be nothing else—she'd recognized immediately as one of the rare breed called Appaloosa, one of those uniquely marked horses prized so highly by the Nez Percé tribe who raised them that the Indians would kill a horse rather than let it get into the wrong hands.

The bay was breathing heavily now, his neck slick with sweat, but she pushed him on. Just to get close to that stallion . . .

And then she entered the dappled light of the grove. A beam of sunlight flashed suddenly on a golden-red rump, then on the dappled, shining hide of the stud. She heard a vicious squeal and the pounding of hoofs, and as she came out of the trees, she saw the stud herding, biting, slashing at a chestnut mare and a small foal, driving them toward the distant hills.

She pulled her bay to a halt, his sides heaving, and watched the three horses gallop away toward the brown, jagged foothills. Her mouth gaped, her breath coming nearly as fast as her mount's.

The Appaloosa stud had been driving off *her* mare, Goldy, and the new foal! Of all the damn nerve!

There was no use following them; her horse was winded and she wasn't prepared for a long chase anyway. She reined her bay around and headed back toward Bitter Creek, musing, caught up in plans to get her horses back.

And then it struck her—it was fated, a godsend. She'd lost her stallion, but here was the perfect replacement— and free for the taking, too. She remembered suddenly that Joe Taggart had had an Appaloosa stud once. Did he still? This couldn't be his, though, because he kept his stud close to the barn for breeding. His stud was much too valuable to let him roam the range.

No, this wasn't Joe's old stud. This was a wild horse, anybody's prize.

She kicked the bay into a tired trot. She had to tell Shad; they'd get a hunting party together, capture the stud. Excitement filled her.

Lara could see the thin straight line of the Bitter Creek fence ahead of her; the late afternoon sun glinted off twists of new wire. She unhooked her canteen and took a long swallow of the tin-flavored warm water as her horse ambled toward home, undirected. The water trickled over her chin and spotted her blue chambray shirt. Carelessly, she wiped her chin with the back of her hand, tilted her hat further back on her head, and then, hand still touching the hat's brim, she froze.

Two mounted horses were riding toward her on the Taggart side of the fence—and here she was on Taggart land! She stopped, waited for them, forearms resting on the pommel. No sense trying to pretend she wasn't there.

The two horses loped easily toward her; the riders became more distinct. One was a woman, riding sidesaddle. Lara tightened her lips derisively—if *that* didn't look silly. The other was a man, tall, broad-shouldered, on a big red roan. Then Lara's heart gave a quick squeeze of apprehension and she straightened in her saddle. No mistaking it—the man was Branch Taggart. Even from a distance she recognized the way he sat his horse, the gleam of fair hair where it showed under the Stetson, the set of his muscular shoulders beneath the vest.

And when they got closer, Lara recognized the woman —it was the beautiful one who'd sat by Joe at dinner that awful night. Shame filled her suddenly and her cheeks stained red. Why did *they* have to be riding out here?

She had to face them now, especially *him,* and the memory of her humiliation came flooding back to fill her with raw embarrassment. But she held her head high as they cantered up. She had her pride.

"Why, hello, Miss Lara," drawled Branch. His blue eyes measured her coolly and she knew, she just knew, that he was mocking her for her stupid behavior that night. She could still feel his hand on her, the burn of the brandy on her lips, her hot, useless tears. She held her head up higher.

"Hello, Mr. Taggart."

"Please, it's Branch." He turned to his companion. "Have you met my cousin, Stephanie Huston? Stephanie, Miss Lara Clayton."

The cool, beautiful girl eyed Lara indifferently. "I don't believe I've had the . . . um . . . pleasure."

The little liar! "How do, Miss Huston," replied Lara sweetly, purposely affecting a Western drawl as if to separate herself from Stephanie and all her kind stood for.

She was aware of Branch's sudden close scrutiny. Glancing quickly at him, she caught a flash of humor in his blue eyes. She tried to ignore him. Stephanie's black mare danced gracefully, keeping the other girl occupied for the moment.

"My fence was cut"—she eyed him coldly, warily— "and I followed my mare and foal onto your land. They were stolen by a wild stud."

"A wild stud!" Branch focused on Lara more intensely. "You don't say. Not common around these parts."

"A wild *Appaloosa* stud," said Lara, watching him closely.

Branch whistled, pushed his hat to the back of his blond head. "You sure, Lara?"

"Of course I'm sure!" she snapped. "I followed him, but there's no way I could keep up. He was driving them up northwest." She gestured toward the hills. Narrowing her green eyes, she said, very deliberately, "I aim to get up a party and catch that stud, Mr. Taggart, and I'd like your go-ahead to cross your land."

Branch eyed her carefully, gauging her spirit. The silence strung out just a little too long. They could have been alone on the vast land. "If that stud really is an Appaloosa"—he stopped at Lara's snort of impatience—"he's got to be out of my dad's stud. There aren't any others around. You know the Indians don't just let them go."

"I'd like to see you prove *that,* Mr. Taggart," countered Lara. "He's wild and he stole my best mare and foal and, like I said, I aim to get him." She gave her hat a tug to set it more firmly on her head.

"Well, guess you can try, Miss Lara," drawled Branch easily. "And you can cross our land any time." He hesitated a moment then. "You say your fence was cut?"

"Yes." Lara's voice was hard.

"Let's take a look." His tone was noncommittal as he reined his horse over to the tangled wires. He dismounted fluidly, checked the wire just as Lara had and looked up at her. "Sure has been cut. Now who in blazes would do a thing like that?"

"I can't imagine, Mr. Taggart," breathed Lara insinuatingly, walking her horse over the low wire, then kicking him into a fast lope away from the two of them. But still, even as the distance between Lara and Branch widened, she imagined his eyes following her, watching her, and she was glad somehow he couldn't see her face.

* * *

Randy McQuade's broad back tensed as he tossed the fifty-pound bag of flour onto the backboard. "That be all, Miss Lara?" he asked solicitously. "We got some new dresses in . . ."

Lara laughed. "Thanks, Randy, but that'll be all for today. I should send Jennifer in to look at the dresses, though."

"You do that, Miss Lara," he replied eagerly.

"Sure will. Bye now, Randy." She walked around to the front of the buckboard, gathered the reins from where they were wrapped around the brake handle, and started to climb up to the high seat, hitching up her blue serge skirt to facilitate her movement.

"Need some help?" lazed a familiar male voice from behind her shoulder, then she felt a strong hand cup her elbow as if to boost her up to the seat.

She turned in confusion, trying to tug down her skirt to cover the white eyelet petticoat, one foot still up on the buckboard's step. Her balance was unsteady, her foot caught on the step, and she teetered backward precariously.

"Whoa!" came the low voice, and strong hands spanned her waist, steadying her. "Don't move—your skirt's caught."

She couldn't do a thing but stand there while he unhooked her skirt. She felt a discomfiting heat of confusion spread up her neck to her cheeks. "Thank you," she finally murmured, her eyes still lowered to the dusty street.

"You're quite welcome, Miss Lara," said Branch Taggart with a precise dry courtesy, as if he were carefully trying to give her no reason to snap at him. But Lara sensed instinctively that behind those hooded blue eyes and politely smiling lips he was laughing at her.

She started to turn back to the buckboard, but she felt his hand on her arm; she stopped, too shy suddenly to face him.

"You're not angry at me now, are you, Lara?" he asked, his voice surprisingly low and intimate.

"No," she half whispered.

"Are you going to start an argument?" His voice caressed her ears, easy and smooth, the way you'd talk to a skittish colt.

She felt herself go tingly and loose jointed all over. Still, her eyes were downcast, unable to meet his. "No."

"Good," he said levelly. "Then I'd be happy to escort you to lunch at the Winchester Hotel, Miss Lara."

"What?" she blurted out unthinkingly, her green eyes rising to meet his precipitously, then nearly bit her lips in embarrassment. She always said the wrong thing when Branch was around.

"I said," he continued deliberately, "that I would be most honored to take you to lunch at the . . ."

"I heard you," she interrupted. "I just . . ." Her voice trailed off. She felt so very foolish.

"Well?" His head was cocked to one side; he was waiting for her reply, his blue eyes crinkled with laughter and the bright May sun.

"I . . . really . . . I don't think . . ." Lara's tongue stumbled, her mind whirling uselessly. She could think of nothing cool or clever or tasteful to say. And yet, strangely, a part of her wanted to accept his invitation graciously, to act like a lady as she had been taught at Mrs. Bryant's; a part of her was drawn to this tall, handsome man's presence. Her mind churned.

"You'll come then. Good." His tone left no room for argument. His hand cupped her elbow again and he led her across the street toward the Winchester Hotel.

Lara said nothing. It was too easy to be led, although why she didn't mind was beyond her. The place on her arm burned where she could feel his light touch through her white blouse.

His voice reached her through a daze. "I'm glad I happened to see you. I meant to find out more about that Appaloosa stud you saw." She was all too aware of his steady blue gaze on her. "By the way"—his voice was quiet, matter-of-fact—"you look very nice in a skirt."

Her eyes flew up to meet his, expecting derision, mockery. But all she saw in their hooded blue depths was admiration. She felt hot all over. "Thank you," she mumbled. Was that all she could say to him?

They entered the coolness of the Winchester lobby and Lara had the sudden presence to straighten her blue skirt and white shirtwaist. Abruptly, she remembered to button the high collar of the blouse—she'd opened it on the ride into town because of the heat—and tried to smooth back her hair, which was caught with a blue ribbon at the back of her neck.

"You look fine," teased Branch, bending his head close to hers, and then she felt like an idiot again.

They were seated at the best table, served expertly. Lara had no idea what she was eating; her stomach fluttered with nervousness and she kept asking herself what she was doing here with Branch Taggart making small talk. Had she lost her mind completely?

"Tell me about the stud," he finally said over coffee. "I'm real curious."

"He was a beauty. Not too big—maybe fifteen hands. But real well muscled. Black." At last she felt comfortable, removed from the social chitchat, onto a subject she knew. "White stockings and a white blaze and the white

127

rump with black spots. He looked at me almost as if he were challenging me. I've never seen a horse like that . . ." Her voice trailed off, remembering.

"He could be one of Satan's offspring," mused Branch, leaning back in his chair easily.

Her eyes whipped around to meet his. "He *could* be, off some wild mare, but he doesn't belong to you."

"Hey, don't get riled up. I agree, he belongs to whoever catches him, and I won't stand in your way. Especially since you need a new stud."

"Don't do me any favors," Lara remarked stiffly. And then she couldn't help saying, "Besides, if you'd fence in your land, you might know whose stock belonged to whom. And letting some of your mares roam the range that way, well . . ."

"We *do* brand our stock," interrupted Branch with more than a hint of amusement. "You talk as if we have no idea . . ."

"Well, you can't possibly!" Now it was Lara's turn to cut him off. "Don't tell *me* that some of your yearlings don't belong to us!" She clasped her hands defiantly on the table. "Every time a fence gets . . . cut . . . and a cow gets loose, I'm sure *you* end up with her calf! That's the problem with open range, for pity's sake! By the time your cows are scattered halfway to Wyoming, Lord knows how many you've lost or have starved or what bull has fathered what calf. Why . . . why, there's simply no way to upgrade your stock on the open range!" she finished hotly.

Branch tossed back his blond head and chuckled deeply. Lara was stunned that he should find the subject even vaguely amusing. "How *can* you laugh?" she demanded.

"I'm laughing," he said lightly, "because you're just like all the rest of the fenced-in ranchers. You think yours is the only way. How quickly you forget why we came west in the first place, Lara . . ."

"Oh?" she challenged. "And why did our families come west? Do tell me."

"To get away from fences. To be free, Lara, to let our cattle graze all the way to Canada if we so choose." The amusement had gone from his eyes now, replaced by determination.

"You're so out of date, Branch. Maybe, originally . . . But now that just doesn't work anymore. Too many homesteaders filing on the best sections of open range, too many rustlers. And now with selected breeding, well, your methods are simply . . . antiquated."

Branch fell silent for a long moment and Lara was smugly satisfied to have scored a few points. Oh, certainly open-range ranching had its points too, but she was right—she knew it. It was old-fashioned thinking. For goodness sake, this was 1891!

"You know something, Lara?" said Branch reflectively.

"What?"

"I agree with you on a lot of what you say. I always have. But I'll be damned if I'm going to fence in because of a few homesteaders using up the good grazing land or a few rustlers. I'd rather fight for my freedom than roll over and say die."

Lara opened her mouth to protest, but before the words were out, Branch raised a quieting hand.

"Hey"—his voice emerged levelly—"what are we doing arguing the same old thing? There is no right or wrong—we both know that. And you know something else?" he asked, his blue eyes softening. "You're one nice-lookin' woman when you're upset!"

"Branch Taggart!" she whispered, feeling her stomach turn to jelly. "Why . . . why you're a terrible cad! Here we're discussing a very serious matter and you pay silly compliments . . ."

"Now, Lara, you promised."

He made her feel foolish. "Sorry," she bit out.

"I'm beginning to understand that you don't need help runnin' Bitter Creek . . . or with that stallion. My opinion of women might just have to undergo a change," Branch reflected, smiling.

"And just what is your opinion of women?" asked Lara, wondering what he had up his sleeve next.

"I've always been of the opinion that they're not meant for hard work or harsh conditions, that they need city lights, parties, smelling salts." His eyes held a faraway look suddenly; they seemed to brood darkly.

"Hogwash," she snapped. "I can do a day's work with any man. Just ask our foreman, Shad Harper."

"I don't have to ask him—I believe you, Lara. You've begun to intrigue me . . ."

She took a sip of her coffee to hide her confusion. His gaze met hers steadfastly, convincingly. She could almost believe he was a fine, upstanding man, a pillar of the community, as Sheriff Lawson had said of his father. She felt her defenses melting; she didn't *want* to keep up her prickly armor anymore.

"Is that another compliment, Mr. Taggart?" she asked smoothly, amazed at her own audacity.

"Why, yes, I guess it is," he replied, as if surprised.

"Well, then, I thank you," she said, wondering that she sounded so relaxed, even a bit coy. She felt her lips curving up into an involuntary smile.

He studied her raptly for a long moment until her smile became fixed and began to fade. She had no idea what to say next—her newly found confidence ebbed as the moment stretched out unendurably.

"Well," he finally said, "I'd best be seein' you on home."

She looked at him quizzically.

"I couldn't let a lady drive her rig home alone when I'm headed in the same direction, now could I?" He rose, pulled her chair out, and led her from the dining room.

"Really, you don't need to . . ." she began once they were out on the wooden sidewalk.

"I'm quite aware that I don't *need* to, Lara. I *want* to. Enough said?" His tone was firm, silencing any further protests.

He tied his horse to the back of her wagon, helped her up, then swung up easily beside her, taking the reins in his capable hands. She couldn't help but notice the way his thigh muscles tensed under the denim jeans, the way his forearms glistened with blond hairs where his sleeves were rolled up—whipcord strong. It was as if she saw every detail with incredible clarity: his profile—strong and masculine—the powerful line of his cheek and jaw, the tilt of his Stetson and the shadow it cast over his blue eyes.

He talked easily as he drove north up the Government Road toward Bitter Creek, carrying the conversation. Lara found herself actually enjoying his voice, the warm sun on her back, the lazy clip-clop of the horses. He was an easy man to be with, she admitted to herself grudgingly.

When they reached the turnoff to her ranch, he swung down lithely, then led his horse around to where she sat on the buckboard seat.

"Well, Miss Lara," he said, suddenly formal again, "I want to thank you for a most pleasant lunch and for the enlightenin' conversation." He hesitated then, as if thinking twice about his next words. "If you want some help with that Appaloosa . . ."

It was tempting to take him up on his offer. She *needed* that stud. But the image of the barn in flames, the pile of charred rubble, was suddenly superimposed on her mind.

"No thank you, Mr. Taggart, we can do it ourselves." Her voice sounded as dry as the desert breeze to her own ears. She hadn't meant it to come out quite like that—or, she thought fleetingly, maybe she had.

For an unending moment Branch stared at her impassively, a slight quirk to one brow, then, before she could see the smile gathering at the corners of his lips, he spun his horse around, leaving her to taste the dry dust that lingered, suspended, in his wake.

Chapter Nine

IT WAS AS HOT AS IT EVER GETS IN THE HIGH TIMBER country of western Colorado. Lara felt perspiration trickle down between her breasts and dampen the waistband of her jeans. Her red cotton plaid shirt clung to her back wetly as she spotted a tall stand of spruce promising shade from the blistering sun.

She nudged her mount toward the welcome sight, noticing a small stream within the stand apparently not dried up yet since winter snow was still melting from above.

It had been over three days now since she, along with Shad and two other hands, had ridden out to track the stallion. She was beginning to despair of ever retrieving Goldy, much less capturing the prize stud. They had been hot on his tracks twice already, and each time he had found an escape route, fleeing higher and higher into the backcountry. If only they could drive him lower, into one of the box canyons—but he was seemingly too wise for that. In fact, Lara had mused, he was a heck of a sight smarter than most people she knew.

Lara would give it two more days and then return to Bitter Creek. She had promised Harriet to be gone less than a week, and even the thought of that short a time spent in the wilderness with three men was enough to upset her mother thoroughly.

Lara dismounted, allowed her horse to drink, then tied her mare to a nearby tree.

Now it was her turn. She peeled off her shirt, tossing it carelessly aside, and knelt by the stream's bank. Quickly, she doused her head and breasts with the icy mountain water, feeling it prickle her skin deliciously. She drank greedily for a minute, then decided to shed the rest of her clothes and refresh herself all over.

Short minutes later, she was shivering from the cold but felt immensely better than she had before.

Almost reluctantly, she pulled her jeans back on and began to tug the shirt on over her damp flesh while tossing her wet, thick hair over one shoulder.

It was then that Lara saw him.

Crouching motionless, camouflaged by the dappled sunlight, not twenty feet across the stream from her, was a mountain lion.

Gasping, Lara snapped her head around; her rifle was sheathed in her saddle, too far away to reach. Her mount skittered nervously sideways, straining at the tied reins. The stealthy lion had taken them both by total surprise.

In a split second her eyes darted back to the inanimate cougar and fixed on him. Perhaps, she prayed silently, he wouldn't attack. They rarely did.

Blood pounded through her veins; a shiver, a cold

hand of fear, crept up her spine, immobilizing her. If only the rifle were nearer.

"Stay absolutely still."

Lara's heart leaped in her breast but she made no move to turn her head around and search for the author of the command. She couldn't have even if she wanted; she was paralyzed with fear.

The cougar lifted his hypnotic gaze to a spot over her shoulder. His lithe body tensed; a tremor rose from his lean flanks; his ears laid flat against his back while his tail began a slow whipping.

My God! Lara realized in horror. He was going to . . .

A deafening shot split the air above her before the thought was done. The cat rose in the air, then fell heavily on his side, twitched, then lay motionless in death. It was a clean kill.

"Oh, my God, Shad." The words fell breathlessly from her lips. "Oh, my God!"

"It's not Shad."

Still crouched, Lara spun around.

Standing ten paces behind her was Branch.

Automatically, her hands drew the damp shirt closed. "How did you . . .?" she breathed, still stunned.

Beneath the slanting brim of his hat, Branch's gaze remained fixed on the damp, clinging shirt that molded itself revealingly to Lara's breasts. "I've been tracking that lion for days. He killed two calves the other night. Lucky for you I was." His eyes rose slowly to lock with hers.

"Yes," whispered Lara, the rifle shot still ringing in her ears.

Shouldering his weapon, Branch began to move forward. Lara looked into his eyes and searched his unreadable face.

Mechanically, he placed his rifle on the ground, then took her by her shoulders. She began fumbling with the buttons on her shirt desperately, her fingers unable to perform the simple function. Branch drew her hands aside firmly and let his gaze fall to her breasts.

A flood of sudden emotion coursed through her as Lara looked slowly down to where he gazed. Beneath the damp cloth of her shirt her nipples stood rigid, either from the cold water or from his perusal—she didn't know.

Moving one hand from her arms, he reached up and flung aside his hat.

"Don't." Her word plunged between them without conviction. Her breath caught in her chest as if there were no air left in the world. She couldn't tear her eyes from his. His face was rigid, unmoving, but she saw a myriad of emotions passing over it, each in turn, as if a faint summer breeze touched a leaf but strangely didn't stir it.

Then suddenly, involuntarily, she was twisting from his grip, panicked. But just as abruptly her quest for freedom was denied when she was spun back around into his steely embrace.

His lips descended to her protesting mouth, and before she could catch her breath, Branch's mouth crushed hers in a brutal kiss.

Lara's head bent backward under the force of his kiss. Why was he purposely hurting her? His lips twisted over hers, forcing her mouth to open. A man didn't kiss a woman like this.

And then his tongue drove into her mouth and a hot flash of lightning bolted up from her belly. Her mind reeled; she sagged against the hard wall of his chest both willing him to stop and contrarily, wanting this to happen.

Branch's arms encircled her, crushing her body against his. The buttons on his shirt scraped the soft flesh of her breasts. She whimpered.

He moved his mouth from hers and sought a spot at the hollow of her throat with his lips. Lara moaned, shaken to the core by his assault. Still the buttons on his shirt pressed into her, but somehow it was not an unpleasant pain. How was it possible?

Her knees were so shaky they felt like they would buckle at any moment and the deep, insatiable agony in the pit of her stomach was growing even stronger. If she didn't stop him from the insane attack in a moment, she sensed, this maelstrom of emotions would swirl her into its depths and there would be no regaining the surface.

His mouth sought hers again. With her flagging strength, she tried to push against his chest. "No," she panted weakly.

Branch straightened, looked into the green pools of her eyes. "I'm going to have you, Lara. If not here and now, then tomorrow. You know that, don't you." It was not a question.

She swallowed. "I . . ."

"Say it, Lara. You want me as bad as I do you. Say it." His voice was husky, deep, frightening her with the intense ring of truth.

She tried looking away; a tremor seized her body, shaking it. "I . . . I don't know what I . . . want," she whispered, surprised at her honest confession.

"No," he stated quietly, "you wouldn't know, would you?" And then, his fingers biting into her arms: "But I do know, Lara. I'm going over there and get my bedroll. When I do, there'll be no turning back. Do you understand?"

Yes. Oh, God. Yes, she *did* understand! The months of loneliness crowded in on her desperate thoughts; the secret yearnings of her heart to know fulfillment rushed in on her like a surging tide. She knew desire. She longed for it—longed to be held, to be wanted.

Through trembling lips she whispered, "Yes . . . I understand."

While Branch disappeared to get his bedroll, Lara sank to her knees. Was she mad? Her breathing was shallow, uneven—her desire had not ebbed. And, yes, she told herself, *yes*—he's a Taggart. But I'll die if he doesn't come back. And then she looked toward the shadowed grove into which he had disappeared, not caring about her previous reluctance to continue this drama to the bitter end.

But he did return, crouching beside her, shaking out the warm blankets next to them.

Lara could not look at him; his motions seemed so cold, so businesslike—as if he had done this a thousand times before.

"You're very practiced at this," she murmured shakily.

Finished, Branch stood. He began to undo his shirt. "One of us has to know what we're doing, Lara," he stated too easily.

Shame gripped her suddenly. "I suppose so," she said quietly.

"You want to back out, don't you?"

He was taunting her. "And if I do?" she breathed.

"I guess I'd have to let you go. But there's always tomorrow."

Lara looked up. His eyes displayed no humor—he wasn't mocking her then. She made her irrevocable decision. It was horrifyingly true—it was inevitable. "What do I do?" Tilting her small chin upward, Lara awaited his answer with as much pride as she could muster.

"Why not let me show you?" He smiled, stooping down alongside her. And then he slipped her arms out of the shirt and her pale breasts caught the warm, flickering sunlight. "You're beautiful," he whispered, easing her onto her back on the bedroll.

Branch's stare burned her naked flesh, but somehow she felt no shame. It was as if she *wanted* him to look at her, to touch her.

As if he read her thoughts, Branch leaned over and carefully kissed a taut nipple, cupping the breast from underneath with tanned fingers. Her heart pounded furiously while she watched his head bent over her, the blond hair catching the dappled sunlight.

Shivers ripped through her limbs as his mouth possessed the ripe breast, then moved to the other. Branch drew the peaks into his mouth, then toyed with them until Lara's breathing became ragged with an unknown yearning.

And then, while his mouth teased her breasts, his hands adeptly slid her jeans down until they, too, joined her shirt and boots in a sighing heap on the ground.

His hand stroked her leg gently, savoring the taut flesh of her thigh. Somewhere in her conscious mind she wondered if he would keep his clothes on, but then his hand slid to her inner thigh and she felt his fingers touch her flesh intimately and all rational thought fled.

Lara gasped aloud as a shock wave spiraled up her belly. Branch drew her body closer to his, encircling her with an arm, then stroked her inner flesh with more insistence.

Again and again, Lara felt the waves of pleasure wash over her, yet still, each one seemed to be growing stronger, building to an unknown crest that she could no longer deny.

Branch's mouth sought hers, then, when she was laboring too hard for breath, his lips moved to her breasts. She twisted mindlessly against the pressure of his hand and moaned weakly for release. When finally it came, she cried aloud unashamedly with the surging force of climax as waves of pleasure rolled from within her.

When she was done, lying next to Branch, she became aware of her perspiration and Branch, too, was covered with a fine sheen of sweat. His mouth found hers lightly, teasing, agonizingly sweet.

He lifted his head; his lips lingered over hers. "That was just the beginning, Lara," he whispered deeply, then stood and slid out of his clothes, tossing them aside to join the others.

Lara turned her head away; a quizzical look gathered on her damp brow.

Naked as she, Branch knelt down alongside her again. "You *are* still a virgin, you realize, Lara . . ."

"Yes," she said pensively. Of course she was. She hadn't thought . . .

And then her eyes fell on his nakedness, on the pure, raw beauty of his man's body—his sinewy arms, the rugged shoulders, the lean waist tapering down to . . .

She gasped. How was he going to . . .?

Branch chuckled. "Don't worry," he reassured, "we'll manage somehow."

She squeezed her eyes shut tightly. All the stories crowded her mind—the pain, the agony suffered beneath a man's lustful body.

But Branch stilled her trembling. Silently, he stroked

her as if she were a frightened child until the shaking subsided. And he kissed her then, filling her mouth with his tongue, kneading her breasts until the nipples again stood pert beneath his hand. The dull ache in the pit of her stomach grew until Lara again twisted beneath his hands, longing to feel the pleasure she knew he could bring to her.

Slowly, Branch spread her legs with gentle hands, then lifted his body over hers until his thighs were between hers.

Unthinking, she lifted her head and saw their bodies. She closed her eyes, waiting, her breasts rising and falling with an odd mixture of desire and fear.

Slowly, Branch moved upward until he was poised above her. Lara felt the pressure and drew in a deep, ragged breath.

"I'll try not to hurt you, Lara," he whispered tenderly, but somehow she knew it would.

Her body went rigid. Branch sighed deeply, probed into her, then met the wall of her virginity. "Relax . . ."

She tried. And then she felt his muscles work and he moved quickly, driving home the instrument of his manhood until a cry was wrenched from her lips.

Branch ran a hand carefully through the tangles of her hair, turned her face around to meet his. "Open your eyes, Lara," he said huskily.

She did, slowly, feeling the pain subside.

"I promise I'll never hurt you again." He began to move within her then, carefully, patiently, until she began to arch beneath him, wondering how she could possibly know the right thing to do.

Branch, she sensed, was treating her with great patience and gentleness. Was this the man with whom she had done battle? This man whose body was joined as one with hers—was he the monster she had thought him?

Lara's thoughts drifted, floating on a cloud of sensation, and with each passing moment she felt the urge to be fulfilled growing once again. This time, however, there would be no stabbing pain to plummet her back to earth.

Together they rode on the swelling tide of sensation until Lara cried out for release and Branch shuddered above her. Her climax this time was far more intense, and afterward she realized that she had actually torn at his back with her nails. Should she apologize?

They lay entwined, unspeaking, until the sun began its dip into the summer sky.

Finally, silently, he rose, took his bandana, and wetted it in the stream. He returned to her, knelt by her side, and gently wiped away the stains of her virginity. Then he leaned down, the muscles of his shoulders cording, and kissed her tenderly on the lips. She closed her eyes, savoring the sensation.

"I'll have to see to the horses," he said quietly, pulling on his jeans.

"Yes." Her voice was a mere breath.

Her eyes followed him as he moved effortlessly through the routine of setting up camp. The slain lion he dressed out near the stream while Lara watched, fascinated, the muscles working in his broad back, the flat plain of his cheek ticking while he concentrated.

Branch fixed them a light supper from his saddlebags consisting of beef jerky, bread, and canned beans. All the while they made only small talk.

"You'll be missed, Lara. They'll come looking for you."

She took a bite of bread. "I don't care."

"You should get on back to camp soon . . ."

She swallowed. "I'm staying here for the night." Her eyes met his steadily.

"Well, I'll be . . ." murmured Branch with a quirked brow.

Twice again that night they came together, their bodies bright with perspiration, catching the moonlight as if pearls had been dropped on their faces, their breasts, their hips. Lara had never known such happiness and not for a moment did she regret it. She never did sleep but instead watched Branch's even breathing, the rise and fall of his lightly furred chest, the pure, undeniable beauty of his body.

When he awoke at dawn, she was dressed, tucking her dark hair up under her hat.

He sat up abruptly. "What're you doin'?"

Lara turned green eyes onto him. "I'm going back to camp, Branch. What else would I do?" She began to mount. It was wonderful, even sweet, but it was over—of that simple truth, she had no doubt.

Suddenly she felt Branch's hand on her arm. He spun her around roughly. "Just like *that!* You're leaving?"

"I . . . what else is there?"

"Good God, you're callous, aren't you?" His fingers dug into her flesh.

"Let go of me, Branch," she whispered dully. "I'm only being realistic. It's over." Her heart ached with regret. She wanted only to be gone.

But he would not let her escape her agony so easily. "Nothing more then," he spat cruelly. "This is it? This is your *reality?*"

What else was there? Didn't he realize that?

"That was all you wanted?" he raged on, gesturing to his rumpled bedroll that lay on the ground in a still warm heap.

"How dare you," hissed Lara abruptly. She stood squarely facing him; her eyes shot green fire. She took a deliberate step backward and slapped his face as hard as she could.

He slapped her back.

Her eyes, tear swollen, flashed up at him defiantly.

He turned away then, unable to look at the place on her cheek that was beginning to redden.

"Christ, I'm sorry, Lara. I thought what we shared meant more . . . I guess I assumed"—his voice came wooden, dull—"that you felt more for me than you do."

Lara's thoughts whirled uselessly. What did he want from her? Avowals of undying love? Surely he knew that what they'd done together was not *love*.

"Whatever I felt . . . feel . . . for you makes no difference. Nothing can come of it. I was leaving when you woke up. If you hadn't, I would have been gone from your life without all this"—she gestured futilely with her hand—"this . . . useless arguing." Her eyes were downcast; she couldn't bear to see the outrage in his face. She wished it were all over, that she could go home and forget everything, wipe it out of her mind.

Branch's finger tilted her chin up so she was forced to face him, but his blue eyes were mild now, mild and vaguely puzzled.

"Did you mean to disappear, to never see me again?"

"Yes, if that's possible," she replied steadfastly.

"I can't believe it," marveled Branch. "You mean, you don't want to get married?"

"Married?" Her rationality turned to utter shock. "Me . . . marry a Taggart?" The thought was so preposterous that she shook her head helplessly. "A Taggart!"

"I can't believe this," said Branch again. "You mean to

tell me that you let me . . . *willingly* let me take your virginity, then you refuse to marry me!"

Lara snapped out of it abruptly. "I could never marry you. Never. You don't mean a word of it."

But Branch was still in the throes of shock and amazement. "By God, woman, you're no damn better than that mare of yours and the stallion! Haven't you any pride?"

Lara stepped into the stirrup, suddenly hurt and defensive, and mounted her horse. "Oh, I have pride all right, Branch," she called. "I have too much pride to marry a Taggart!"

She told the first real lie of her life when Shad asked her where she'd spent the night.

"It got late . . . I got lost, I guess, so I slept on the ground."

"We've been half out of our minds—up all night—and believe me, your Mama would be good an' mad, Miss Lara." He shook an angry finger in front of her face.

"Not if we don't tell her." She felt a sick mixture of anger and guilt suddenly; she was aware of the men's glances that walked on her with many tiny feet as she strode away haughtily.

However, there was one good side to her day—one of Shad's men managed to separate the mare and foal from the stallion and brought them back to camp. The stallion, Lara assumed, would trek deep into the high country and not come down until his urges overcame his caution once again. As far as the Claytons were concerned, he was gone for good.

Wearily, she rode behind the men back toward Bitter Creek Ranch. At least Goldy and the foal were back, she thought, but then she recalled Branch's words and a dark cloud settled over her. She was no better than the mare and the stallion. What he referred to, she knew, was the act of coupling—an act of pure, primitive desire.

And like the mare, she was sated—sated, but returning home alone.

Chapter Ten

UNCHARACTERISTICALLY, JENNIFER'S KNOCK FOUND LARA lying on her bed, fully dressed, doing nothing but daydreaming. It was odd how lethargic she'd felt since she got back from recapturing the mare. It was as if life itself had shifted focus just a touch, so that the things normally important to her receded into insignificance and the things that she'd always scoffed at suddenly loomed huge, threatening.

"Come in," she called to her sister.

Jennifer closed the door behind her and proceeded to the flowered chintz armchair, where she fluffed her skirt unconsciously before sitting down and folding her slim white hands in her lap.

"Well?" asked Lara, puzzled by her normally talkative sister's behavior.

"*Must you wear those pants?*" asked Jennifer finally.

"Yes, I must if I'm to get any work done around here."

"Oh, Lara," sighed Jennifer, "that's *not* what I came to talk about."

"Then what did you want to talk about?"

"You."

"Me?" A vague thrill of alarm writhed in her innards.

"There's talk"—Jennifer looked pained and took a deep breath—"that you and Branch Taggart spent the night alone in the hills."

"Talk?" Lara's voice was a little too high; it almost cracked. "Whose talk?"

"Oh, you know, the ranch hands . . ."

"Ha! Gossipy old men!" The vague alarm blossomed into full-fledged anxiety. "No one listens . . ."

"Yes, they do. What do you think's going to happen the first Friday night those men go into Rifle for a good drunk? Oh, Lara, you're such a fool, such a naive fool." Jennifer had concern in her big blue eyes. "Why do you insist on making everything so difficult?"

"It isn't true! You can't believe them!" cried Lara. "I spent the night alone. I was lost and it was too late to get back to the others. I told Shad . . ."

"I know what you told Shad, Lara, but things look awfully suspicious. Everyone knows Branch was up there, too. What else are people to believe?"

"I don't care what people believe! I was alone and no one can prove otherwise!" Then Lara's voice lowered. "Has Mama heard this . . . gossip?"

"I don't think so. They wouldn't dare let slip in front of her."

Lara felt relief flood her. "Thank God."

"Well, I just thought you should know so that at least you'll be more discreet in the future," said Jennifer matter-of-factly. "He's a darn good catch and I don't blame you a bit, if truth be told."

"Jennifer!" Lara's voice held shock, indignation. "I didn't . . . I mean, I was alone. I was!"

"Okay, I believe you, but I don't care one way or the other. Still, it's not the best sort of reputation to get started even if there's not a grain of truth in it."

Jennifer left, closing the door quietly behind her. Lara felt cold, then hot, then cold again. How low, how disgusting—to be the object of scorn and pity, the fallen woman. Why, she'd be ostracized by the whole town, discussed by every old biddy, smiled at knowingly by all the men. She knew how loose women were treated in a small Western town—she'd had a friend from school . . . it was too awful to even contemplate. She'd keep that night of bliss a careful secret. No one would ever know except her and Branch, and she prayed that he wasn't the type to go around boasting.

She rolled over onto her stomach and buried her face in her pillow, feeling tears of despair near the surface. Oh, why had she been so stupid! She'd never let it happen again, never!

And yet she had to admit to herself that she didn't really wish that it had never happened. Oh, no. For a short time that night she'd been totally fulfilled, totally happy. She had known a closeness, a oneness with a man that she was unable to deny. And Branch Taggart was the only man who had ever really broken through her awkward shyness.

Later that afternoon Lara finally emerged from her room and pitched in with the rest of the hands to help clear away the last of the rubble of the burned barn. It was dirty work, raking and shoveling, emptying endless loads of burnt timber into a pit they'd dug to bury it all. Idly, she wished she had that Appaloosa stud to put in the new barn; her mind conjured up the line of valuable horseflesh she could raise with him. Bitter Creek had never really made money on their horses—only on the cattle—but that could change. After all, how many people had Appaloosas? Very few. How on earth Joe Taggart had gotten his was a well-kept secret.

Lara worked tirelessly alongside the men until long summer shadows fell across the cleared area. They were nearly done.

She straightened from the back-breaking labor, stretched, then rubbed at the dirt in her eyes. Later she would wonder how she ever saw it—it must have been pure chance—but as she stood there working the dirt from one eye, her stare fixed on a spot near her feet, she saw a bright-colored stone. It lay half buried near what used to be the entrance to the barn.

Her fingers reached down, touched the stone, and picked it up. It was a large turquoise, a valuable one, shot with red. A stone that would be worn with pride in a cowboy's silver-worked belt buckle or hat band or perhaps even his horse's bridle. She turned the polished stone slowly in her fingers, bringing it into the light, where she could study it more closely.

Had it been her father's? Shad's? One of the other hands'? It was a lovely piece with a marvelous splash of red twisting like a branch up through the stone. Very distinctive.

"How odd," she thought aloud. Why would it be here? Whose?

And then, suddenly, as if a bolt of lightning had struck her, Lara was staggered by a thought.

"It belongs to whoever set the fire," she gasped, shocked by the revelation of her own voice.

It could belong to no one else!

But suddenly her words seemed irrational. It *could* belong to someone who had been at Bitter Creek after the fire. Who?

Branch had been here. But she tucked that thought away; she had never seen him wear anything remotely like this piece. Noah? She almost laughed. A New York dude with *this*? How many people had been here? Very few. Her brow furrowed in concentration. It belonged to a man; a woman would not wear such a large piece of jewelry.

She sauntered over to where Shad was working, trying to look casual. "This yours, Shad?"

The foreman leaned on his pitchfork, wiped the sooty sweat from his brow with a forearm, and peered nearsightedly at the stone. "Sure ain't. Jewelry ain't my style."

"Does it belong to any of the other hands?"

Shad laughed. "You think any o' them there cowlovin', bandy-legged coots could afford anything like that? Them fools put all their dough right in the bartender's pocket."

"You sure? Maybe you better ask them all."

"Okay, miss, I will. But sure's a snake rattles, it ain't none o' theirs."

Lara walked away slowly, trying to quell her mounting excitement, trying to keep the obvious from flooding and clouding her thoughts. The stone belonged to whoever had set the barn on fire. It belonged to a Taggart.

The next day she made an excuse to ride into town again. She'd slept badly, consumed with the mystery of the turquoise stone. It didn't belong to anyone on the ranch. Shad had brought her the news that none of the hands claimed it and she'd even asked her mother and Jennifer if it looked familiar. She had already known what their reply would be, but she asked anyway. She didn't want a shadow of a doubt to tinge her discovery.

But she had to talk it over with someone; she was bursting with excitement. She threw on the first thing that came to hand—a faded blue shirt that Craig had outgrown years ago and her leather skirt. She had no time to think of her appearance this morning. She pushed her hair impatiently under her hat and ran downstairs. She hadn't the time to hitch up the wagon—a horse would be faster.

"I'll be back this afternoon," she said to Harriet as she grabbed a biscuit on her way through the kitchen. "I'm off to Rifle."

Harriet shook her head. That girl. She had a bee in her bonnet this morning, that was for sure. "Pick me up a bottle of that mint syrup at the druggist, will you Lara? I've run out."

"Sure, Mama."

"And a blue hair ribbon for Jennifer. She's lost hers."

"Okay." This last was flung over Lara's shoulder as she ran out of the house on her way to the corral.

Lara hitched her horse in front of Zimmerman's drugstore, determined to do her errands first so she wouldn't forget anything. She slapped her hat on her thigh as she stepped up onto the wooden sidewalk, shaking the dust out of it, and set it back on her dark head firmly. It occurred to her that she looked a bit seedy but she shrugged it off. People around Rifle would have to accept her as she was.

Walking toward the drug counter, she was aware that her boots made a dull thumping noise on the bare plank floor. She sounded like a cowboy, not a lady at all. And then, as if to drive home the point, she noticed a beautiful blond woman examining the display of imported perfume. Lara couldn't help staring at the back of the beautifully coiffed hairdo that was piled in ringlets and coils on the woman's head. Nor could she avoid a stab of envy at the exquisitely cut white linen suit that the woman wore. Even from the back it exuded style. It wasn't until the woman turned around that she recognized her—Stephanie Huston. Branch's distant "cousin."

The two women's eyes met and locked. Unbidden, Lara felt the blood rush into her cheeks, staining them pink underneath the dust smudges, but she could not explain her reaction, even to herself. And then, in the same long moment, she heard a familiar male voice from the next aisle over.

"You ready to go, Stephanie?"

That low, caressing drawl—the lazy tone—it was Branch!

Lara's heart jumped and her knees grew suddenly weak.

"Come say hello to your neighbor, Branch." Lara heard the woman's voice ring out clearly.

And then, while she remained frozen in her tracks, Branch appeared from around the corner of the aisle, tall, dressed in snug-fitting jeans and a red and white checked shirt that enhanced his deep tan. How arrogantly handsome he looked!

She realized that she was trapped between the two of them; she felt an edge of sheer desperation as if she were a small, helpless animal, a varmint caught in a snare.

Then she heard Branch speak. "Lara?" Apparently he caught himself then, seemingly embarrassed. He cleared his throat. "How are you, Lara?" His tone was carefully noncommittal.

"All right." She half choked on the words. "Fine, I mean." Was that really her voice, so high-pitched, so out of character?

And then Stephanie sashayed past her toward Branch, her high-heeled shoes clicking loudly on the old plank floor, her perfume cloying, assailing Lara's nostrils. She locked her arm through Branch's possessively and for a fleeting moment Lara thought, or imagined, that Branch seemed ill-at-ease.

"You sure you're okay?" Those blue eyes perused her slowly, measuringly.

"Yes." If only she could move her legs. If only she could flee past them without making a cowardly spectacle of herself. She felt Stephanie's eyes taking her in. Her head grew light, throbbing. She was so keenly aware of her disheveled clothes, the grimy smudges of dust on her face and her stained cowboy hat. Why, compared to Stephanie, she must look like an urchin.

Lara cast her eyes down; she couldn't bear another moment of seeing that look of condescension in Stephanie's eyes, the closed, guarded look in Branch's. If only she could gather a shred of dignity around her. Again she was aware of the flush on her neck and cheeks. Even her embarrassment was plainly evident. Suddenly she wanted to shriek out, "I may not look like you, but I was good enough for Branch to take to bed! Did you know that? Did you? Did you know he even asked me to marry him?" But Lara remained silent; she couldn't make such a fool of herself. Instead she just stood there, enduring the excruciating humiliation of the long moment, her teeth worrying her full lower lip.

Mercifully, Branch broke the awkward silence. "I'll be seeing you then, Lara." His words, so simple, so casual, hit her like stones. Vaguely, she was aware that Branch was trying to save her reputation, but shouldn't there be something more between them? Something more than these ordinary words that he would say to any casual acquaintance?

Then their eyes met for an interminable span of time. Heedlessly, she felt his deep blue gaze burn into hers. She drowned in it, desperately, wildly. And then she wrenched her eyes from his with a pain that tore through her body as if she were giving birth.

She heard her own voice answering him. "Nice to see you again, Branch." And she finally found the strength to move, walking away from them both, a cold, false smile uptilting her lips, her green eyes averted from their faces. When she was finally past them, Branch's faint male scent lingering on her senses, she could still feel their eyes burning holes in her back. And it was only then it occurred to her—why hadn't she thought about the piece of turquoise stuffed into her skirt pocket? Why hadn't she pulled it out and thrust it into Branch's face? Would he have recognized it? Of course he would. And then, while she asked the druggist for the mint syrup, she was suddenly glad she'd momentarily forgotten about the stone; it would have been foolish to accuse a Taggart out in the open. She'd have to be clever—far more clever than that! Oh, what an idiot she was to have allowed their encounter to rattle her so!

As she walked out of the drugstore later, however, she was relieved to look up and down the street and not see them again. And then anger welled inside her when she recalled his casual words. What a smooth customer he was! Well, soon she'd have her day, when she proved the stone belonged to one of the Taggarts—and that day would come.

She forced herself to forget the humiliating, awkward

encounter in the drugstore—why let a silly thing like that cloud the achievement of finding the turquoise—and then she could barely wait to tell Noah, to show him the stone. Noah was clever; he'd help her devise a plan. She knew he'd do anything he could for her.

Rushing, she pushed her way into the *Rifle Reveille* building, and her face brightened when she saw him sitting behind his rolltop desk, that crazy comma of sandy hair falling over his brow. She was seized by a feeling of affection for him.

Her glance swept the office. She'd never been in a newspaper building before, but it was exactly like she had pictured it to be: stacks of yellowed old issues were piled behind the long front counter in the reception area; on the other side of the counter was Noah's desk, hopelessly cluttered, and in the rear of the long, narrow building was the printing press. The building smelled of metal, ink, and old dusty papers.

"Lara, what a pleasant surprise," Noah said, rising to his feet, coming around the counter.

Lara plunged in; she couldn't wait another moment. "I've found something very interesting, Noah." Her hands trembled nervously as she reached into her pocket for the stone, then held it out to him.

"What's this?" His face studied hers. He was obviously puzzled by her excitement.

"Look, Noah—look what I found." Again she pushed the stone under his nose.

"Hey, slow down. You're not making a scrap of sense. What is this?"

Lara took a deep breath. She felt Noah's arm come around her shoulders as he led her over to the bench by the front plate-glass window. She sat down, still very aware of his touch but strangely unaffected by it.

"I found this turquoise stone on the ground, right where the barn door used to be. It doesn't belong to anyone on the ranch—no one. Do you understand what that means?"

"Lara, you are a little crazy—you know that?"

She looked up at him with anger in her face, shaking off his arm. "That's what Branch Taggart said that night I rode out to their house. Are you going to be just like him? Are you?"

"No. I didn't mean anything by it. I'm sorry. Let's start out all over again." Noah's expression showed he really was sorry; she allowed herself to be mollified by it.

She handed him the stone, explaining, "It's the Taggarts'. This piece of turquoise, I was trying to tell you—it belongs to one of them. I found it out at Bitter Creek."

"But how can you be sure it's theirs?" He turned it over in his hand, studying it.

"Aside from the fact that I've already checked with everyone else who was out there, I just know it is!" Here she was, practically screaming at Noah, who was only trying to help her, and it was really Branch Taggart on whom she wanted to vent her wrath.

"Okay, okay," he soothed. "Suppose the stone does belong to a Taggart, or maybe to someone they hired—suppose you're right about everything. Just what does it mean?"

"It means—well, it's so obvious! It means a Taggart was at our place, sneaking around sometime when no one saw them, and lost this stone. Don't you see? It means the person who lost this is the person who set our barn on fire!"

"All right, suppose—*theoretically*—that the stone does belong to whoever burned your barn. How're you going to prove it?" Noah's pale eyes rested on her gravely, almost sorrowfully, as if he wished he didn't have to discuss this distasteful subject with her.

Suddenly Lara's anger was gone, replaced by confusion. "I . . . I don't know how, Noah. I thought you'd help me think of something. That's why I came to you." She turned her green eyes up to meet his beseechingly.

"I wish you'd come to me for a different reason." He spoke softly, almost inaudibly.

She could tell he was tormented; the pained look on his face told her that. But had he given up trying to gain more than her friendship? She couldn't tell. And did she really want him to? What if he were available? He was, after all, appealing. But the question that flew around in her mind confusing her the most was, would he help her?

Finally Noah spoke. "The stone—I'd nearly forgotten. Listen, Lara—why not take it to Deputy Lawson. Ask him."

"I can't. He won't help me—he's made that perfectly clear."

"He might . . ."

"No. That's out entirely. My only hope is to find the piece of jewelry the turquoise came out of."

"Small task," mused Noah.

"Yes," she replied, feeling suddenly dejected. "Like looking for a needle in a haystack." She gave a weak laugh.

"Look," said Noah, resting a hand on her shoulder, "someday I'm sure this will all be cleared up. These things have a way of coming out in the wash . . ."

"After I'm dead and buried and the Taggarts own Bitter Creek," said Lara hopelessly. "Don't you see?"

"What I see is a beautiful young girl who shouldn't be bothering her head with these matters."

"Then who will?" asked Lara heatedly. "What on earth difference does it make that I'm a girl or what I look like? Why must you complicate things? It's so simple to me. It's justice, that's all."

Noah regarded her steadily. "You're right, really. It's uncanny—I've heard suffragettes in New York say things that sounded very similar. I always thought they had to be terrible amazons to believe that, but I may have to alter my thinking."

Then Noah's expression changed from one of musing to one of more intensity as he gazed at her. She wondered what was going on behind his pale eyes, behind that intellectual-looking facade.

And then Noah's hand came up to take off her hat, a warm affectionate smile crossing his lips. Then he did a funny thing, she thought. He wet a finger and rubbed gently at a dusty smudge on her nose. It seemed, at that moment, that he was going to kiss her—his mouth was so close, his arm around her shoulder. She saw desire in his eyes.

"Noah," she whispered. "Please . . . don't . . ." And then, over his shoulder, through the plate-glass window she saw that bright white suit, Stephanie's suit, and Branch walking slowly past the window with her. Branch was smiling at Stephanie, his head bent close to her blond hair, his sculpted lips split in a flashing smile. It registered somewhere in Lara's consciousness that they made an exquisite couple, Stephanie so lovely, Branch so overwhelmingly handsome, so tall and self-assured.

It was as if he sensed Lara's hypnotic gaze on him. And then—it could only have been an eye blink of time— Branch lifted his head, and slowly, inevitably, his eyes turned toward the window, as if he already knew what he would find there.

At the same instant that her breath snatched in her throat, their eyes met and locked. For an endless moment Lara's eyes met Branch's blue gaze through the window. There was no Noah holding her so intimately; Stephanie blurred into a splash of indistinguishable, glaring white.

There was only Branch. And Lara. Her mind went blank. It was as if she were engulfed in a weightless void.

The moment stretched out poignantly until Branch's ice blue gaze was wrenched away from her, shifting narrowly to Noah, resting on him heavily, endlessly.

Branch's features were cast in stone when his glance came back to rest on Lara. She felt her body shiver involuntarily, as if a cold hand pressed on her flesh.

And then the instant passed. It was over. Branch was leading Stephanie past the window, his head turned away from Lara's view.

An overwhelming emotion gripped her then, filling the void. It sent all thoughts of Noah or the turquoise stone flying out of her head. There was only room for one thing in her thoughts: the way Branch had looked at her through the window. And then her mind found the words that described his look.

He had regarded her with disgust and accusation. It made her feel guilty and—she realized, appalled—it made her feel soiled.

Chapter Eleven

"PLEASE, SAY WE CAN GO TO GLENWOOD SPRINGS." begged Jennifer, her round blue eyes ready to fill with tears if needed. "Lara wants to go. She told me. Please, Mama." She crossed her fingers at the tiny fib.

"All right. I suppose there are a dozen errands I need to take care of anyway. And it *has* been a long time since we've all gone somewhere together, hasn't it, Jenn?" Harriet's green eyes began to brighten at the thought. "We can have lunch at the Hotel Glenwood, and maybe even look at dresses at Mrs. McKeever's, to the Natatorium, and catch the evening train back."

"Can't we stay overnight? Please, Mama?"

"We'll see."

Jennifer did not feel the need to press anymore. She'd gotten her main desire—anything else was incidental. A whole day away from the ranch in a city. Well, a small city, to be sure, but at least there was more to see than on the ranch or in Rifle. Now, the question was, what should she wear? The pale pink if it was a sunny, hot day, which was most likely; the cornflower blue if it was cloudy.

When Lara rode in that afternoon from doing the daily ranching chores, Jennifer pounced on her before she got off her horse.

"Lara, we're going to Glenwood Springs on Friday. Mama agreed! Aren't you excited?"

"What for?" asked Lara in her flat way.

"To do errands and shop and have lunch and *see* things!"

"I have things that need doing here."

"Now, if you're going to ruin our day before it even starts . . ." Jennifer's sky blue eyes narrowed warily.

Suddenly Lara looked enthusiastic. "No, wait, I didn't mean it. I'll go with you—of course I will. There are things I'd like to do there too." Her green eyes stared out across the sun-blistered wood of the corral. "I'll really look forward to the trip," she finished, realizing that this was finally her chance to talk to the sheriff of Garfield County.

"And wear something pretty, one of your city dresses. Promise."

"I promise. We'll all look like fashion plates and be soaked with sweat all day under our petticoats and corsets. Why do we women have to put on *those* things?"

"Because we look pretty in them," replied Jennifer smugly.

"I guess so. Well, once in a while won't hurt," admitted Lara, forced to agree with her sister.

So it was that on Friday morning Shad drove the three grandly dressed women into Rifle and saw them off on the eastbound train. They got off an hour later at the small but busy station right on the river in Glenwood Springs.

They noticed immediately that the new Grand Avenue bridge was being constructed across the Colorado River just a block from the station.

"Goodness, I never can get over the way the place grows!" exclaimed Harriet, looking around her. "Every time I come it's so much bigger. Why, I hardly recognize it. Look, they even have electric lights." She pointed to the spot above the street where there were indeed lights strung. "Why, I reckon Denver City has no better than that."

Directly across from the station was the island in the Colorado River that held the famous Indian Hot Springs. They could already smell the sulfur-laden gases that bubbled up from the center of the earth through an age-old, bottomless volcanic crevasse.

The spanking-new Bath House had just been completed, a heavy red sandstone, turreted edifice with bath-house facilities and the five-hundred-foot-long Natatorium, which was a huge, faintly steaming bathing pool.

It was quite a gathering spot for celebrities who came to hunt in the high country, foreigners, all sorts of adventurers, even royalty from time to time. People came thousands of miles to breathe the clear mountain air and soak themselves in the curative waters. The town made a good living off the ancient Indian Hot Springs, selling bottles of the smelly water—Yampah Water—labeling it as a cure for every ill that beset man.

But the Clayton women had too many errands to do before indulging themselves, so they made their way up hot, dusty Grand Avenue, stopping off along the way to do their errands. Harriet bought a bolt of rose silk for a dress, Jennifer purchased some new silk stockings and a precious hat with a plumed feather, and Lara ordered a sack of medicine with which to worm the cattle. They had everything sent to the station, then they stopped for coffee at the new Parkinson Drug Company on the corner and simply watched the people go by.

It was fun, Lara had to admit, to get off the ranch and forget about it for a day, to dress up, almost like at a masquerade ball, and look like a real lady for a change. She was wearing her very finest summer cotton, a white muslin with sprigs of pink rosebuds scattered on the fabric; it had a round yoke of white pleated organdy and long, fitted sleeves. The frilly lace collar, although flattering, was somewhat irritating around her neck, but she did manage to shade herself from the hot sun with a matching parasol. She felt terribly elegant, strolling down the avenue in her finery, white net gloves and all. Even her hair was up in a coronet of thick black braids, with a ringlet over one shoulder. Jennifer had kindly seen to that.

The morning had flown past, but the ladies decided to visit the Natatorium for their swim first and then have lunch in the restaurant of the Hotel Glenwood later, a popular and respectable gathering place, unlike the fifty or so saloons that lined the streets. Ladies—at least, *nice* ladies—didn't even dare look into a saloon.

The marble floors and costly decorations of the Bath House were most impressive. The three women changed into their black stockings and ruffle-skirted bathing costumes, then left the Bath House to emerge into the hot sun of noon and the even hotter water of the pool.

"Oh," breathed Harriet, up to her waist in the water, "I'm not sure I can stay in this!"

"Come on, Mother, we'll go on down to the cool bath," said Lara. "Come on, Jenn."

"If you must. They do say the hot water is healthy and good for the complexion."

"Your complexion is already lovely, dear," said Harriet, patting Jennifer's arm.

They sat on the shallow steps of the cooler pool. "My, this is restful," sighed Harriet. "I *am* enjoying myself. It's been too long since we've done something like this, girls, hasn't it?"

"Much too long," agreed Jennifer, smiling.

"Yes," murmured Lara. "It really is."

"I'm beginning to think about lunch," sighed Jennifer, her eyes half closed against the sun's glare, her dark golden eyelashes lying on her cheeks.

"Mmm," answered Lara drowsily.

"Lara, Mama, look!" hissed Jennifer abruptly. "It's a prince, I think, or a duke or something!"

Feigning disinterest, the three pairs of eyes casually moved to the pool's end. A swarthy man was being helped down the pool steps by two dark-visaged men, obviously servants. He did have a very foreign air about him with a long black waxed mustache and a neat goatee and longish black hair. He was obviously looking for a cure, as one of his legs was badly swollen and gouty.

"Goodness," whispered Lara. "I wonder where he's from?" A garble of an unintelligible language reached their ears. The prince was angry and chastising one of his servants. The women all stared, wide-eyed now.

"I guess," stated Harriet smugly, "it's not such a backwater place to live after all—not if people like *that* come here from all over."

Finally, they reentered the Bath House to shower and change, redoing their hair carefully, feeling somewhat drained by the hot water, but ever so healthy and cleansed.

"Now for lunch," said Harriet firmly as they walked back up Grand Avenue.

It was a warm summer afternoon in Glenwood. The small city of twenty-five hundred souls bustled with cowboys, housewives, businessmen, sheepmen, railroad workers. The saloons were busy, racketing with loud voices, tinkly piano music, women's strident laughter.

The Hotel Glenwood lobby was shaded and quiet this summer afternoon and, since it was late for luncheon, they didn't have long to wait for a table. Idly glancing around at the decor, Lara's eye was caught by a man sitting at a low table in a far corner of the hushed lobby. She could not help but stare. He was a brutally sensual-looking man: a lumpy, perhaps broken nose, fleshy jowls, heavily hooded eyes, very long blond-gray hair that snaked out from under a flat brimmed hat with a wide silver band. She could see his face and part of his body, as he was sitting, but his companion's chair faced him and cut off a portion of her view. He wore, Lara noticed, a buckskin shirt, outrageously beaded with six-inch-long fringe trimming the arms and the yoke and a heavily encrusted turquoise medallion around his neck. He was altogether a most eccentric, outlandish figure— one that you'd find most difficult to forget. Even from across the lobby Lara sensed the dangerous aura that surrounded him in spite of his foppish appearance.

His companion leaned forward then, as if in earnest speech. The eccentric-looking man nodded, not speaking, a smirky grin on his face.

The other man leaned back, finished speaking, and absentmindedly pushed his Stetson back on his forehead, pulling out his tobacco pouch.

Lara gasped silently.

She recognized the companion instantly—the fair, crisp hair, the line of the jaw, the casual way he lit up a cigarette. She'd recognize him anywhere!

What on earth was *he* doing here, in Glenwood Springs, talking privately to such a strange character? What indeed? Private business, Cattlemen's Association business? Perhaps.

It was then that the maitre d' returned for them, ushering the three ladies out of the lobby and into the dining room, where their table was waiting, thankfully banishing the pair of men from Lara's sight.

She hardly saw the menu at first. Her mind searched for an answer to the puzzle of Branch's presence, but the reasons continued to elude her. Then she had to give it up and guess that Branch Taggart had his own business and his own friends, some more disreputable than others. It was certainly not her affair. She had to put it out of her mind.

They had a pleasant lunch, especially since the three women could not help but notice the admiring glances that came their way from the men in the dining room. Jennifer absolutely bloomed, two pink spots of excitement on her cheeks. Even Harriet seemed quietly pleased by the attention. Lara was at first embarrassed but soon grew used to the stares and whispered comments. Then she felt proud that she was part of such an attractive ensemble. Unbidden, she felt her back straighten and her lashes lower provocatively. This man-woman game had, perhaps, its own reward.

It wasn't until they'd finished dessert that Lara allowed herself to remember Branch and the eccentrically dressed man again. Then the stranger's image came into her mind with utter clarity for a split second, just long enough to recall his silver and turquoise hat band and medallion.

A cold whisper of gooseflesh ran down her back. Silver and turquoise. Automatically her hand reached into her reticule and felt for the object there, as if to comfort herself. Was it possible . . .?

"Now what shall we do?" Harriet was asking, patting her pink lips with the linen napkin.

"The dress shop, of course." Jennifer's eyes shone.

"I don't need another dress," Lara put in absently, "after St. Louis. Perhaps I'll look for the Langtrees' store and say hello. I did promise, after all."

"Oh, the lady from the train. Would you like us to come along?"

"Goodness no," replied Lara quickly. "You want to look at the dresses. It'll take you all afternoon. I'll meet you back at Mrs. McKeever's before you know it."

"All right, dear. Don't wander too far and be careful," said Harriet dutifully, her mind already on the racks of beautiful silk dresses.

Lara did stop by the Langtrees' Emporium and said hello to Edna. The woman was glad to see her, pressed some flower seed packets and jelly onto Lara, while appraising her from head to toe. "You're looking well, my dear. It couldn't be easy . . ."

"I'm very glad to be home, Mrs. Langtree," said Lara firmly, "and I love ranch life. I do hope you're enjoying it here."

"Oh, my, I can't complain. Mr. Langtree works hard and we're saving our pennies. Maybe we'll be able to retire someday and go back home."

Home! thought Lara, amused. Edna Langtree could live here for fifty years and still call Chicago "home." Some people didn't adapt easily.

The visit had taken only minutes. Lara hastened back to Grand Avenue and quickly found the place she was looking for: GARFIELD COUNTY SHERIFF, said the sign, and under it, in smaller letters: TOM PRICHARD.

She walked in, stopped at the heavy oak desk, and let her eyes adjust to the dim light inside the building.

"Sheriff Prichard?"

"Yes, can I help you-all, ma'am?" drawled a pure Southern voice.

"Well, I hope so," she began. She introduced herself, told him where she was from, and began on the tale of the burning of their barn. All the while Tom Prichard watched her with faded eyes in his kindly, almost gaunt face. When she finished her story, he said nothing, but began tamping, filling, and lighting a battered old pipe he pulled from one of his pockets.

"Well, now, miss. Got any ideas how the fire might have gotten started?" he finally asked.

"A very good one, Sheriff Prichard," replied Lara grimly. "I think our neighbors, the Taggarts, set it deliberately or hired someone to do it."

"And why ain't Ned Lawson looked into it?" A puff of smoke rose from the pipe.

"He doesn't believe the Taggarts could be guilty. He wouldn't help me."

"Just what d'you-all aim fer me to do, miss?" he asked, squinting against the smoke.

"I have something I found on the spot where the barn burned," began Lara, reaching into her reticule, holding the object out in her palm for Tom Prichard to see. "It doesn't belong to anyone at Bitter Creek. I checked. It belongs to whoever set that fire, Sheriff Prichard."

The sheriff took the turquoise stone, turned it over

slowly, examined it endlessly. "Odd piece. Comes outta some jewelry, I reckon."

"Yes. Don't you see? The man who wore that jewelry lost it that night and I think I know who it was!" she announced triumphantly.

"Who, miss?"

"Well, I don't know his name, but I just saw him over in the Hotel Glenwood talking to Branch Taggart." And she described the man as well as she could, down to the last detail of beads and fringe and lank gray-blond hair. "You can't miss this man. He's a very special type."

"Yeah, miss, he sure is."

"What?" Lara raised a slim, puzzled brow.

"Well, you just described Colt Farnsworth down to the last little bitty detail."

"Colt Farnsworth?"

"Yeah, he's a sorta jack-of-all-trades. You know, hires out to the best price. Been around for years. Carries a fancy Henry rifle and those pearl-handled forty-fives."

"You mean he's a hired-gun killer?" breathed Lara, wide-eyed.

"Well, he generally works on the right side of the law, but mighty close to the edge, mighty close. He'd probably kill his own mother for the right price. But I gotta say, he's real smart—so smart I've never been able to catch him doin' somethin' I could hang him fer. But I'm bidin' my time." His pale eyes drifted from Lara's to a spot somewhere outside the small barred window. "Yes, someday I'll git him."

"This may be your chance. He wears all sorts of silver and turquoise jewelry. I'll bet this is his."

"Mebbe. I could pull him in fer questionin'. Can't hold him, though, lessen I find some hard evidence. And he's too damn—excuse me, miss—smart fer that."

"Keep the turquoise. Maybe it'll help you get him. Sheriff Prichard, I *know* someone set that fire. It wasn't an accident and I want the man caught."

"I'll see 'bout it, miss. Send you word through Ned Lawson if'n I find anything interestin'." He put down his pipe finally, letting it smoke thinly on the scarred desktop, hefted the turquoise stone, and examined it with a pale, shrewd eye. "Yes, interestin' piece."

Lara left the sheriff's office feeling better than she had for a long time. He was going to help her now that she'd given him her evidence and the lead to follow.

Colt Farnsworth. A strange deadly man. A heavy, garishly colored but poisonous serpent. A *friend* of Branch Taggart's? Not likely. She was glad she'd decided to talk to the sheriff, glad she'd thought of it when Jennifer first told her about coming to Glenwood. Someone, at least, was on her side now.

She hurried down the boardwalk toward Mrs. McKeever's Dress Shop, ready to face the racks of dresses, blouses, skirts, petticoats, nightgowns, chemises. She felt as carefree as a bird.

She might even decide to buy something frilly and useless, just to celebrate her new mood.

The next day passed so quickly that the three women could never have said where it went. It began with a visit to an old friend of Harriet's, one Myrna Oldfield, who had moved to Glenwood when it was merely a collection of sod huts. Her husband was now a wealthy man, having invested in real estate, silver, and cattle, and he had built his wife a dark and fussy Victorian house of brick and wrought-iron work and one tall, octagonal tower.

The ladies had lemonade in the shady gazebo while

Myrna's two collies frisked on the nicely kept lawn that ran down to the river. It was a scene, Lara thought, from one of the ladies' magazines she'd seen at Mrs. Bryant's. Even the Clayton women fitted into the idyllic picture: Harriet in pale gray silk draped over a red and white striped underskirt, Jennifer in yellow, with a daringly low neckline, and Lara in a candy-striped, ruffled dress with lots of tiny buttons running down the fitted front to where the skirt was draped back to a graceful bustle.

Clarence Oldfield, Myrna's twenty-five-year-old son, sauntered across the grass shortly to meet the ladies, having heard of his mother's visitors. He was a mild-looking young man with pomaded hair, done up in the latest city style with a high starched collar, striped vest, and white linen suit. He obviously thought he looked quite spiffy and postured ridiculously for the ladies while Myrna clucked over him with motherly affection.

Fortunately, Jennifer soon had him wrapped around her little finger: pouring her lemonade, retrieving her lace hanky, fanning her devotedly. Lara watched with amusement. It looked so effortless when Jennifer did it.

"Mama, have you heard what Clarence is doing this afternoon? He's just told me he's going to the first game of the Glenwood Polo and Racing Association! Why, I had no idea this little old town had *polo* teams!" Jennifer batted her lashes at Clarence and adjusted the neckline of her buttercup yellow dress. His eyes followed her hand as if glued to it. "Could we go to see it, too, Clarence? I've never seen polo."

Blushing, the young man looked at his mother, then over to Harriet. "Well, I suppose so. It's awfully hot and dusty out there, though."

"Mama, please," begged Jennifer.

"Polo," mused Lara aloud. "I'd like that." Her curiosity was aroused.

"If you wish to go, girls, you may. I think I'd rather stay here where it's cool, if you don't mind, Myrna," replied Harriet.

"I'd love to have you, Harriet—you know that," said her friend. "Now, Clarence, you take good care of those two precious girls."

"Yes, ma'am, I will."

Clarence drove them out to the polo field in his mother's carriage after lunch in the gazebo. The girls' skirts puffed like giant posies in the seat and their parasols caught the wind, nearly blowing out of their hands. They laughed a lot and Clarence seemed to become more himself away from home, showing a dry wit whenever he forgot Jennifer's bewitching presence for a moment. Lara rather enjoyed him, knowing he wasn't really interested in her, only Jennifer. He was a pleasant companion with whom she didn't have to play games.

He introduced them to several friends at the hot, dusty field outside of town. They were mostly young men his age, very concerned with their appearances, mostly well off, dropping names of their Eastern colleges like confetti. Lara found them too young, too citified, and foppish, but Jennifer seemed to adore every one of them. Still, they seemed to find Lara attractive, although much quieter than her sister, and the group immediately dubbed the pair of girls Snow White and Rose Red.

The strings of polo ponies rested in the only shade available—a grove of cottonwoods—and the spectators had to stand in the hot sun, enduring choking dust. But it *was* exciting. The game caught Lara's fancy instantly. Harvey Lyle and the Devereaux brothers had started the

Polo Association, explained Clarence, and had taught local cowboys and pack-trip guides to play so they could indulge in their passion for the game. Surprisingly, the tough little cow ponies made good polo ponies and a well-trained one sold for the outrageous price of one hundred and twenty-five dollars.

The mallets flashed, the white ball rolled wildly back and forth, horses galloped up and down the long field, whirling, stopping, spinning, sometimes falling in a tangle of men's and horses' limbs. Miraculously, no one was hurt. After the game, on the arm of one of Clarence's friends, Lara strolled over to where the ponies were tied and took off her net glove to stroke a wet neck, a velvety nose. She couldn't help but picture the Appaloosa stud under a saddle, racing up and down the field. He was just the right size and build for the game. At over a hundred dollars a head, his offspring could bring in lots of money to the ranch. How she longed to jump on one of these ponies' backs and get the feel of a trained polo pony!

Perish the thought. She gave a sidelong glance at her darkly handsome escort and almost burst out laughing. What would he think if she suddenly dropped her frilly parasol, hiked up her candy-striped skirt, and hopped up on one of the horses? He'd probably faint dead away and Jennifer would never, never forgive her! Sedately, she took his arm again, acting the little lady, and walked slowly back to where Jennifer held court, surrounded by the gallant future hope of Glenwood Springs.

When it was time to go home to Rifle, all three ladies experienced a tinge of sadness. They had had *such* a marvelous time. All the way back on the train, Lara was unusually talkative, spewing all sorts of schemes for raising and training polo ponies. Jennifer wept quietly but prettily over a romantic note that had been delivered to her that morning at the hotel. It had been sent by Clarence Oldfield, promised undying love, and had contained a pressed flower that Jennifer held crushed to her breast dramatically.

Shad was waiting with the buckboard in Rifle and saw to the transfer of their luggage and boxes and packages from the train. He cocked an eyebrow at the number of parcels and pursed his lips tellingly but said not a word.

As they waited, still dressed in their finery, a commotion began further on down the platform. They could hear men's shouts and the drumming noise of horses' hoofs on the wooden side of a railroad car. It seemed that some men were trying to unload a horse that had no desire to leave the security of his stall. Finally, three men clinging to his thick neck, a powerful buckskin was led down the ramp, where he stood blowing and flicking his ears at the new scene.

Then a man came up to claim the half-wild beast and Lara drew in her breath in recognition. It was Colt Farnsworth—his outrageous fringed and beaded shirt, his silver jewelry, his long pale hair and fleshy face were too startling to mistake. And the pearl-handled pistols, the bandoliers crossing his wide chest completed the picture.

He led the horse past the gaping people who had gathered to watch the excitement, ignoring them all as if they were insects and of no account to him whatsoever. Then, as he drew abreast of the three Claytons, he stared at them flamboyantly, taking in every detail of their appearance slowly, thoroughly, sensually, then smiled a lazy, knowledgeable grin and tipped his flat-brimmed black hat to them in an audacious, mock-polite manner.

Lara was faintly aware of Harriet's shocked gasp as she watched the man lead his horse past them, swing up into the saddle, and lope off down the street toward the Government Road.

"Who was that strange man?" asked Harriet.

"I can't imagine," Lara replied, shading her eyes with a hand, following his diminishing form as it galloped ominously toward her home.

Chapter Twelve

IT WAS THE SAME SORT OF AWAKENING THAT LARA HAD experienced on the morning of the fire: something was terribly wrong. She drew herself up from a deep sleep, instantly alert.

There was a cracking, a sharp noise that split the air as if wood were being broken.

My God, she thought, the barn was half finished—it couldn't happen again!

But this time quite a different sight met her eyes when she rushed to the window. It was the Appaloosa stud. He was in the corral; a broken fence rail lay in the dust.

Instantly Lara knew what was happening; he was after the mares, he was trying to lead them off!

"Damn you!" she cried uselessly out the window, and then quickly spun around.

She was dressed in a minute and racing through the

front door into the yard in less than two. But it was too late; Goldy had jumped the broken rail along with the stallion and was already following him through the brush to the east of the corral. The only sight that gave Lara any comfort was that of Goldy's foal, struggling unsuccessfully to free himself like his mother had done. The other mares had been left behind and were milling in the corral in confusion.

"She won't go far this time, Miss Lara," grumbled Shad from the bunkhouse, still tucking in his shirttail.

Shad was right. Goldy would not be led too easily away from her foal; no doubt she would be back in the corral by nightfall. Still, the stallion would be reluctant to let her go—he would kick her, nip her, savage her.

Lara's heart clutched at the thought. There was only one hope—she would have to follow them and try to help the mare make her escape. It shouldn't be too difficult this time since Goldy would move slowly, unwilling to stray so far from the foal.

"Let's mount up," she called to Shad through the dawn, who nodded his assent without hesitation.

A short while later, having separated from Shad when they lost the path the horses had taken, Lara was approaching the boundary fence. She rode along the fence line for a time—it was still just barely light—and the going was slow as she strained for signs of the renegade pair. But then suddenly Lara saw tracks where the unshod stud had surveyed the fence, then circled back to collect the waiting mare. A further look at the fence line even provided Lara with proof that the two had indeed leaped over the barbed wire and headed off toward the north face of Wolf Butte, which loomed to the northeast, massive and eerie in the awakening sky.

Lara hesitated. She should head back to find Shad,

but, on the other hand, the delay might ruin her chance for success.

Her decision made, she urged the horse into a careful lope along the wire until she came to an old gate. She was losing precious time now and felt frustration gnaw at her. If the stallion headed up toward Wolf Butte on the opposite side from the Taggart ranch house, then surely Lara would lose them, since the land was so sere and rocky that the pair would leave no tracks. She wondered suddenly, startlingly, if the stallion knew that, too.

The sun rose quietly, chasing the deep shadows back into their places beneath the rocks; Lara followed the faint traces of their tracks, praying she wasn't misreading the signs. After all, there were lots of riders on the range and it hadn't rained for some time.

And then the worst that could happen happened; her horse threw a shoe and went dead lame.

Forcing aside her frustration, Lara reviewed the options: she could try to ride the long, slow trail back to Bitter Creek, or she could swallow her pride, cross the short distance between herself and the Taggart ranch house, and borrow a fresh mount.

The very notion of the latter galled her.

Still, did she really have any choice if Goldy were to be found?

Swallowing her fierce pride, Lara turned the horse and headed toward the Taggarts'.

It hadn't been five minutes since her horse had thrown the shoe when Lara sensed that she was not entirely alone on the range. The sun was low on the eastern horizon still, and somehow she had the chilling impression that someone, or something, was watchi her. Shielding her eyes against the strong morning rays, she searched the brush-spangled hills to the east.

And then she saw him.

Atop a bluff, at least a hundred yards to the east of her, sat a lone figure on a large, thick-necked horse. The man was as motionless as an ageless monument carved of stone—and yet he gave the impression of gazing in her direction. Goose bumps rose unbidden on her flesh. She rode on doggedly, still heading toward the Taggarts'. She told herself he could be anyone: one of the Taggart ranch hands, a drifter, even a traveling preacher.

Her path took her closer to the man as it curved around the bluff, but not so close as to afford her a view of his features. Still she realized there was something about him that tugged at her memory. He sat erect in the saddle, his flat-brimmed hat parallel to his wide shoulders. Neither one of the pair moved. Even as the wind stirred the grass, waving it before the horse's sturdy legs, it did not seem to touch them at all. It was uncanny, as if they were not of this world. Her shoulders hunched up tensely of their own accord.

With grim determination Lara passed beneath the bluff, trying not to give this stranger overdue credence. One last time she glanced furtively in his direction, took in his appearance, and nagged at her memory to recall where she had seen him. Then the sun glinted coldly off the brass plating of his sheathed rifle, off the myriad bullet tips in his bandoliers.

Abruptly she had it. Even his attire gave him away: the buckskin shirt and pants with the long fringe. And, yes, even from this distance she could see his jewelry winking in the sun, too.

What was that awful man doing out on the range at this early hour? Had he been at the Taggarts' or was he *watching* her? And why hadn't she heard from Sheriff

Prichard about him? He had promised to send word through Ned Lawson.

Lara heaved a sigh of relief when she was out of his sight at last. Still, for some time she looked over her shoulder every few feet—just to be sure.

She told herself that this Farnsworth, this sinister apparition, could be here for a hundred reasons. Even if, as she suspected, he was a hireling of Branch's, it might well have nothing to do with Bitter Creek. The man might work for the Cattlemen's Association—he might be tracking for the Taggarts or just hunting. Still, there *was* the turquoise stone.

And then it all came flooding back to her: the fire, the loss of their prize stud, her anger, and the furious ride out to the Taggarts' home. It was almost like reliving a nightmare to be heading toward Wolf Butte again. She could hardly believe she had the nerve to make the trip, to actually invade the Taggarts' home once more.

She passed below the long base of Wolf Butte, but today its shadow did not chill her; it fell to the west of the high rock, off to her left.

She rode up the long entrance way lined with cottonwood trees; it was a déjà vu scene but with one major difference—today was bright and sunny and she was no longer the desperate, hysterical girl she'd been that night. Everything was under control.

Then, before she could change her mind, Lara was knocking at their front door.

Amazingly, her request was honored smoothly as the youngest Taggart, Guy, answered her knock. "You sure can borrow a mount, Miss Lara, and don't worry about your own horse—we'll see to her."

Lara thanked the pleasant-looking, fair-headed Taggart boy and was assured that their foreman, Sam Fuller, would fix her up immediately. He then invited her inside while she waited, but Lara chose to remain on the porch. She'd been fortunate enough not to run into Branch yet—why push her luck?

Guy disappeared for several long minutes, then returned, telling her that Sam was waiting for her. For a fleeting moment she was about to ask Guy what Farnsworth was doing on their range, but then she thought better of it. If Guy *did* know anything, he certainly wouldn't tell her! Perhaps, she thought, she should just come right out and ask if Branch was around—she could demand an answer from him. But then, where would that get her? And what if Farnsworth had nothing at all to do with the fire? Wouldn't she be making an utter fool of herself?

Sam did indeed meet her at the back of the house by the corral. His tall, lanky form was folded against the fence, a cigarette dangling from his mouth, his hat pulled low on his forehead.

"So you've swallowed your crazy talk, miss, and decided to be nice," he said as she walked toward him.

Lara was surprised at the nasty tone of his voice. Did Sam still carry his grudge against the Claytons so close to his heart?

"Come on, Sam. I'm here to borrow a mount, that's all. Guy said it would be all right."

"Yeah, I know. He told me to fix you up. And since I just work for the Taggarts, I guess I have to do what he says."

Lara could not help but see the glance he shot her from under the wide brim of his hat—a look of pure malevolence that nearly set her back on her heels. Could he really hate her so much? She'd only been a kid when his daughter—Craig's wife—had died; she'd had nothing to do with it.

"Sam, please. If it's any trouble for you, I can saddle the horse myself. I'm in a hurry—just show me where the tack is . . ."

"Oh, no, miss. I saddle the horses around here. I want to be sure it's done right. No accidents or anything—you know what I mean? Fer all I know, you ain't got the common sense to know the difference 'tween a saddle and a bridle!"

"Sam Fuller," Lara gasped, "that's an unkind thing to say. You've got no reason . . ."

"Hell, no worse than what you said to them that night at dinner—a little better, in fact."

"Don't remind me, Sam. I'm sorry about all that. Forget it."

"I guess Guy forgot it anyway," Sam said as he slid between the poles of the corral into the group of horses. "He even had a lunch made up for you. It's there on that bale of hay." Then he called, "Here's a good one for you. Brownie. A real sweetheart. He'll give you a good ride." He led a pretty bay with two white stockings up to the gate. Lara was instantly embarrassed. Guy had gone to the trouble of providing lunch! Why? Why should he even think of it, or care? And then Lara realized Sam was waiting for her to open the gate. Suddenly it crossed Lara's mind to wonder if Sam would deliberately give her a dangerous horse. She didn't dare ask; it would only antagonize him further, and Brownie looked docile enough as Sam led him up to the hitching post.

"Here." He thrust the lead rudely into her hand. "Tie him up while I get the saddle." And he disappeared into the barn.

Lara stroked Brownie's soft muzzle while she held him;

he wrinkled his nose and snorted, shaking his mane. She could smell the warm, horsey aroma of him and she breathed it in deeply, willing herself to relax—the delay here was unavoidable. And then she wondered again at Guy's kindness—sometimes it almost seemed as if the Taggart men were human after all.

Sam Fuller broke into her reverie rudely, heaving the heavy saddle onto Brownie's back with a whomp and shouldering her aside to tighten the girth. He turned to her finally, after giving the straps one last yank, and said, "Ready for your hunt, miss? Sure you can handle him? He's a bit high-strung." And an oddly glinting grin broke the weathered brown of his face.

"Yes, thanks, Sam," she said, then swung herself lightly into the saddle, tucking the lunch bag into one of the saddlebags, refraining from throwing out a retort to Sam's insinuations.

Sam stood back, hands on hips, still grinning in that smug way. "Stirrups all right?"

"Yes." Then, giving him a little of his own, Lara nudged Brownie around just enough to coat Sam in a fine layer of dust, feeling oddly satisfied by her childish display of temper.

She set out across the pastureland near the barn rather than following the dirt road. She wanted to head out toward Wolf Butte and the narrow trail that she recalled wound up from its base. The view from there was endless. You could see almost as far as Rifle. She made her way across the range, passing herds of white-faced cattle and a few brood mares with half-grown foals. The morning sun felt warm on her shoulders and Brownie moved effortlessly and willingly underneath her. She found him to be well trained and responsive. So much for her earlier suspicions. She kicked him into a rocking lope across a smooth field and felt the wind catch her hair and tug at her hat brim. A few fluffy white clouds formed on the horizon as the morning advanced. Lara slowed Brownie as the land rose and became rougher as it approached the trail up Wolf Butte. The horse had to pick his way through the prickly, stiff sagebrush and around large boulders fallen from the butte in far-off times, times so long ago as to be unthinkable. The pungent smell of sage drifted up around her as Brownie brushed against the bushes, bruising the thin silvery leaves.

At the foot of Wolf Butte she came across the trail. She turned onto it where it wound up a gully that meandered around and up the side of the steep butte. There was more underbrush here because the gully held a stream most of the years. There were pinyon, a few aspen trees, scrub oak, some bushes with bright berries; ground squirrels chattered and fled before Brownie's hoofs. A fat brown marmot sat on a rock unmoving and a brilliant black and white and iridescent blue magpie scolded her.

If it hadn't been for that renegade stallion, it would have been a peaceful, idyllic ride. When she came across a tiny trickle of the stream, Lara let Brownie stop and drink. He'd climbed steadily for an hour and dark patches of sweat were beginning to show on his shoulders. She patted the side of his neck with affection. And to think she'd suspected Sam of picking her a bad horse! Brownie was a sweetheart.

She reached the top of Wolf Butte—a flat mesa with little shade. She then rode the perimeter of the mesa, staring around her, trying to spot two small creatures far below: her mare and the stud. Finally, her stomach gnawing with hunger, she found a flat place and dismounted to quickly eat the lunch Guy had so thoughtfully provided. She was starved and thirsty. How stupid of her to have ridden out that morning without food.

There was a fat ham sandwich, some homemade brownies, and a canteen of water. And even a carrot for Brownie. Had he told the cook to make it for her? And why go to all that trouble? After all, she was a Clayton.

While she rested for the moment, Lara's musing turned to Branch—a man whose motives eluded her, a man who would see her family driven from the land, then turn right around and smile at her. Perhaps he really didn't know anything about the fire. It must have been his father. That *must* be it, surely. Otherwise, his actions made no sense.

Images of Branch—their encounter in the glade—flooded her mind. It was as if she had been transplanted to another world that day, a beautiful, glorious world of their own making—a world where nothing dreadful could happen.

No, Lara realized, she would never, *never* regret that day. But then, what about the other Branch, the one who doted over his too-sweet blond cousin and looked at Lara as if she were soiled goods. She loathed him for that. And for all she knew about their affair, maybe he had even boasted about it himself!

Rising to her feet quickly, Lara shook off the conflicting thoughts. They were tearing her apart; she mustn't let them confuse her again. The view—that's what she'd come up here for after all. She only had to gaze out at the panorama spread before her. The rangeland stretched away, delineated sharply at the horizon into blue above and brown below. No muted pastels or misty greens. It was all spare and clean cut here, with writhing buttes jutting up to cut the flatness, the sky endless, infinite blue, the earth warm and dry below it. It was often a hard, severe, bitter land, but it was beautiful in its own way and Lara loved it. It was home.

Her eyes traveled over the vista, searching, probing the dots of sagebrush, the stunted pines far below. Still no sign of Goldy or the stallion. Perhaps she had misread their direction or perhaps she was looking directly at them and her eyes couldn't distinguish a clump of brush from a horse's body—it was a long way down.

Blocking the blinding rays of afternoon sun from her eyes, Lara guessed it must be getting late—at least three or so. The last thing she planned on doing was spending the night on the top of this mesa. She would have to admit defeat, at least for this day, and make her way back to Bitter Creek. Goldy would return—her foal was back in the corral. Lara just hoped the stallion would not harm the mare for insubordination.

Her glance swept over the vista one last time for good measure and for a minute her eyes came to rest on what she thought was a man on horseback—it could be that Farnsworth, she found herself thinking—but as she gazed on the bluff miles to the north and far below her, she realized finally that it was nothing more than two large rocks, one behind the other in its shadow. Funny how the eye can play tricks, she thought.

Finally, she remounted Brownie to begin the long ride back down the narrow, rocky gully. She let him have his head; he was surefooted and could easily find his way down without any guidance from her. Daintily, unerringly, he picked his way among the ruts and stones on the gully floor. She was so weary she felt she could almost doze off; her body moved in rhythm with the horse, mesmerizing her.

Slowly, gradually, she became aware that Brownie's

gait was different—he had slowed, his ears perked forward, quivering, and his head held high, as if he were searching ahead for something. Abruptly he stopped short and Lara could feel his whole body quiver as he stood in the middle of the gully, legs braced, waiting for something that obviously terrified him.

It was then that she heard the noise, a distinctive rattling sound—a snake! But where was it? Must be still in its lair, just disturbed by their passing. Nothing new in that.

She patted the horse's neck only to find it sticky with nervous sweat. "It's okay, boy—it's just an old snake trying to rile you. Nothing bad. Let's go." But Brownie wouldn't budge. He stood, trembling, the sweat staining his shoulders and neck dark, his ears pointed toward the rattling. She tried to turn the horse to the side, but he refused to move. She was afraid to get off because he might pull away from her and hurt himself in his fear. The gully was narrow. There was no way to turn the horse off the trail, in the other direction from the rattler, anyway.

Then, suddenly, they both spotted the snake simultaneously, lying next to a smooth rock, coiled in defense. It was crossing Lara's mind that horses generally pay little attention to snakes around these parts when Brownie exploded under her.

She felt herself lose her seat; as if in slow motion, she arched up in the air above the frantic, bucking horse and then the ground came up to meet her. There was a sudden stab of pain in her head, a starburst of pain, then darkness.

By the time Branch finished raging at his youngest brother, Guy was thoroughly cowed. "I can't believe you let her ride off alone like that! Are you completely irresponsible?" he finished, turning on his heel and storming out of the study.

Then, to further blacken his mood, Branch found out that Lara had ridden Brownie up into the hills. He gave Sam Fuller the same enraged lecture he'd given Guy.

"But," Sam defended, "how was I to know she was going way off like that? I warned her Brownie was high-strung. How was I to know?"

Exasperated, Branch went to saddle his own mount, calling back to Sam, "You know Brownie frightens easily! You can hardly control him yourself if he as much as sees a cottontail!"

Angrily tugging the brim of his Stetson down to shade his eyes, Branch reined his horse around so hard the unsuspecting beast reared into the air. Branch swore under his breath and headed the confused animal out onto the Wolf Butte trail in the direction Lara was purported to have taken.

That damn little twit may be able to wrap her mother around her little finger, thought Branch, but on Taggart land things were different. A woman knew her place and stuck to it!

Now there was no doubt the green-eyed hellion had gotten herself in trouble—no thanks to Sam Fuller, he remembered, but still . . .

He followed the trail toward Wolf Butte, then saw Brownie's tracks lead off to the narrower trail that wound its way up to the top of the mesa land.

"Hell," he grunted, knowing the steepness of the trail and Brownie's disposition.

He kicked his mount into a canter even though the way was hard going at best. He thought about Guy's stupidity: providing Lara with a thoughtfully prepared lunch, then letting her ride out on just any old mount. Just plain stupid! No doubt the boy was so infatuated with her that he couldn't even think straight!

A sudden anger aimed at Lara pounded through his veins. Damn her sparkling green eyes—like a witch, you never knew quite how to read her. And her mouth—the full lower lip that seemed to pout even when she smiled. And when was the last time he'd seen that pouting mouth?

"As if you don't know," he muttered bitterly into the wind. With Noah Ackroyd was where—all but falling into his arms, and right in front of the window for everyone to see! And here he had thought her innocence was quite real, uncontrived—certainly not another Stephanie, whose parents shipped her into the mountains once a year to still the wagging tongues of Denverites.

Lara. The name whirled around his brain painfully, yet tasted sweet on his tongue. And shouldn't he have known better than to fall under her spell? He'd been *that* route before. The fleeting moments of bliss were all too soon gone, turning into painful memory. So why, then, had he lain with her that night up in the high country? She'd bewitched him so thoroughly with her pride, her naiveté, her natural fearlessness . . .

And he had told her that day that he would let her go. What a laugh! It was a good thing she'd stayed on her own volition or he would have forced her.

Branch slowed the mount's pace, turning him into the steep, narrow ravine that ascended to the top of Wolf Butte. From here on in the going would be slower.

So what had gone wrong that next morning—what had put the burr under Lara's saddle?

Branch admitted to himself that he probably should have talked to her about their situation the previous evening. Perhaps she was wounded somehow when he hadn't mentioned marriage then. But he did offer the next morning. He owed her that much whether or not a marriage suited him. It was a simple code of ethics and she should have damn well known it without him having to offer in the heat of argument. He was, after all, a gentleman.

"Damn," he swore aloud. What did it matter? She had Noah, and when she broke the poor fool's heart, she'd find another—just like all women.

Suddenly Branch's horse skittered sideways. He pulled up on the reins. Around the pile of boulders to his right, heading hell-bent-for-leather toward home, came Brownie.

Branch's heart bucked—the horse was riderless.

Furiously he forced his mount forward, up the trail, letting Brownie pass them. His horse danced, wanting to join Brownie, fighting for control of the bit over Branch's commands. And all the while Branch suffered a fear—the black fear that a man keeps hidden in the secret places of his soul.

Branch fought his fear. He urged the nervous mount on up the trail, trying to keep Lara's image from driving him mad. The fear surfaced again, like a writhing serpent encircling his being, squeezing him. Again he willed it down.

How far up could she be? Brownie must have been on the trail taking the shortest route home. She couldn't be too far . . .

And then Branch saw her and the fear coiled, seized at him, totally engulfing him.

Lara was lying on the trail, sprawled on her stomach, a dark pool of blood spreading in the dust from beneath her head.

He had to waste precious time tying his horse or it

191

would have bolted for home. He silently cursed the begrudged time. Finished, he turned to Lara, kneeling down beside her.

For a fleeting moment his hands reached for her but then hung suspended in midair: the fear was unbearable.

She's all right, he promised himself. It's only a head wound—they bleed a lot . . .

The fear subsided grudgingly. He reached again for her and carefully rolled her over. In an agony of suspense he put his ear to her heart. She was breathing! He let out a long, ragged breath, then tore the bandana from his neck and pressed it against the wound.

Lara groaned. Her breasts rose and fell weakly beneath the dusty shirt. One thing for certain: she had to be taken off this mountain and fast.

Branch scooped her into his arms tenderly, leaning her head against his shirt. He called on all his reserves to mount the horse while still cradling her against him. The wound had stopped bleeding and the last thing he wanted to do was to disturb it.

The ride back to the ranch stretched out forever and yet he was reluctant to see it end.

At one point Branch nearly laughed aloud at his notion: this was a helluva way to tame the girl, but if it worked . . .

He glanced down at her dark head, then found his lips brushing the tangled mass. No, he thought, there was no way to tame Lara—she was too much like the land that had borne her.

Chapter Thirteen

THE BEAM OF SUNLIGHT STRUCK LARA'S CLOSED EYES AND she could feel the brightness through her closed lids. She stirred under the colorful quilt, rolled away from the light, then tried to doze off again. But she was half awake—just close enough to the edge of consciousness to know that she would not really sleep much longer and to feel nagging worry—something she had to remember.

Then her heart lurched with remembrance and she sat bolt upright. Instantly, her head throbbed while her eyes took in the strange room. It was a cheerful room—white stucco walls with dark oak beams running across the ceiling, bright yellow ruffled curtains on the deeply recessed window, and a tiled floor with a beautiful Navajo rug. A graceful pottery vase with a dried array of grasses in it sat on the Spanish-style dresser and the mirror that hung over it had an intricately carved antique frame. It occurred to her that she would admire the room very much under normal circumstances, but right now . . .

It was all returning to her in a rush of jumbled images: the accident, waking up in the Taggarts' house, the doctor's cool fingers on her head. The doctor must have given her some laudanum—he'd said the stuff was for pain and she'd taken some because her head hurt so. That was it. Otherwise she never would have been able to sleep in this room, the Taggarts' guest room.

How long had she been there? She had the awful lost feeling that a block of time was missing, but how much time she couldn't say. She tried to sit up, but her head ached, so she stopped after struggling to a half-upright position on the pillow. Her body ached all over. She put a hand to her head and felt a bandage and under it a lump like a goose egg.

It was then that the thought first occurred to her—who had brought her here? She searched her mind—she couldn't exactly remember. She must have been half conscious. But there remained in her mind a clouded impression of strong arms holding her, a familiar voice reassuring her.

Somehow she knew who it had been. She felt a tired exasperation. Why did Branch always manage to be in the right place. Why was he always extricating her from fixes? It was as if he followed her around, which was ridiculous.

The door opened softly; she barely had time to turn her head toward it.

"She's awake," said a strange male voice, then, precipitously, two young men stood on the threshold, staring at her. One was Guy, the brother she'd already met; the other was obviously the middle Taggart boy.

"Hello again," said Guy, smiling sheepishly at her.

"I'm Robert Taggart," the other young man said, introducing himself soberly. He was brown haired with a serious, solid look about him.

As the two men approached her bedside, Lara was instantly aware of their likeness—oh, they looked different enough, but there was a distinct aura of maleness, of total self-assurance. There was no doubt in her mind that they were very much Taggart men.

"How do you feel?" asked Robert.

"I'm not sure yet." She tried to smile.

"Branch made us swear not to pester you, but we couldn't resist," said Guy conspiratorially. "We haven't had anything like this happen in this house for years. It's an occasion."

"So we just peeked in to see how you were," went on Robert, "and you were awake."

"What time is it?" asked Lara.

"Around six o'clock in the evening, I reckon . . ."

"You mean I slept all afternoon?" she asked, aghast, trying to rise. But her head swung with dizziness and she felt nausea rise in her stomach. A sharp pain shot through her side. Strong hands pushed her back against the pillows and she was vaguely aware that she kept saying, "I'm sorry to be so much trouble . . . I'm sorry . . .," as the darkness engulfed her once more.

She had strange dreams—the Appaloosa stud galloping away from her across the hills, always just out of reach. She felt a terrible frustration and a sharp sadness. And then the stud turned his head toward her and his eyes were mocking and laughing at her, and they were blue eyes, as blue as Branch's, and then he was Branch, but the eyes were no longer mocking and cruel. They were kind and full of deep concern and they floated over her in the ragged-edged darkness.

Once she thought she heard a familiar low voice talking to her, calling her name, and then, too, she thought she felt a hard, warm hand hold hers, but it was all confused and mixed with her dreams.

When she was truly awake again it was dark, but a kerosene lamp sat on the dresser and shed a yellow light over the room.

"Lara?" The voice was low and husky, full of relief.

She turned her head painfully. Even the dim light was enough to make her blink. Branch sat on a chair next to her bed, leaning forward, a worried crease on his brow. "Thank God you're awake. I was afraid . . . How do you feel?"

Lara gave a wan laugh. "Everyone keeps asking me that. I'm not sure. I haven't been awake long enough . . ."

"Everyone?" asked Branch, his mouth turning down at the corners grimly.

"Your brothers . . ."

"They disturbed you?"

Seeing the flash of anger in his eyes, she said quickly, "I invited them in. I was awake for a short while and they were very pleasant. Honestly, they didn't disturb me."

Branch muttered something under his breath, then seemed to catch himself. "Well, you sound all right." He smiled then. "The doctor said nothing was broken, but you have a concussion. I reckon your head is going to hurt pretty bad for a time."

"I guess I should thank you," she fumbled, suddenly shy.

"It's just lucky I found you. That damned crazy horse nearly killed you. It's our fault. We owe you an apology." His voice was gentle with her; it was hard to believe all those cruel words had been spoken, just as hard to imagine the passion that had ignited between them.

She shifted restlessly. Quickly he bent over her, helped rearrange the pillows behind her head. His hands were as gentle as a breeze. He touched her cheek softly. She closed her eyes in tired acceptance.

"Lara?" His tone was low and intimate now, strange to her ears. The sound lay on the air with dulcet heaviness, echoing and reechoing silently. She could feel her whole being begin to reach out to him, melt into the gentle sensation that embraced them as if they were alone, totally alone in the universe.

"Here you are!" The words came from the doorway. "Oh, Lara! How on earth are you?" The taut line between Lara and Branch was suddenly snapped as if it had been cut with a coldly honed blade.

Jennifer rushed into the room, filling the air with her perfume, her presence, her worried questions. "Oh, you poor thing! Where does it hurt?" she cried. "Mama sends her love. She wanted to come, but I thought I better . . ." She turned to Branch. "That ranch hand you sent to fetch me was so nice, and he tried so hard not to upset us. But, oh! How we worried! Although I can tell now that you're going to be fine. Isn't she, Branch?"

"Yes, Miss Jennifer, I think so." He leaned close to Lara's ear. His breath tickled the tendrils of her hair. "I think I best leave you in your sister's capable hands. I'll be back later."

Jennifer plumped herself on the chair by the bed. "What *happened?*" she asked, wide-eyed. "The ranch hand only said that you'd been thrown and had hit your head. I couldn't imagine *you* being thrown!"

"I was following the Appaloosa and my horse went

lame. I was closer to the Taggarts' than I was to home, so I stopped to ask if I could borrow a mount. I was so close! I could have caught him! He was heading right toward Wolf Butte. Anyway, the horse Sam Fuller gave me was kind of crazy. He spooked and threw me. That's all." Lara reached out and touched Jennifer's hand. "I *am* glad you came. This house is all full of *men!*"

"That's why I came, sis." Jennifer winked. "I've never been in the Taggarts' house before and I thought it was a propitious moment to make my entrance, don't you?"

"Jennifer!" scolded Lara, then she relented. "Well, at least you made a better entrance than I did. I barely remember anything." She tried to straighten up and winced with pain.

Jennifer took a cloth and wet it in the washbasin. "Here," she said, placing it on Lara's forehead. "You poor baby." She bustled around the room for a moment, examining everything. "Looks like you've got old Branch eating out of your hand—lucky girl," she flung over her shoulder as she patted her hair into place in front of the mirror.

"Oh, Jenn! Don't be silly. He was merely being . . ."

"What?" interrupted Jennifer. "And don't say polite, Lara. He wasn't being merely *polite* when I saw him just now." She sat by the bed once more and leaned forward. "The man they sent over with the message said Branch followed you and found you and brought you back. Don't tell me he isn't madly in love with you."

"Oh, drop it, Jenn. I don't feel like arguing," Lara sighed.

"Oh, honey, I'm sorry. Would you like a glass of water? I even brought some of Mama's mint syrup."

"I want to go home, Jenn."

"Home? But I just got here. Look, you can't go home.

You can't travel. You're hurt. The doctor left directions that you are on no account to be moved from this house."

"I want to go home," repeated Lara stubbornly. "I can't stay here."

"Why not? I'm the perfect nurse *and* chaperon. It's about time we made friends with the Taggarts."

"Friends! Friends with the Taggarts! I'll never be a friend of theirs. There are things you don't even know!" Suddenly Lara remembered Farnsworth, his shadowy figure motionless on the tall bluff. There was lots Jennifer didn't know about.

"But they're treating you like a queen! They want you here! They've even asked me to stay for a few days. Lara, don't be stubborn."

"I can't stay here!"

"That's ridiculous. You *will* stay. It's settled."

"What's settled?" asked a familiar, drawling voice at the door.

"Oh, nothing," replied Jennifer hastily. "Just girl talk."

"I just stopped by to let you know dinner is ready. Lara, I can have a tray sent up to you."

"Oh, no, please. I couldn't be such a bother . . ."

"Don't be silly," began Jennifer.

"It's no trouble," said Branch.

"I won't be treated as an invalid," Lara said more strongly. "I feel much better. I'd like to join you, to thank your father for his hospitality."

"Are you sure you're feelin' up to it? You've had a pretty bad shock." Branch stood in the doorway, a worried crease on his brow.

"I insist. Now if you'll give me a few moments to freshen up, I'll be ready . . . Oh! I don't have anything to wear but my . . ."

"I brought a few of your things," said Jennifer. "When did I ever go anywhere without a change? The bag is out in the hall."

Branch unfolded his arms, cast Jennifer a concerned look as if to say, "Watch Lara carefully," then disappeared.

"Lara," began Jennifer, "are you sure?"

"I will *not* be waited on by the Taggarts," said Lara firmly. "I will not be any more beholden to them than I have to."

"All right," sighed her sister, "I'll get your clothes."

While Jennifer was gone, Lara swung her legs carefully over the side of the bed and pushed herself to her feet. For a moment she swayed as the blood left her head, but she told herself it was only because she had been lying down for so long. She walked across the room to the washbasin and splashed cold water on her face. Peering at herself in the mirror, she was shocked by her paleness and the livid bruise that spread out from under the bandage on her head.

She tried to brush out her hair, but the tugging hurt. What she really needed was a long, hot bath.

Jennifer returned with the carpetbag. "What about the pale yellow? I brought that one. It's easy to get into, anyway."

"Anything, it doesn't matter. Will you help me with my hair?"

It took a while to get Lara into a chemise, a petticoat, and the crisp, summer dress. The corset was out of the question—her ribs were too bruised. Finally, she was as presentable as Jennifer could make her.

The walk down the hall to the steps seemed endless. Lara had only reached the top of the stairs when the ache in her ribs made it impossible for her to catch her breath. Maybe it had been a mistake for her to attempt dinner tonight—she wasn't even hungry. Her head swam sickeningly; every step seemed to jar her head until it pounded so loudly she was sure everyone could hear it.

She stopped to catch her breath on the stairs, reaching a hand out to steady herself on the banister, but suddenly a cold sweat broke out all over her body and everything seemed to be receding, receding down a whirling tunnel. Vaguely, she heard Jennifer's cry of alarm and she felt her knees begin to buckle.

Then suddenly strong arms were lifting her, steadying her, and she was aware of her head resting against a solid male chest and aware, too, of a faint but well-remembered masculine scent surrounding her.

He carried her easily down the rest of the stairs and she didn't even protest. It was awful to let herself feel so secure in Branch's arms, but she hadn't the strength to deny herself the comfort.

Carefully, he set her down on a sofa at the bottom of the stairs. "Better?" he asked.

"Yes, thank you," she mumbled, embarrassed by her display of weakness, unable to raise her glance to meet his.

"Do you want me to carry you back up?" Branch hovered over her. "I think it might be best."

Her head came up abruptly. "No. Really. I'm all right now." The back of her legs still tingled where his arms had supported them—she dared not let it happen again.

She stood up, fought the weakness in her limbs, and walked firmly toward the dining room, leaving Branch to exchange a wry look with Jennifer.

Joe and his two younger sons were gathered at the

other end of the dining room around the whiskey decanter, waiting: Joseph Taggart, straight as a ramrod, still tall and ruggedly aristocratic; Robert, solid as the earth; and Guy, blond and full of fun. With them, in the center of the group, stood Stephanie Huston, stunning in a beaded black evening dress that showed a great deal of her white, swelling bosom. The moment she saw Lara she glided over to her and greeted her effusively. Her bell-like voice seemed to penetrate Lara's head and cause it to ache again.

"Oh, my dear," Stephanie was cooing, "you are so brave to join us. Why, you look wonderful. I can hardly believe you're up and about. It would have taken me weeks, I'm sure!" Her white hand fluttered like a bird, landed on Lara's arm briefly, flickered away; her pink lips curved in an ingratiating smile; her eyes remained as cold as blue ice.

Later Lara was to marvel at the fact that she got through dinner at all. Stephanie was determined to remain the queen bee, acting as hostess, drawing every man's attention with practiced deliberation. Her strident voice pounded unceasingly into Lara's head.

It was only Jennifer's ability to charm them all that made the meal bearable. Her soft, womanly beauty shone in the formal setting of the Taggarts' dining room, her natural allure and high spirits the perfect foil for Stephanie's diamond-edged sophistication.

It did not escape Lara's notice that Stephanie's cleverest remarks and most scintillating smiles were all for Branch. It was obvious enough to be slightly embarrassing. Jennifer kept shooting quizzical glances in Lara's direction as if to say, "Defend yourself—say something!" but Lara was very quiet, uncomfortable at being a guest of the Taggarts and feeling so ill that she could barely touch her food.

At last, thankfully, the fine meal was over, the ladies rising to leave the men to their Havanas and whiskey.

Stephanie's hand fluttered to Branch's arm, touching him lightly, her pink lips open in a coy smile. "You won't be long now, will you, Branch, dear? It gets so lonesome in this big house without you men! Why, doesn't it?" She turned to Lara and Jennifer, including them briefly, condescendingly in the conversation as they left the dining room.

But Branch merely smiled absently and went to stand over Lara. "Let me carry you upstairs," he offered softly. "You're not well."

"No, please," she murmured. "Don't bother yourself. I'll do just fine. Jennifer will help me."

"I insist," he said somewhat gruffly then, his blue eyes the color of a moonless evening sky. "Don't be so all-fire stubborn, Lara."

"I'm not being stubborn," she hissed back. "I'd rather not . . ."

"What?" broke in Branch. "Have me touch you? Is that it?"

"Yes," she admitted, meeting his angry gaze staunchly, holding his eyes with her own.

Branch raked a frustrated hand through the rumpled thickness of his hair. "Look, Lara . . ." he began, but was interrupted by his brother, Guy, who emerged from the dining room, wearing a big white smile.

"I'll carry you up to your room, Miss Clayton. I guess we'll each have a turn at it."

"Really . . ." Lara started to protest, feeling stifled by all the male domination, but Guy gave her no chance. He swept her up into his arms and bounded up the stairs as if she weighed nothing, grinning at her self-consciously all the time.

She was unaware that Branch stood at the bottom of the steps, a look as black as a thundercloud on his handsome face, and that Stephanie's expression was smugly content and even the tiniest bit triumphant.

"Thank heavens *that's* over," sighed Jennifer as she helped Lara undress. "I was nearly ready to scratch that woman's eyes out!"

Lara looked at her sister questioningly. "She certainly is rather obvious, but why should it bother you? They all thought *you* were absolutely wonderful."

"It bothers me because she's after Branch and you won't defend your claim."

Lara sighed. "He's not mine, Jenn. I don't want him. Can't you understand?"

"Frankly, no." Jennifer pulled Lara's nightgown over her sister's head, then brushed out Lara's hair. "There, you're all ready for bed. You could use a good night's sleep. Everything will look better in the morning. I'll be right next door if you need me."

Thank the Lord for Jennifer, thought Lara. Somehow just the notion of her sister's proximity lifted her sagging spirits. She lay in bed, dozing off, and decided that she'd go home tomorrow no matter what. Branch's presence was unbearable.

Then a new thought brushed her mind as she lay in the quiet darkness: the piece of jewelry from which the turquoise was missing—if it weren't Colt Farnsworth's—was most likely somewhere in this house. If she were really brave, she'd search for it, prove her suspicions to the world, but somehow she knew she could not do it. It would be utterly dishonest and petty after the kindness

204

they had shown her. But then, she couldn't help but ask herself, why were they being so kind—even Joe Taggart, her father's eternal adversary? It could be, she realized bitterly, that they sought to woo her into selling Bitter Creek. If vinegar didn't work on her, then they would try honey. Perhaps that was behind all their sweet talk.

Lara's heart sank. If that were true, then all of Branch's kindness had merely been contrived to coax her over to their side along with Jennifer and her mother—Branch's kindness and, she reflected dismally, his seduction of her, too.

Her last thought before drifitng into a restless slumber was that the Taggarts could burn down the new barn, the house, everything, but her family would still have the land, and if she had anything to say about it, they would never give that up.

The snick of the door latch woke Lara instantly from a tangled dream. "Who's there?" she managed to whisper, her heart beating against her ribs like a caged bird. Somewhere in her consciousness a voice told her it was only Jennifer.

But there was no answer, merely the faintest whisper of a movement, a shadow that was blacker than the inky darkness of the room.

She parted her lips, not quite clear as to whether to ask another question or to scream, but a hard hand suddenly covered her mouth, choking off all sound.

She had a moment of blind panic, a fear realer than that of the shifting nightmares she'd been having. She tried to reach up and fight the hand on her mouth but found her arms imprisoned beneath the quilt.

"Lara, be quiet," came the words then, half growled, half whispered. "Stop struggling."

Then she knew who it was and her panic subsided, replaced by a new, even more terrifying anxiety. He removed his hand from her mouth; she became aware of his quiet breathing very close to her.

"I'm sorry I had to do that. I was afraid you'd wake someone up . . ." His tone was almost hesitant, as if he were not sure of why he was there, of what exactly he was doing.

"What are you doing here? You nearly scared me to death!" Although her voice was angry, she knew that was not truly what she was feeling. She was fully awake now, aware of his masculine odor, the threat of his size as he loomed over her. Slowly, her eyes began to adjust to the darkness.

"I'm sorry I scared you." His finger reached out to touch her lips with gentle care. "Did I hurt you?"

"No, you only frightened me out of my wits."

Then his hand was on her breast, warm through the thin fabric of her nightgown. "I can feel your heart beating . . ."

And so could she as the sensations of his touch sent her mind reeling.

"Do you have any idea how bad I want you?" he asked lazily, with a casual drawl. "I couldn't even bear to see my own brother touch you. My own brother!"

His hand was shifting upward, seeking the satin tie that held the bodice of her nightgown together. "No, don't . . ."

"Why not? We've had each other once. I can't do you any more *harm*." His voice was sarcastic. He leaned close in the darkness and kissed her throat just where it hollowed above her collarbone. "I've been wanting to do that all evening."

"But Stephanie . . . ?"

206

"Never mind her," said Branch, digging his fingers into her tangled, heavy black hair, pulling her head back ever so gently. His lips closed over hers, draining her of all strength and will. His touch eroded her resistance with its demanding sweetness.

His head drew back; she could just distinguish his features, shadowed in the darkness. His eyes were merely dark pools. A stray gleam of moonlight outlined a lean jawline. He wore no shirt and his bare chest touched her arm.

"Why are you doing this?" she breathed, shaken, melting. "Why can't you leave me alone?"

"Damn it! I don't know why!" He gave a short, harsh laugh. "Fate seems to be throwing us together. We may as well give in to it."

And then he kissed her again, fiercely, until she moaned under him with pain and desire. Somehow he was lying next to her on the bed and his hands touched her everywhere: brushing her taut nipples, stroking her legs under her nightgown, tickling, teasing, manipulating, until the core of heat within her grew and spread, aching.

He drew her nightgown over her head and stared at her for a long time, seeing how the moonlight collected in opalescent pools in the hollows of her body.

He pulled off his jeans and slid his hard, lean body next to hers. His mouth traveled from her forehead over her face and neck, down to her breasts, lingering to savor their ripeness, then lower still, licking a lava-hot trail of desire down her belly and across her hips. His tongue found a spot on her hip that caused Lara to gasp aloud in delight. He explored the area, then moved his head to her other side, tracing his lips over her flesh until her nails dug into his shoulders and he raised his head with a deep chuckle, tormenting her.

Lara stroked his head, ran fingers through the thick mass of blond hair until he lowered it once again over her belly. The tension within her mounted until her hips were writhing of their own volition. Then his head lowered further still and found her core.

"Branch!" she whispered, horrified. "No, you can't . . ."

"It's all right, Lara. Let me." His voice was husky in the darkness. "Let me show you." And she hadn't the strength or will to stop him.

The sensations became wilder, unbearable, swirling her to greater heights, until she thought she could rise no more. Then he stopped. She almost cried out in frustration, her whole being tensed, waiting. It was as if he teased her, preparing her for the greatest height, leading her on. When he finally penetrated her, she felt the spiral beginning again, so powerful, so fast, that she was surprised, and then her whole body pulsed with release and joy.

She lay spent but Branch was still hard inside her. He began slow, sensual movements within her and soon she was reaching for the sweet agony again, gasping, slick with sweat, mindlessly pursuing fulfillment. Her body took over, feeling only the darting pleasure, the building, the journey to the edge as his shaft filled her, then left, then filled her again. She reached the edge, the agony for release almost unbearable, and shuddered, falling into the depths of sensation. Branch joined her this time and they were swept together into the exquisite oblivion.

When it was over, Branch's body still lay, sweat-slicked and relaxed, so close to her that she could feel his heart beat. Her head rested on his shoulder, one of her legs sprawled over his. She felt utterly content.

She traced a line with her finger along his arm. The

hard, masculine flesh thrilled her. Its very strangeness felt so right under her hand.

"Seems like you're made for me," she heard him say finally, breaking the sighing tranquility of the night. "You're good for me . . ."

She remained silent. Tiny shoots of reality began to sprout, working their roots into her thoughts as if into the winter-split crevasses of a boulder.

"You won't try to ride off from me this time, will you?" he asked, nuzzling her neck, running fingers over the sensitive spot on her smooth hip.

She gave a short laugh. "I'm hardly in the position to right now."

"No, and I'd like to keep you in this position for days, weeks . . ." His voice had an edge of humor to it.

Lara wished the thoughts would stop invading her peace but she had to know—she couldn't let him this near and keep wondering.

"How do you know Colt Farnsworth?"

There was a long, uneasy silence in the darkness. Finally Branch replied, "He works for the Association."

"You mean the Cattlemen's Association?"

"Yes. Occasionally, when we've had trouble with rustlers, I have to deal with him." His tone was level, easy. Silence fell between them again and she felt every nerve in her body grow taut. Then he asked with exaggerated insouciance, "Why?"

"I saw him this morning . . . on your rangeland. I've heard he's . . . he's a rather disreputable character . . ."

"He is, Lara." Branch's tone remained noncommittal. "Sometimes, as ranchers, we have to deal with his sort. He is an excellent tracker and I reckon he has always done right by the Association."

Lara digested his words. He sounded sincere enough

and what he said made sense to a point. Besides, she reminded herself, there were lots of men around these parts who wore silver and turquoise jewelry. Still . . .

She felt the proximity of Branch's body, so close, so near to her that her own cool flesh was warmed by his. She felt torn. She wanted desperately to stay here with him, but . . . "Branch?" she whispered. "I can't stay here."

He stiffened. "Not even one more night?"

"No more nights like this, Branch," she said more firmly.

"Why not? Marry me and we'll have every night . . ."

"Is that all you want me for?" she asked, rising up on one elbow.

"You've gotta know better than that . . ."

"I know that if I did marry you it would be the easy way to get control of Bitter Creek Ranch since burning us out didn't work."

"You damn stupid . . . !" Branch sat up precipitously. "Is *that* what you think?"

"Yes." Such flat, irrevocable words.

"Why won't you believe me?" he asked tightly.

"Branch, I know about your first marriage." She heard his quick intake of breath. "You don't want to marry anyone, not really, unless it's for some other reason, like the land. You don't want a wife. You want a female body and a dowry, that's all. Marry Stephanie. She'd believe you wanted her. She'd say yes."

"Stephanie is not a subject we need to discuss."

"No. She's none of my business."

He was silent for an endless time. "It's that Noah Ackroyd, isn't it? What would he say if he saw you here—like this?"

"Oh, Branch," she sighed hopelessly, "it's not Noah, it's not anybody. It's just *us*. We could never fit together."

"You're a fool, Lara. No match was ever made in heaven. You're foolish and you're young and you're too damn idealistic," he growled, rising from the rumpled bed and pulling on his pants. His dark form padded noiselessly to the door. He opened it, stopped for a minute, and turned as if to say something. Finally, he ran a hand through his hair, turned away again, and was gone.

Alone in the dark, Lara felt suddenly drained and hurt. How easy she made it for him, giving her body freely—a loose woman. And yet he had asked her to marry him—she sighed inwardly—but for all the wrong reasons. Branch might desire her physically, but surely that was all. He'd had his fill of marriage. It showed sometimes in his eyes. No, he couldn't possibly want another wife. What he wanted was Bitter Creek, and she mustn't ever let herself forget it.

Chapter Fourteen

THE ROOM WAS BRIGHT WITH MORNING SUN BY THE TIME Lara awakened; it was perversely cheerful in the face of her inner turmoil. Her mind, disoriented and dull with sleep, was immediately filled with the memory of Branch's nocturnal visit. For a split second she wondered if it had all been a dream, but that was cowardly—she knew that he had really been there, touched her, said those things. And she knew too, that she had responded to him, opened herself to him wholly; and she'd been as much at fault as he.

She lay in bed, half dozing, going over the whole thing in her mind—every nuance of his voice, every move of his whipcord-strong body—and she knew that she'd have done the same thing again in the same circumstances. God, she was weak.

She heard a timid tap at her door then, giving her a slight start. "Yes?" She patted her cheeks quickly for color, then ran hasty fingers through tangled hair. "Come in," she said finally.

The door swung open. A breakfast tray preceded Concepción's stout figure. "You must be very hungry, Señorita Lara," said the cheerful servant, clucking her tongue.

"Thank you," Lara replied, "but I'm not really." While Concepción fussed with the pillows, then propped the tray on Lara's knees, she had the vague impression that the servant was avoiding her eyes.

Did she suspect? Did *everyone* in the Taggart household suspect what had happened in this room last night? She felt her stomach roll sickeningly and her appetite disappeared completely.

"Would the *señorita* care for a bath?" asked Concepción, smiling kindly.

Lara nodded. "Yes, please." Then: "Have you seen my sister today?"

"Oh, yes. She went riding with the *hombres*—they wanted very much to show the *señorita* the ranch," giggled Concepción knowingly.

Lara opened her mouth to ask if she had seen Branch but decided against it. And then she hoped Jennifer wouldn't dally too long, since suddenly she very much wanted to be on her way home—as early as possible.

She left breakfast untouched and bathed instead—a long, soothing bath to relax her still aching body while she tried to sort out the troubled thoughts plaguing her. Everything in her life seemed topsy-turvy—nothing was as it should be. One moment a smile would tug at her full lower lip, remembering the oneness she and Branch had experienced, but then the next moment she felt near tears, reminding herself that he was using her and she had allowed herself to fall into the same category as a common saloon dancer. Next he would be giving her gifts for her favors! She savaged herself unmercifully with the thought.

Yet emerging from the confusion of her thoughts was the one single undeniable fact: she was rapidly falling in love with him. It was a terrible truth she could no longer hide from herself. With great effort, she put the thought from her. Later, when she was away from here, she would think more on it and find a way to rid herself of this love.

She dressed in the only other outfit Jennifer had thought to bring along: a white blouse with a high frilly collar and a blue and white seersucker skirt. She combed out her thick, damp hair, taking great care not to disturb the bandage, and pinned the heavy mass into a loose, full bun at the back. She noticed that her coloring was still pale and that her eyes appeared glassy—no doubt a hangover from the injury. All in all, she realized dismally, she looked terribly out of sorts.

Concepción returned, scolded Lara about not eating breakfast, then informed her that Señor Branch and Señorita Stephanie were lunching on the sun porch. Would Lara care to join them? It would do her good.

She followed the servant down the stairs, thinking that there was no time like the present to inform Branch that she was leaving as soon as possible. Even now Lara was not certain that she could face him at all, and especially with that Stephanie around.

Stephanie. Was there something between her and Branch? He certainly had brushed aside all her questions concerning the blond woman. Perhaps he really cared for Stephanie and was protecting her reputation. And then she had a thought that stabbed her with hot agony: My God! Had Branch taken her to bed too?

Approaching the double doors in the dining room that led out to the sunny porch, Lara felt suddenly, miserably uncertain. It must show. All the blood had drained from her face.

Mechanically, her feet carried her the few remaining steps; she was somehow out on the porch, shielding her eyes from the bright sun, approaching Stephanie and Branch.

He rose immediately, led Lara over to a wrought-iron chair next to his, then seated her as if she might shatter like a porcelain doll. She was all too aware of the spot on her arm where his hand had just touched her so gently.

Glancing toward the blond woman, Lara permitted herself a brief moment of self-satisfaction; at least Branch treated her with respect in front of Stephanie.

Stephanie's eyes narrowed. "My, my," she trilled, "you seem quite recovered."

"I do feel much better today," Lara agreed, meeting Stephanie's glare with as much assurance as she could muster.

"Then you'll be leaving?" replied Stephanie, resting a possessive gaze on Branch, who seated himself next to her.

Suddenly, she recalled why she had come down here in the first place. "Why, yes . . . I really must be going . . ."

"Nonsense," interrupted Branch. "You're staying right here until the doctor says otherwise." It was then that Lara noticed—or perhaps she only imagined it—that Branch had not taken his gaze from her, not even for an instant. Her heart gave an involuntary lurch, one that she forced herself to ignore. Even while she argued with Branch about leaving, her thoughts were turned to Stephanie, now standing over him, her hair coiffed perfectly in a blond bun at the back of her head, her petal-pink dress crisp in the morning light. Stephanie had everything in her favor—everything: a wealthy Denver background, an Eastern education, beauty and sophistication. How could Lara hope to compare . . .

". . . and that's final," she heard Branch say.

There was no point arguing; she would just have to leave when he was busy elsewhere.

Lara glanced up from the cup of tea and met Stephanie's eyes; she quite obviously had caught the woman unaware, for the look on Stephanie's face was one of cold loathing. The moment stretched out tensely and Lara refused to tear her eyes away. Why should she back down? And then, mercifully, Sam Fuller appeared, seeking Branch's presence out at the corral.

Branch rose, reached over, and squeezed Lara's hand. "I'll be back shortly. Just stay here in the fresh air and rest. Stephanie will keep you company. And no more talk about leaving!" He straightened, then turned to his distant cousin. "You talk some sense into her, Stephanie."

"Oh, I will Branch, dear . . . I will."

Branch must be blind, Lara thought, or he would never leave the two of them alone. Didn't he realize . . . ? But then she supposed that men had no time for such petty female emotions. She thought of getting up and going back to her room—anywhere—but a spark of curiosity and plain female stubbornness kept her seated there. She'd be damned if she would retreat in the face of Miss Huston's nastiness!

For a time they both remained silent, sipping gentilely from their teacups as if to see which one was the more ladylike. It was a silly game and Lara knew it, but she played according to the rules just to prove she could do it.

Stephanie was studying her, a condescending, contrived smile on her pink lips. Finally, when Lara was beginning to fidget under the steady regard, Stephanie broke the awkward silence.

"You know, Lara, you're a very attractive woman . . . I think Branch likes you a little."

"Really . . . I think you're quite mistaken . . ."

"Oh, don't worry, Lara. I've had better competition than you. And I've always prevailed. You forget, dear"—the woman's voice dripped acid—"that I was here before Branch's unfortunate marriage and now I'm here again."

"You . . . love him?" The words tumbled out of Lara's mouth before she could stop them. She should have known!

"Call it what you like." Stephanie smiled, a twisting of her lips that failed to reach her eyes. And then: "At least he *respects* me!"

"What?" Confusion furrowed Lara's brow for a split second.

"You heard me correctly, little *Miss Innocence*. I haven't been so stupid as to lie in his bed like a . . ."

"No!" Lara cried, feeling a sudden shame consume her. "No . . ."

Stephanie laughed. "You see, Lara," she continued on patronizingly, "I have waited, bided my time, as it were. He'll tire of your little independent act soon enough and, believe me, a man would hardly marry a woman whose bed he has already . . ."

"Hello!" came a feminine voice from the direction of the double doors. "What a marvelous ride I had!"

Lara was horrified, unable to gather her wits. She'd never seen a sight more blessed than Jennifer's sudden appearance.

Her sister swished her riding skirt coquettishly, tossed

her velvet feathered hat on the table, and plumped herself into a chair. "Robert and Guy are just the most *wonderful* hosts!" She picked up a roll from a basket, tore off a bite, and popped it in her mouth. "You look ever so much better," she said to Lara, then popped another bite in. "I'm simply famished."

Stephanie remained motionless, eyeing Jennifer with mild interest. Finally, she rose and stood behind her chair.

Licking her fingers daintily, Jennifer turned her focus onto Stephanie. "My, what a *lovely* pink dress. It flatters your skin so divinely. Very nice."

Stephanie raised a winglike brow. "Why, thank you, Jennifer." Her voice was wary.

"Oh, yes, you do have lovely skin, Stephanie . . . although . . ." A twinkle lit Jennifer's eyes, lighting them to a robin's-egg blue shade.

"Yes? Although what?" remarked Stephanie.

"Although, if it were me, I'd stay away from pastel colors . . ."

"Why?"

"Oh, you know," Jennifer's gaze lifted slowly to lock with Stephanie's. "Light colors tend to show off those awful wrinkles around your eyes and mouth that we women have to be so careful of in this dry climate."

Lara gasped audibly. There was a grating sound as Stephanie's grip tightened on the back of the chair, causing it to scrape across the flagstone. Jennifer laughed lightly, completely delighted with herself.

Fury flashing from her eyes, Stephanie quickly collected herself, saying she had something to see to, spun around, and disappeared inside with an angry rustle of skirts.

Jennifer chuckled. "Oh, don't look so shocked, Lara. I was standing in that doorway for a full minute before I came out. I heard everything."

"But . . ."

"But nothing! She asked for it! And if you don't start standing up for yourself . . . Honestly, sis, I don't know *what* I'm going to do with you!"

Lara sighed. "How can I when she's right? Oh, Jenn . . . what she said is . . . true." Her eyes fell away in shame.

"I know—at least about you and Branch. But I'm sure she's dead wrong about a man not wanting to marry a woman . . . afterward, that is." Jennifer studied her sister for a moment. "Has he . . . has he offered marriage?"

"Yes," whispered Lara. "But he doesn't feel anything for me. Not really." Hot tears burned behind her eyelids. "He wants Bitter Creek, Jenn. I should have realized it all along. I should have known it that day up in the woods." Lara dabbed at her eyes with the napkin. "I was so overcome by him . . . so stupid!"

"No you weren't. It could have happened to anyone, Lara. Alone . . . in the woods with a man like Branch . . ."

"But *you* wouldn't have been up there alone searching for a wild stallion! Maybe Stephanie is right on that account, too. She called me independent . . . said I was playing games."

"Oh, posh," exclaimed Jennifer. "She's just too cityish. She's probably never had an independent thought in that made-up head of hers anyway. She's just green-eyed jealous, that's all."

"Oh, Jenn." Lara felt her spirits lifting. "Do you really think so? I mean—do you think I even compare to her?"

"Of course you do. And in truth, you're far prettier. Why, I wasn't kidding for a moment when I made reference to her wrinkles. She's probably only twenty-five, but I swear she looks forty! It must be the hard living!" Jennifer winked wickedly.

"Honest?"

"Cross my heart." Jennifer made the motion over her heart exactly the way she had when they were children, her expression one of exaggerated solemnity.

Then suddenly the awful tension that gripped Lara released its hold and the whole episode seemed absurd: Stephanie's pettiness, the victorious gleam in Jennifer's eyes, her own paralysis. She giggled tentatively. Jennifer eyed her curiously for a moment, then began to giggle, too. The two women sat on the porch in the sun for a long time, alternately laughing then wiping away the tears then laughing again.

When Branch appeared on the porch once more, he stopped short and eyed the two women lazily. "You know," he stated, "I reckon I haven't heard this much laughter around here for a long time. Don't let me stop you." He leaned his tall frame against the door, his arms folded casually.

Jennifer continued her giggling, but Lara was instantly sobered. "We were . . . well, we were . . ." she fumbled, her eyes downcast.

"Go on."

"It's nothing, Branch, really," said Jennifer, sparkling. "Just a silly little-girl joke." Jennifer rose. "Well, I think I'll take a nap . . ."

But when she was gone Lara remembered that she had not told Jenn that they were leaving as soon as was possible. Faced with Branch, her resolve hardened again.

She had to get away from Wolf Butte Ranch and its overpowering aura of male domination.

She turned toward Branch, met his unreadable gaze. Suddenly she felt shy beneath his close scrutiny, but that was ridiculous. After all, he'd seen her . . .

"Do you know something, Lara?" He unfolded his arms and walked toward her.

"What?" Her hands twisted nervously in the folds of her skirt. If only he didn't have this effect on her.

"I've never seen you really laugh." His tone was deep, pensive. "I never thought anything could make you lovelier . . ." For an endless moment he just stood there, towering over her, and Lara's thoughts became utterly jumbled. On the one hand, she wanted to feel his warm breath stir her hair, to have his lips touch hers. But then reason told her how wrong her fantasies were. Branch Taggart was her enemy. He'd been at the root of all her troubles at Bitter Creek—he wanted her ranch and that was all. Men were different; they were capable of using people in cruel ways.

Her glance lifted timidly to his face.

"Why, there you are!" came Stephanie's voice, causing Lara's heart to leap. And behind her stood, of all people, Noah Ackroyd! How . . . ?

"Mr. Ackroyd," said Stephanie, emerging from the doorway, "came to see you, my dear. Wasn't that thoughtful?" Her eyes burned viciously into Lara's.

Noah strode directly over to Lara. "I stopped out at Bitter Creek to visit . . . your mother told me. Are you all right?"

"I'm fine, Noah, really. I'm afraid you made this trip for nothing." She tried to smile. Noah Ackroyd . . . here?

"Thank heavens!" Then Noah turned to Branch,

shaking his hand. "It's been a long time. I hope you don't mind the intrusion . . ."

"Certainly not, Noah. Good to see you again." Branch ended the handshake as soon as etiquette would allow.

Lara was instantly uncomfortable, well aware of the chill in Branch's manner, the way his lips turned at the corners in a cruel smile. Oh, God, she thought, if only there were some hole she could crawl into and hide! She never dreamed Noah would come here!

"I just think it's so sweet of you to visit Lara, Mr. Ackroyd," cooed Stephanie. "Such a long ride! Why, it shows true . . . friendship." The word fell off her tongue like a slow caress.

Lara cringed inwardly.

"Why don't you play hostess, my dear cousin," Branch grumbled curtly, "and see to some refreshments for our guests."

If Stephanie was put off, she never flinched. No doubt, thought Lara, she knew she'd scored her point. And Branch—he was behaving quite horribly—hardly the gentleman host.

Noah and Branch talked in a stilted manner for several minutes while Lara tried to collect her thoughts. The one thing she knew was that she simply had to get away from here! She had to get home!

Her eyes flew up to Noah's face. "How did you get here?" she asked abruptly.

"Why . . . I brought my horse, Lara."

"Good. Jennifer has the buckboard here. Perhaps you'd be kind enough to drive us home. We can tie the horses to the back." She knew her voice held a hysterical edge—she couldn't think clearly and Branch was making her so nervous.

Confused, Noah replied, "Why, of course, I'd be happy . . ."

"Lara." Branch's tone knifed through the air. Her stare flew up to meet his. "I think you ought to explain to your friend, Noah, that the doctor thought it best for you to remain here for several days. I intend for you to obey his orders."

Lara was so stunned by the suppressed anger in his voice that words refused to come to her. She'd never seen him so cold, with such barely contained fury. In spite of the warm sun on her shoulders, goose bumps rose on her flesh.

Woodenly, she came to her feet. She had to get away! "I'm not a prisoner, Branch," she breathed. "I'm going to get my things now . . ."

Branch took her arm firmly. "You're not leaving with . . . *him*. If you insist on going, I'll drive you back."

It struck Lara suddenly, in spite of her mortification, that Branch was not asking her or even suggesting a solution—he was blatantly commanding her. "No," she whispered stiffly, pulling her arm away. "Noah will drive us."

She could see the muscle working in his tight jaw, the rage boiling within him. It made no difference. She was leaving with Noah and wild horses couldn't stop her now.

While Noah waited in embarrassed confusion on the porch, Branch followed Lara inside to the bottom of the steps. She was actually afraid to turn around and face him, yet she knew their confrontation was not over. She felt miserably sick to her stomach and her head was beginning to ache again.

"Wait a minute!" He barred her path up the steps with an arm. "I think you owe me an explanation."

Nausea half consuming her, Lara tried to push past him. "I don't owe you anything!" She choked on the words.

"The hell you don't! What's going on between you and that Eastern dude?"

"You mean *Noah* . . . don't you?" Lara finally turned to face him. "Whatever is going on between us is *my* business, Mr. Taggart!" And she could hardly believe the hasty statement even after she'd made it.

"Then there is something!" Branch took hold of her arm threateningly. "And won't Jennifer be in your way on the ride home?" he asked sarcastically.

"Stop it!" Lara cried. "You're acting like a child!"

"Am I?" He squeezed her arm painfully, his fingers like a steel vise. "Do you really think I'm a *child?*" His eyes splintered anger at her.

"Noah's just a friend. Please, Branch, let go of me . . . I want to go home. Please."

"Please nothing! You just want to be with him! Admit it, Lara."

With what little dignity he had left her, she looked accusingly down at her arm where he gripped it. "You can't keep me here, Branch. I don't want to be near you when you're like this." And then, before she could stop her thoughts from becoming words, she said tiredly, "I'm not your wife. I'm not running off with a man, Branch. I just want to go home."

Suddenly his face contorted darkly. He dropped her arm as if it were a hot coal. "No," he growled harshly, "you're not my wife, Lara." His face closed into a mask of stone. "You can see whoever you please. Don't let me stand in your way."

His bitterness was more than she could bear. She had

the awful feeling that, in his mind, he was comparing her to Jewel. But he was wrong, so very wrong. "A man like you should never have married in the first place," she whispered. "You don't trust women and I'm not going to stand here and be insulted by you—not another minute!" She turned toward the steps, feeling a wave of dizziness wash over her.

"Lara . . ." he said thickly, his tone full of pain.

But she couldn't turn back around; she couldn't face him. The thing he had accused her of—being with Noah *that* way—was too much for her to swallow. She had her pride.

"Lara . . . I didn't mean . . . you aren't like her. I don't know what came over me . . ." But his voice held little conviction and she sensed an inner turmoil within him.

Her eyes were bright with unshed tears. "Just let me alone, Branch." Deep in the pit of her stomach she felt sick with a mixture of misery and confusion. How could Branch even think she would look at another man after what they had shared? How could he compare her to Jewel? Were all women whores in his eyes because of one bitter experience? "I don't want to see you again, Branch," she whispered ardently. "I don't want you near me . . . or to touch me. I'm not a cheap little plaything for any man!"

Later she would be tormented by the agonized look that had come to his eyes then. What had he been about to say to her? But at that moment, as he took a hesitant step toward her, Jennifer appeared at the top of the stairs.

"Lara!" her sister called, concerned.

"Pack your things," Lara said in a broken voice. "We're going home now."

It seemed like a stage play to Lara after that long moment. She suddenly became an actress. After she had collected her thoughts, packed, and returned downstairs, she thanked Joe Taggart and his sons for their hospitality. She stood in the entranceway and smiled dully at Stephanie; her words sounded to her own ears like lines being read from a script.

And Branch played his part, too. He reappeared and carried their bags to the buckboard. He then chatted with Jennifer politely, almost too easily. He smiled at Lara stiffly and wished her well as they stood next to the buckboard, the sun catching in his hair.

They said good-bye and for an endless, pregnant instant, Lara felt as if, perhaps, there was something else that needed to be said, but the moment passed futilely.

Once out of sight of the ranch house, Lara's thoughts dwelled painfully on their farewell. She vaguely recalled thanking Branch, promising to take care—so polite, so smiling, so false.

Branch had displayed no emotion whatsoever. His eyes had been cool, an ice-blue color that told her nothing. And then he had said, "Good-bye, Lara," and she had not missed the finality in his tone.

It was over; she should feel relieved. Instead she shuddered to recall how uncomfortable it had all been.

Jennifer and Noah, sensing Lara's mood, rode along in strained silence. But Lara was too involved in her own misery to notice their discomfort. Over and over she told herself that Branch cared nothing whatsoever for her and that he had used her cruelly to try and gain control of Bitter Creek. And then she would tell herself that *she* was the one who had played the game so poorly—*she* was the one who had fallen at his feet and behaved like a wanton. And she could not help but wonder what their relationship might have come to if she hadn't fallen into his bed so easily.

The feud, even the burnt barn, seemed suddenly small in comparison to her broken heart. She hurt all over inside and she detested herself for loving him. She had been a fool. But now it was ended. And now she had to learn the hardest lesson of all—to detest him, too.

Chapter Fifteen

"WHO DO YOU THINK CUT THAT FENCE THEN?" CRIED LARA in exasperation. She paced up and down in the kitchen in front of the table where Harriet and Jennifer sat impassively, absorbing Lara's mood. "It's been cut before in the same place and now our best yearlings are all over God's creation! And you don't even care!"

"Of course I care, Lara," soothed Harriet. "It's just that I can't *do* anything about it. Shad will take care of it."

"Shad! Shad! He can't do everything! Those Taggarts won't ever stop! We'd need armed guards patrolling the whole fence line twenty-four hours a day!" For a fleeting moment Lara almost blurted out her suspicions about Colt Farnsworth, but she held her tongue—with no more evidence than she had, they would think she was imagining the whole thing.

"Why do you insist on blaming the Taggarts? They've been nothing but nice to us," continued Harriet calmly.

"Only on the surface," muttered Lara darkly. "They want you to sell."

"And I still might. Joe knows that. He'd never do anything dishonest."

"How on earth can you say that?" cried Lara. "Look what he's already done!"

"You've no proof. I refuse to believe it. I know he wouldn't do it. Your judgment is clouded on this issue, Lara. You've taken your father's feelings to be your own. Why don't you look at it more objectively?" finished Harriet steadfastly. "Now get control of yourself—you aren't helping matters any."

Surprising everyone, including herself, Lara sank onto a chair and burst into tears. Harriet and Jennifer exchanged rueful looks over her head; Harriet rose to comfort her.

"You're just overwrought, dear. You're trying to do too much. And it's been barely a week since your accident. Leave everything for a while until you feel better," coaxed Harriet softly, patting Lara's head. "Go on upstairs and take a nap. Jennifer, go with her and see she's all right."

Lara felt ridiculous as soon as she reached her room. Crying like a vapid female—how silly, how useless.

"Go on down and help Mama," she said to her sister. "I'm fine. I'll just rest awhile. I guess I'm tired."

"You've been tired a lot lately," commented Jennifer.

"I guess it was the accident. . . . But it sure seems I should feel better by now." Lara tugged her boots off and lay back on her bed, one forearm flung over her eyes.

"Lara," said Jennifer drily, "I think it's more than that. I reckon it's going to take you longer to recover from this 'accident' than you think."

"What on earth do you mean?" asked Lara lazily.

"I mean"—Jennifer eyed her steadily—"that you must be pregnant."

There was a moment of stunned silence in the room as if life itself had been snuffed out momentarily. Then Lara sat up and let out a long, ragged breath, her eyes staring wildly, unfocused. "My God," she whispered, turning a stricken gaze onto her sister. "No, oh no!"

"I'm afraid it's 'yes.' Think about it, sis."

Lara's thoughts spun frantically in her brain; it couldn't be! Just because she was a little tired . . . But then, she remembered miserably, she had been sick to her stomach an awful lot lately. And she had missed her time of month—although that had happened before. Still, could it mean . . . ? It just couldn't be!

Finally, terrified to admit the truth, Lara put her face in her hands and collapsed on her bed in a boneless heap.

Jennifer rose and went to sit on the edge of the bed, patting her sister's back. "There, there. It's not so bad. He'll still marry you. I know it. Everything will be fine."

"Fine!" Lara raised a pallid face to Jennifer's. She looked desperate. "You don't understand! I can't even bear to be near him. I'd never marry him, never! I couldn't stand it. And he feels the same way too!" She laughed hysterically. "Marry a Taggart! How can you . . . ?" And then she began to sob, great gasping, tearing sobs that frightened Jennifer.

"All right, all right," soothed Jennifer. "You don't have to marry him. We'll think of something. Don't worry. It'll work out. You'll see."

Slowly, with quiet, tranquil words, she calmed Lara until the two sisters sat on the bed with their arms around each other and Lara's sobs had turned to heartbroken hiccups.

"We have to tell Mama," Jennifer finally said.

"Oh, no! I can't! I'm so ashamed." Lara's voice was broken, near to hysteria again.

"She's your mother. She loves you. You don't have to be ashamed. She'll know what to do. You know, Lara, you can't hide it."

"I'll go away somewhere," came her muffled voice.

"Don't be silly, sis. We're your family. We'll take care of you."

"Oh, Jenn." Lara turned her face into her sister's chest like a child and found a small degree of comfort there. Her family, at least, would stand by her.

It was worse than she had expected to tell her mother. But, surprisingly, Harriet took it very calmly, almost as if it were an everyday occurrence.

"Is there any hope of a marriage, Lara?" she asked finally after a long silence.

"No." Lara's voice was barely audible.

"I see," replied Harriet. "Can you tell me who it is?"

"I'd rather not," came Lara's muffled reply.

"I wish you would. It might help us make some decisions." Harriet gazed at Lara pensively. "Never mind. I have a notion who it is anyway. You know, Lara, he'd make an excellent husband . . ."

Lara returned her gaze with stricken eyes. "Oh, Mama! You don't understand . . . I can't!"

"It's your choice and we'll stand by you, but you must understand fully what you're doing. It won't be easy."

"Oh, Mama, what will I do?"

"It's not too difficult," said Harriet with studied placidity. "We'll go to Denver City. Then, when the baby is born, we'll come back, if you still want to by then, and say you were married there and your husband died—oh, we'll make up some fatal disease for the poor fellow—

and you'll be a young widow with a child. Now stop worrying about it. You aren't the first . . ." Harriet bent over her youngest child, her heart nearly breaking with pain, and kissed her forehead, thinking of the irony of it all. Her own daughter, caught in the same trap. "You aren't the first."

The train wheels echoed the beating of Lara's heart—*click-clack, click-clack*—all the way to Denver City. In spite of the awesome, mountainous scenery, her mind was filled with a dull pain, a gray cloud of futility. She was thankful, vaguely glad of her mother's and sister's support but too dulled to feel anything strongly. She was to have Branch Taggart's baby. She'd accepted that fact, but the reality of it had yet to sink in.

She'd gone through the motions of packing, leaving directions for Shad, arranging for Noah Ackroyd to check on things and keep them posted. But it wasn't until the enforced idleness of the train ride that she'd allowed herself to think.

She would return someday—of that fact there was no question. But what would Branch do when he saw her in the Rifle Dry Goods store one day with a baby? He wasn't stupid—he could count. Wouldn't he know it was his child? Or—most likely—would he believe so ill of her that he would assume it was someone else's? He had no right to know the truth anyway—Branch Taggart didn't give a damn about her or her family. And her thoughts kept turning, twisting uselessly, like a ball of tumbleweed sent willy-nilly by the capricious wind.

And even as they settled themselves in Denver City, Lara's mood did not brighten. There were teas, dinner parties—a whirlwind of activities to occupy her thoughts. But all the while Lara felt stifled, even frightened that one day she might let slip the "lie" and shame her mother and sister. And then the social gossips would take that damning piece of evidence—the proof that she was never married—and tear at it like ravenous wolves.

It seemed the lie of her marriage hung over her head waiting to pounce on her at any moment. She wondered how she could live with it much longer.

Even Jennifer, although for the most part thoroughly enjoying herself, took note, one hot summer's day, of Lara's mood. "You walk around here like the living dead, Lara," she said scoldingly.

"I feel like I'm dead, Jenn. I feel like we've lived here forever."

Jennifer went on that day to regale Lara of the fact that she and their mother were quite content and that everyone had been so nice to them since their arrival. "Don't you care about anything? Don't you realize how accepted we've become?"

Myrna Oldfield of Glenwood Springs had given Harriet the names of several of her husband's business connections in Denver City, so they had not been altogether alone in their new venture. The women of Denver had welcomed them warmly, always happy to add respectable people, especially female ones, to their list of acquaintances. There was still a shortage of women in the raw but growing high-plains city.

So they had fallen into a routine, at first searching for a house to rent, then settling into the newly built, shingled and gabled town house. Then Harriet began to entertain —only small afternoon teas and private dinners. She explained to her new friends that she couldn't do anything too elaborate as her daughter had been recently widowed, poor dear, and she'd always glance warningly at Lara. Harriet's time was filled with charitable deeds, afternoon visits, and discussions of flower gardens, and she seemed to thrive on it.

It was a sweltering day in August when they received the invitation to Mrs. Hammond's annual dinner and dance evening. Jennifer lay in a hammock on the porch fanning herself and reading the engraved invitation over and over.

"Just think! It says supper at midnight! How romantic. Formal dress, too. Oh, everyone will be there! It's just too exciting!"

"Well, I'm not going," stated Lara, grumpy from the heat. "It'll be boring."

"Boring! She thinks it'll be *boring!* With *every* eligible young man in Denver there . . ."

"You mean with Alfie there," retorted Lara. "He's the only one you are interested in."

"Yes, Alfie is a dream. And I adore him. But there are so many others, all dying for a new girl. Lara, you could have your pick if you played your cards right. The grieving young widow. Oh, yes! Wear your black dress." Jennifer pushed the hammock with one dainty white-stockinged foot until it swung gently.

"I'm not interested in those men."

"Well, you have to be interested in *some* man, some-where. Why not at Mrs. Hammond's?" She sat up in the hammock, her cheeks flushed from the heat. "Maybe Alfie will propose that night. Maybe with a full moon and flowers and champagne punch . . . Oh, Lara, I'm so happy I could cry!"

"I'm sick of hearing about Alfie," complained Lara. "He's so frivolous."

"And rich and sweet and *so* polite."

"And spoiled rotten," Lara put in.

"So what? I'll spoil him, too." Then Jennifer remembered. "What about that one who sent you those flowers—what was his name?"

"Richard Temple," muttered Lara, wiping at the sheen of perspiration on her upper lip. She seemed to feel the heat more lately.

"Yes, young Mr. Temple. What about him?"

"I'm not interested."

"But he's young and attractive and he's going to be a lawyer soon, isn't he? A wonderful career. He seemed to like you, Lara, and Mama thought he was ever so nice."

"You think I should encourage him?" asked Lara. "The poor sap. He'd be getting his money's worth, wouldn't he?"

But Lara did go to Mrs. Hammond's, for lack of anything better to do, and the milling crowd, the music, the piles of food and eager young men did cheer her up. Whereas Jennifer had worn an off-the-shoulder white organza dress, Lara wore a black beaded gown with a round neck and fringe of black jet. Harriet insisted that she wear black to indicate her widowhood. "And, besides, you look lovely in black, dear. So mysterious. And you're barely showing yet. No one will know."

Lara was forced to sit with the married women in chairs lining the dance floor, while Jennifer capered off to flirt and dance with Alfie and a dozen other scions of Denver society. In a way, Lara envied her; in another way, she was glad to sit quietly and watch—it was easier.

She sat through the waltzes and sipped her punch, feeling the heat of the dancing crowd build and dampen the tendrils of hair that escaped from her pompadour. She fanned herself slowly with a black silk fan, smiling at Jennifer whirling by on Alfie's formally clad arm.

The voice, when it spoke her fictitious married name, startled her. "Mrs. Parks?"

Looking up, she saw it was Richard Temple, handsome and debonair in his black formal attire.

"Mr. Temple." She nodded politely.

"Won't you please call me Richard?" he asked in his soft voice. "May I sit down?"

"Of course." She indicated the empty chair offhandedly with her closed fan.

"Mrs. Parks," he began.

Lara all but winced. She detested the dishonesty behind that name. "Please, call me Lara, I insist."

"Lara." He tasted the word, rolled it expertly on his tongue. His dark eyes drank her in as if she were cool water to a man dying of thirst. "Would you care to dance?"

"I think not, Richard. It's a bit awkward due to my mourning, you see."

"I understand perfectly. Perhaps then a stroll on the terrace?"

"I'd like that. It's so hot in here." If the old biddies talked about her, so what. She felt the sudden need for fresh air. He gave her his arm and they made their way through French doors out to the flagstone terrace. The sudden cool air felt wonderful; Lara put her head back and breathed it in.

"You're so beautiful," Richard said finally, his voice emerging, disembodied, from the velvety darkness. "I thought perhaps, seeing as you're so recently a widow, I shouldn't speak so soon, but I'm afraid you'll decide on someone else and I couldn't bear it."

"Richard, please." She started to move away, upset by the intensity in his voice.

"I'm sorry if I insulted you, but I've fallen in love with you . . ." His voice was infinitely sad in the darkness.

"You hardly know me . . ." she gasped.

"I know enough, Lara. I'd like to speak to your mother."

"I forbid it!" Her voice was stronger than she'd intended. "Don't be ridiculous," she finished more quietly.

"You don't love me."

"Of course not. I hardly know you." She was beginning to feel exasperated.

"Just tell me there's hope," breathed Richard soulfully.

"There's always hope," replied Lara drily. "Now I think we best go in before my reputation is absolutely ruined, Mr. Temple."

But before she could escape from the terrace and lose herself in the crowded ballroom, the sound of a woman's voice arrested her progress: a rather familiar, penetrating voice that stopped her in her tracks as if she were struck with paralysis. A man and woman were silhouetted in the French doors, profiled by the interior candlelight, and the woman was berating the man for something. Lara missed the words, but the voice was unmistakable.

It was Stephanie Huston.

Lara thought desperately. Here was the one person who could and *would* destroy her well-built facade of lies, who would take great pleasure in ruining Jennifer's chances for a good marriage, her mother's new life. She couldn't hide on the terrace, she couldn't avoid passing the couple at the doors; even now, Richard was taking her arm and leading her straight toward them.

Why was that dreadful Stephanie witness to all her humiliations?

Well, she'd have to brazen it out, match wits with Stephanie. The blond woman was forward and devious, and certainly Lara could measure up if forced to. She lifted her small, determined chin, stiffened her spine, and

237

carved a gracious smile on her lips. Gracefully, she let her black-gloved hand rest on Richard's arm and glided beside him toward the doors. She held her fan opened coquettishly in front of her fringed bodice; her heart pounded drumbeats in her ears.

"Why, Stephanie Huston," she cried sweetly, stopping short on Richard's arm, feigning great surprise. "I do declare! I had no idea you were back in Denver City."

Stephanie whirled abruptly from her companion, her blue eyes wide with . . . what? Lara wondered. Surprise? Shock? Amazement?

"Lara?" The word left her round, pink mouth before she could think, but, to her great credit, Stephanie recovered very quickly. "Lara—umm—Parks, isn't it now? My dear, how nice to see you here. I recall now hearing that your family was here in Denver. And that you'd recently been married." Stephanie raked Lara meaningfully with a glance, pausing long enough to give her words great significance. "And is this Mr. Parks?" She tapped Richard playfully with her fan.

"Goodness no, Stephanie. Poor Mr. Parks died shortly after we were married. Typhus. It's been so horrible." Lara's green eyes, as hard and scintillating as Burmese emeralds, held Stephanie's narrowed gaze. "This is Richard Temple. Miss Stephanie Huston, an old friend of mine from back home."

"So nice to meet you, Mr. Temple," intoned Stephanie, her smile toothy but as meaningless as a desert shower. "And you *must* meet my fiancé, Rudy Sheffield. Rudy, darling, come here and meet an old friend of mine."

Her fiancé! Suddenly Lara felt a flood of relief, which she strove to suppress instantly. This wasn't the time.

A tall, balding, very distinguished man emerged from the shadows to bow exquisitely over Lara's hand and to shake Richard's. He had a British accent and Stephanie explained that he represented an English company that was a major shareholder in one of the huge ranches of eastern Colorado.

The two couples strolled back into the ballroom, making polite small talk. Stephanie, her cheeks flushed, her voice high, asked the men to "please fetch us some of that *heavenly* punch," and raked Lara again with a cold eye.

"You're looking well, my dear. Absolutely *blooming.*" The emphasis on the word left Lara no doubt as to what Stephanie was referring.

"Thank you. I adore your dress. It is *so* flattering, the way those ruffles hide any . . . imperfections of the figure. Don't we women have to resort to all sorts of wiles to look decent? I declare." Lara fanned her hot face. Noting Stephanie's look, she wondered if they'd be rolling on the floor in a split second in a cat fight.

"And how is dear Branch?" asked Stephanie, trying another tack.

"My, I haven't seen him in ages—not since I met Mr. Parks. I can't say."

"And is Mr. Temple your new beau? I believe his family is well connected."

"Goodness, no. Why, I'm still in mourning. I couldn't possibly encourage a beau."

"If you don't mind my saying so, Lara, you look quite different from the ragamuffin you were before. It suits you." Stephanie gave her a critical glance. "Branch might just be interested now, you know. Now that you're a widow, that is. As for me, I've got Rudy and am quite satisfied. I've lost all desire for a man who would rather spend his time with a bunch of cattle than me. So, Lara, I won't stand in your way."

"You never were in my way, Stephanie, dear," trilled Lara, well into the role now. "Oh, here are the boys. How delightful! So nice to meet you, Mr. Sheffield, but I must be off. Mama asked me particularly to keep an eye on Jennifer. Good night, Stephanie. Come, Richard."

And she glided off, a cold sweat of anxiety on her upper lip, a hot flush of victory on her cheeks. She prayed she'd beaten Stephanie at her own despicable game.

Now to get rid of the clinging Richard Temple.

There was no putting him off, though. He called and brought presents to Harriet—candy and satin pincushions and handkerchiefs—and sat watching Lara endlessly from the overstuffed gold sofa. She received an embossed note from him every day he was unable to call, and Lara's room was filled to overflowing with flowers that he sent her.

It was becoming more and more difficult to be polite to him and Lara tried every device possible to avoid him, but still he appeared, a constant, irritating pest—like a fly or a mosquito, she often thought. So tiny in itself but able to drive you insane en masse.

The monotony of her existence was infuriating. She rode, occasionally, a rented hack, but she longed for the open range and her own no-nonsense gelding. She actually pounced on the mail every day, just in case there was something from Rifle regarding the ranch. And so it was that she read the forwarded letter from Sheriff Prichard first, thanking her lucky stars that Harriet hadn't opened it and begun asking some ticklish questions. But the letter was disappointing; he only said that he had questioned Farnsworth but was unable to prove the turquoise was his. He wrote, too, that Ned Lawson in Rifle was keeping an eye on him since Farnsworth was still in the area. There was one interesting part to the letter; Farnsworth had admitted that he was on a job in the Rifle area, but he refused to name his employer.

That set Lara to thinking. At least it occupied her mind with something other than tea dances and shopping excursions.

She fretted and worried over Shad's infrequent letters and Noah's more frequent ones until Harriet almost decided to keep them from her. She spoke endlessly of the bulls, the calves, the Appaloosa, the winter hay supply.

And then one day a very special letter came, forwarded by Shad, and the two sisters gathered around while Harriet read it, slow tears dropping on the ink, blurring it.

Dear Mother,

Please forgive me for not writing to you before, but I've had my own way to find and my demons to exorcise. I am now living in San Francisco and want to let you know that everything is going well in my life.

Tell Dad I forgive him . . .

"Oh, my Lord," whispered Harriet, "Craig doesn't even know that Frank died! Oh, Lord!"

"Go on, Mama. What else does he say?" pressed Lara.

Harriet read the long letter to them. They were all elated to hear that he was remarried and his wife was expecting a child in the autumn. He wrote that he was attending medical school there and working on the side with an excellent doctor who paid him well. Craig sounded very busy and the three women discussed the undertone of his letter. He was still glad to be away from Rifle, from sad memories, but all in all he sounded quite happy and promised to visit with his new wife and child as soon as time permitted. At least they knew where he was now, and there was the good chance that he would lead a life to which he was better suited.

So Craig was happy, Harriet and Jennifer were happy in their newly rented Victorian—everyone, it seemed, was content but Lara.

She broke the news that she was going back to the ranch on Sunday morning in the middle of September and sat silently through Harriet's resulting tirade, staunchly adamant.

"But you're showing," exclaimed Jennifer. "Everyone will talk."

"I don't care anymore. They'll just have to accept the existence of poor dead Mr. Parks."

"Won't it seem awfully quick to everyone in Rifle?" asked Jennifer sarcastically.

"I don't care. Let them talk. I can't live here anymore."

"But what about Richard?" asked Harriet finally. "He wants to marry you."

"Well, I don't want to marry him. I've never given him even an ounce of encouragement. He's one more reason I have to leave. He torments me—he's sucking my blood!"

"Well, I don't think the time is right. What will people say?"

"Oh, tell them I've gone to visit my in-laws. You know, those ever-so-nice people, the Parkses." Lara smiled tightly. "We've made up my husband's family. Let's not let them languish for lack of their daughter-in-law's visit."

"Oh, Lara, you're so stubborn," sighed Harriet.

And so they had to give in and send her off on the train from Union Station. Harriet had insisted absolutely that she could only go if Noah were to meet her at Rifle and drive her to the ranch. So she had duly wired him and now waited impatiently for the train to pull in to Rifle with its wonderfully familiar bawling stockyards, its busy main street, its nearness to Bitter Creek Ranch, its entire gamut of memories.

She was glad to see Noah through the dusty window of the car, his tall, gangly form sweetly familiar to her as he waited patiently on the platform. A rush of feeling shook her; she was home. And then she realized with sudden clarity that she would have to face Noah and the town of Rifle and the entire valley with her all-too-obvious lie.

She sat a moment longer in the train, steeling herself, gaining control of her fears, before rising and straightening her back, preparing a smile, readying all the words she'd have to use. Pulling her green cloak around her, she finally stepped down off the train.

Noah walked toward her, smiling, pushing his glasses up on his nose nervously, his hair falling over his forehead.

"Lara," he said simply, and stood and looked at her for a long time before he bent and chastely kissed her forehead. "You look wonderful."

"Thank you." She kept her cloak wrapped around her although the September day was mild.

"I've got the buckboard here. Shad brought it in yesterday. I'll get your luggage . . ." He hesitated, unsure. "I'm glad you came back."

"So am I, Noah—more than you can imagine," she said fervently.

It was when he was handing her up on the buckboard that it happened, although, she was to think later, she couldn't have kept it to herself forever in any case. Her long green cloak fell away from her body and she felt Noah's eyes on her, felt his sudden start of surprise, his shocked stare that he couldn't hide in those first few heartbeats of time.

Their eyes met for a numbing second, his revealing full awareness, hers defiant. And then the moment passed and Noah was whispering, "Lara," in pained comprehension and she had to tell him that it was all right, that she had learned acceptance.

He drove in silence for a time, staring straight ahead as if fearful of looking at her. Then, still watching the rutted road in front of the buckboard, he said, "I'll marry you, you know."

His tone was oddly relieved and at the same time apprehensive. Lara felt like cringing at the ridiculous situation—first Richard Temple and now Noah. Instead, she put a gloved hand on his sleeve. "There's no need for that, Noah. I'm a respectable widow, you see." Her words were tinged with faint irony.

"Widow?" he repeated blankly. "But when were you married?" he said inanely. And then, "Oh . . . I think I see . . ."

"That's right, Noah." Lara shifted her glance away uneasily.

"I still want to marry you, Lara. It doesn't matter."

"Noah, it's my problem and you don't need to feel responsible."

"The father . . ." He was obviously embarrassed to allude to the sensitive subject. "I mean, there's no hope?"

"None," she stated flatly.

"Well, then, you have to marry me. I'll take care of you . . . and the child."

"Would that really be enough for either of us, Noah? There's still your fiancée. It wouldn't be fair to anyone. Don't be noble. It only complicates matters."

Then Noah turned to her, almost angry. "You've always been too stubborn for your own good. I've a mind to force you, you silly girl!"

"I'm not a girl anymore, Noah."

He gave a disgusted snort and drove in silence. Lara took the opportunity to drink in the scenery, the gilded hues of autumn that touched the valley, the pungent aroma of sagebrush, the clear pellucid blue of the Colorado sky. Oh, yes, it was good to be home.

And all the time a part of her mind was considering coldly whether she should marry Noah; the logical part of her brain analyzed, weighed alternatives. Was it fair to rear the unborn child without a father, with a lie for a name? Did Noah really love her or was he merely being protective? Marriage to Noah Ackroyd was not a distasteful thought. He was a good man—intelligent, kind, with a sweet way about him. It might even work.

"How is the ranch doing?" she finally asked to ease the tension between them.

"All right. Shad knows his job." His voice was almost sullen. The rejected suitor.

"Only all right? I thought we were going to have a really good year."

He hesitated then, as if he knew what was coming. "There have been some losses." He looked at her quickly as if to gauge her reaction. "Fences broken, that sort of thing. Not much, but too steady to miss. Shad's had men out on the fence line at night, but they've never seen anything."

"The Taggarts," she said flatly.

"There's no proof, but I must admit it's getting to be a

ticklish situation. The ranch hands have been in some pretty rough brawls in town. The valley's beginning to take sides."

"And just whose side are you on?" Lara asked without really thinking.

Noah shot her a quick sidelong glance. "Yours, of course. Although, as a newspaperman, I have to remain neutral. That will never change."

"Damn them," Lara muttered under her breath. "They must be getting impatient."

"Lara, you don't know that."

"I know it just as surely as I know they'll never get our ranch," she said finally, her green eyes hard and narrowed against the autumn sun.

Chapter Sixteen

AFTER THE APPALOOSA STUD HAD RAIDED THE TAGGART corral in mid-July, Branch and his two brothers had ridden up into the high country and returned victoriously a week later with three stolen mares and the magnificent stallion.

It was a prize worth its weight in gold and Branch was pleased with their catch: his black markings were exquisite and hopefully some of his offspring would bear the same unusual coat and the gentle disposition of the breed.

And then Guy had thrown a wrench into the plans for the stud. "Y' know, Branch," he had said one day at dinner, "the Claytons could really use that stallion after theirs was lost in the fire. And remember back in June, when Miss Lara went looking for him? It only seems fittin' that we . . ."

"Yes, Branch," broke in Joe Taggart, "I quite agree

with Guy. Giving the stallion to the Claytons would be the neighborly thing."

Branch raised a quizzical brow. "Neighborly? Now when did you ever . . . ?"

"When Frank Clayton died," replied Joe pensively. "You think on it, Branch. I've given you a free hand to run things around here now and the last thing I'm goin' to do is interfere, so I'm only suggesting that you think on it."

Branch mumbled something noncommittal, then, "The decision doesn't have to be made for a while anyway. If you'll recall, Dad, the whole family just up and left for Denver a few weeks ago. Who knows when they'll be back, or if . . ."

Branch had put the idea of giving the Claytons the stud clean out of his mind as the summer advanced. He had absorbed himself in the running of the vast Taggart holdings and tried to forget all else.

September came and went along with the first early snowstorm in the high country. It was time to think about fall roundup since the snow line would soon march down the hills and invade the valley. He kept himself busy from sun up on the range until late at night in the study while he pored over the accounts. And when he wasn't busy at the ranch, there were the Cattlemen's Association meetings, town hall meetings. He could have let Robert or Guy do a lot of the work, but somehow he felt better when he was busy every moment of the day; then he had no time to think. Often it was brought home to him why Joe had thrown in his hat and let Branch take over— running the Taggart ranch was an immense, time-consuming job. Still, Branch wondered if he would end up the same as his father—alone, content to pass the time of day tending his prize apple trees.

It was a bright, crisp October day when Branch, along with Guy, rode into Rifle to pick up a few supplies.

Branch had just finished stacking the sacks of staples into the buckboard when Guy came loping up to the wagon. "Know who I just saw?" came his exuberant voice.

Branch tipped his hat back and leaned against the rear of the wagon. "Now how would I know?" He struck a match on his boot heel and began to light a cigarette.

"Miss Lara, that's who! She's back!"

The match never reached its destination; it burned so long in the air, hanging motionless, that it seared his fingers.

"Damn, Branch," said Guy, "you don't seem any too pleased. I thought you liked her. I sure do."

Cold, unreasonable eyes met the younger man's confused gaze. Branch remained silent, lit another match, and this time managed to light his cigarette through cupped hands. "Where'd you run into her?"

"Oh, I didn't actually see her face to face. I was just walkin' past the *Reveille* window and there she was." Guy smiled. "I'd a gone in to say hello, but I promised you I wouldn't be long."

Guy chatted on while Branch fought down a sudden, choking rage. She was back. Back and already seeing Noah Ackroyd. God, how he wished she'd stayed gone.

". . . so now you can give Miss Lara the stallion," finished Guy excitedly.

"Maybe," Branch grumbled, "and maybe not."

He'd wanted to ask Guy how she looked—he wanted to know a lot of things—but the words stayed silent on his tongue.

A week passed, the time curiously jerky: minutes dragged and hours flew. He heard gossip about a marriage and a dead husband. She now called herself Mrs. Parks! When he had heard the gossip, Branch was unable to speak of Lara much less think of her without boiling inside with resentment.

She sure had fooled him, and for a while there he'd almost been ready to marry her! He'd nearly fallen into that same trap of living hell as he'd been in with Jewel. Actually, he told himself, he had gotten off easy with Lara.

Mrs. Parks. And supposedly her husband was dead. So what? he asked himself in anger. But deep in his heart he knew he was just mouthing empty words to assuage his ruffled pride; the truth was that he still wanted her— wanted her so damn bad it ached all over. Sure, he'd accused her of seeing Noah Ackroyd, but later, after giving it some real thought, he had felt certain that Lara was not that kind of woman. She was different somehow: not only beautiful in that pure way, but she was a real part of the land. Lara, he had come to admit, loved the land as fervently as did he.

And then she'd up and gone to Denver City and married. Just like that. It didn't make sense. Before he'd even heard about a marriage, he'd asked himself endlessly, why? Why would she just take off like that? It couldn't have been his angry words that day when Noah had come to Wolf Butte. Lara was not stupid. So why then? He couldn't imagine sweet, sedate Harriet Clayton convincing Lara to leave. The girl was far too stubborn— he should know.

Why then? All summer he'd turned the question around in his mind and come up with a blank. But one thing was sure—it stuck in his craw like a sickness—she couldn't have cared for him in the least if she'd gone off and married like that. And no doubt she'd had a time of it with Mr. Parks! Were all his women to betray him?

And now she was back. Supposedly a widow. Desire and anger coiled inside him, each fighting for ascendancy, neither winning. What in hell was he supposed to do now?

It was his father who again brought up the subject of the stallion. "I hear Lara Clayton is back at Bitter Creek," said Joe, sipping on an after-dinner brandy.

Branch felt that familiar stab of pain pierce his chest. He slowly swished the amber liquid around the brandy glass he held, staring unfocused at the swirls. "So I understand," replied Branch tightly, wondering if his father knew it was now *Mrs. Parks.*

Joe cleared his throat, leaning forward in the study chair. "It might be a good idea to rethink this business about the stallion." His shrewd blue eyes bore into Branch's. "If you see fit to give her the stud, she might think more favorably on our offer."

"What offer?"

"To buy them out. I'll never stop thinkin' on it, Branch," said Joe firmly. "I want that land joined to ours. We need the water . . ."

"Lara will never sell and she's the one with all the say about it." That was an understatement! thought Branch.

"I want to join the lands together," Joe went on, unmoved by Branch's assertion. "And I want to give them more than a fair price. For Harriet's sake. I owe her," he finished thoughtfully.

"You owe Harriet Clayton?" asked Branch, bewildered.

And then Joe Taggart went on slowly, his seamed, leathery face contorted with an odd sort of agony, to tell his eldest son and heir a story that had been kept buried for twenty-one long years—a story that contained a recently confirmed truth from Harriet's own lips that he should have admitted to himself years ago. He should have known when he looked into the child's blue eyes and seen his own . . .

"You'll give the Claytons the stallion?" asked Joe when he was done.

"I'll take him over tomorrow, I reckon." Branch sat back in the soft velvet chair and eyed his father carefully. Nothing more had to be said between them—it wasn't their way to destroy a notion by dissecting it. No, a man kept those things quiet. But he couldn't help wondering how they had kept it concealed for so long. He sipped slowly on the brandy. No wonder at all Frank and Joe had hated each other so deeply. And then a lot of things, a lot of questions that had bothered Branch for many years began to tumble softly into place.

The stud was a problem.

It had been a long while since he had been out on the open range and the familiar sights, the distinct smells of sage and aspen and pinyon drove him half crazy with longing to be free. He fought the lead that Branch had secured carefully. He kicked and bucked with rolling frantic eyes, huge and white rimmed. Branch felt sorry for him.

At one point on the ride over to Bitter Creek he called over his shoulder, "It's your fault, boy! If you hadn't been so damn anxious to lead off our mares, you wouldn't be in this fix."

It was early morning. The hint of frost lay across the sere land, just barely tipping the brush and dusting the stunted pinyons in a silver halo. In a way, this was Branch's favorite time of year—color seized the high country and river valleys with an artistic hand. The cottonwoods turned a lazy yellow, the aspens were set ablaze with brilliant gold and orange shades, the buck-brush turned a fiery red. In another week the color would be gone and the earth would smell of damp, dying leaves. Some animals would begin to make their winter dens while others, the deer and the elk, would begin their trek into the lower valleys as the deeper snows advanced on them. In Rifle, on the Colorado River, the Canadian geese would find haven on the smooth water until they were forced to continue their southern journey.

As Branch rode across the vibrant landscape, he thought about the bounty provided here for man. He reviewed in his mind the spoils from their autumn hunt, which hung dressed out for the winter in their shed: rabbit, an antelope taken further north near Wyoming, two deer, and a bull elk. There was more than enough to feed them. He thought about the oncoming roundup and the final harvest. His mind dwelled on all the essentials—everything. Everything but Lara, the recently widowed Mrs. Parks. He wondered how she felt about the dead Mr. Parks, whoever he was, and if she suffered. He tried to picture her as a grieving widow, but he couldn't. It didn't fit the Lara he knew.

But then, the familiar ranch house and the Claytons' new barn loomed before him. Branch steeled himself. This was purely a business venture on his part, a way to woo the Claytons and perhaps secure the promise of a future sale, and to hell with Lara Parks.

There were a few ranch hands in the corral area and they looked up curiously, guardedly, while Branch rode into the yard.

"Well, I'll be!" shouted Shad Harper, approaching the stud with great care.

The horse was all but in a frenzy now, smelling the odor of mares in the corral, seeing the fence separating them from him. He raised his shining black head and gave a trumpeting whinny.

Branch cautiously handed Shad the lead while others joined in to help get him into the barn. "He's pretty worked up," said Branch, dismounting, glancing toward the quiet ranch house in spite of his self-made vow not to.

"What a beauty!" Shad called, tugging on the stud's lead, carefully watching his lethal hooves. "Miss Lara will be pleased as punch! Mighty nice of you, Mr. Taggart."

And then she was there. Branch didn't have to look in the direction of the house; he sensed her presence as does a tree that is touched by a summer's breeze but remains unmoving.

He turned slowly to face her. His heart thudded painfully. She was running toward the stud, clutching a thin white cotton dressing gown around her, her hair flying loose in wild disarray around her shoulders. He'd forgotten . . .

Then, for a split second, he thought she was going to throw herself into his arms, but of course that was ridiculous. She'd never do that willingly. But she did stop in front of him, a strange, searching expression on her face. One of her hands reached up inadvertently to brush a wisp of black hair away from her solemn face. She looked so young he could almost not think of her as a woman and a widow. And yet he knew there was more passion and strength in that slim form than in anyone he'd ever known. It was as if she'd never been gone, never married, as if he'd only seen her yesterday, not months ago. How could a woman stick in his mind like that? It tore his guts out just to be so damn near again.

Her emerald green eyes bored questioningly into his. "Is he—is he *really* for us? Really?" she asked hesitantly.

Branch began to speak, then had to clear his throat. "Yes," he grumbled. "He's all yours."

Lara looked over Branch's shoulder toward the barn. "Oh, Branch," she breathed. And then she went toward the barn, still clutching the loose folds of her robe about her.

Taking a deep breath, he followed her flowing form to the barn, where Shad and the men had stabled the stallion. When Lara entered with him trailing on her heels, the hands stepped back.

"He's really a beauty, ain't he, Miss Lara?" said Shad.

"Oh, yes," she breathed. "He's wonderful."

Then the men, one by one, their eyes traveling from Branch to Lara and back, seemed to disappear into thin air, and Branch was left alone in the barn with Lara.

The stud was circling the stall, judging his new confines, occasionally testing the strength of the wood with his hard hooves.

"He sure hates it, doesn't he?" Lara's tone was tentative, as if she were as uncomfortable as Branch. She was leaning against the stable door, raising a quieting hand toward the stallion. "Shhh . . ." she coaxed gently.

Branch watched her pensively: the small pointed chin, the full lower lip, the way the revealing thin cotton molded itself to her frame. It was no damn wonder at all men desired her, wanted to possess every inch of her. He shouldn't have been surprised to hear of her marriage, and yet each time the thought struck him the pain only increased. And it didn't even seem to matter that her husband was dead.

It crossed his mind that she seemed somehow fuller in the figure than when he'd last seen her in June. Her breasts looked heavier and her hips more curved. Even her stomach was slightly rounded. Had the easy married life in the city gotten to this small woman so quickly?

His eyes swept her again, more boldly now. She leaned her weight against the wooden rail, spoke softly to the wild-eyed stallion; the gown molded itself closer to her body. A deep furrow etched Branch's brow, his thin lower lip curved downward at the corners.

And then, as if a bucket of ice water had been thrown in his face, Branch knew. My God! It was so obvious!

"Jesus. Lara." His deep, disbelieving tone caused her to look around. "Jesus," he rasped. "You're . . . pregnant!"

Lara's eyes fell away, stared back at the stallion. She said nothing.

"You're pregnant!" His tone was scathing now. No wonder she'd married so hastily!

Still she remained silent.

Branch took a step nearer and forced her around to meet his eyes. "You are, aren't you?" came his husky voice filled with utter contempt.

"Yes," she whispered.

"Your husband's?" he spat, then thought for a long moment. "Or some other city slicker's in Denver? Whose is it, bitch? Was it a marriage of *convenience?*"

Her head snapped up defiantly. "Let go of me," she hissed.

"*Whose* is it?" He shook her then.

"None of your damn business, Branch!" Lara flew into a tirade, her eyes glistening wetly. "Just leave me alone!

And you can take the stallion with you!" she finished with a cry.

Branch dropped his hands as if stabbed. He whirled away abruptly. "Keep him, slut. Consider him a payment for past favors!"

Her involuntary gasp of shock stabbed Branch with an awful pain. Blindly, he remounted, kicked his horse viciously and galloped away toward Wolf Butte.

He never slowed the horse's pace until he was several miles from Bitter Creek and from Lara, but not an inch removed from the agony that knifed through him.

His mind spun with painful thoughts; he rode his lathered horse like a man lost in a vast empty desert. How could she? And then to come back to Rifle and flaunt her condition in his face! That little bitch! And to top it all off, she was so far gone that a blind man could see. Everyone would guess exactly why she had gotten married so suddenly. Hadn't she a shred of pride?

And then suddenly, like a man swimming up from a suffocating, bottomless quarry who finally sees daylight, Branch sucked in a breath. Yes, he realized abruptly, she was pretty damned far along—several months, longer? Then . . . then she'd been this way all summer . . . all summer. Since . . . June?

Was his thinking straight? How many months was a woman pregnant before she showed?

His heart lurched in his breast. Oh, God! What had he said to her back there? Bitch, slut. What had he accused her of?

He reined his mount around harshly. He had to know. He had to be certain. A man couldn't live without knowing—the torment would kill him.

Dismounting back at Bitter Creek, Branch tossed his reins to Shad. "Where is she?" he demanded harshly.

Shad grinned and nodded his white head toward the house.

Branch never thought to knock. He barged his way into the house rudely. "Lara!" he shouted. "Lara! Where the hell are you?"

No reply. He searched the ground floor. He returned to the foot of the steps. "I'm comin' up, Lara. You can't hide from me forever." He took the steps by twos, opened one bedroom door—Jennifer's—then stood before another.

He tried the handle. Locked.

"Open this goddamned door!" he stormed. No reply. "All right, then." He backed up, put his boot to the wood, and tested it. And then he kicked in the door. The frame around the lock split, cracking loudly, and the door flew open.

Lara lay on her bed, face down, her frame rocking with sobs. Branch went to the bedside, stood over her.

"The child's mine," he stated in a breaking voice. And then: "Well?"

Finally, receiving no reply but more sobs, Branch reached down and gently turned her over. Lara's eyes sought his; her tears rolled hotly across her cheeks wetting her hair.

"Say it, Lara. Tell me, for Christ's sake, tell me!"

"Yes!" Her head rolled to the side, away from him. "I hate you," she whispered through a wavering sob.

"God," he moaned. "Then Parks married you anyway? Did he know?" He raked a heavy hand through his hair. "That you were carrying *my* child? Tell me . . . For God's sake, tell me!"

"There was no *Mr. Parks*," she cried. "It was all a lie! Oh . . . Oh, I hate you so much."

"No more than I hate myself." How could he have been so stupid, so blind? So that was why she'd gone off to Denver City so suddenly—she'd been carrying his child. Oh, Lord, his mind cried, why hadn't she come to him at once? Did she really hate him so much?

For endless moments he merely stood there over Lara's bed, his hands hanging limply at his sides while he watched her. And he had compared this woman to his dead wife. What in hell was the matter with him? His gaze traveled over her frame painfully; his hands balled into fists and he knew a self-loathing greater than physical pain.

And then—perhaps he only wanted to hear the words—Lara whispered, "Hold me. Please, just hold me."

A flood of emotions surging through his chest, Branch eased his weight onto the bed next to Lara, then carefully, almost reverently, pulled her to him. He longed to crush her body to his but took great care not to. He ached to explore the places on her smooth flesh that he still sensed would bring a cry from her lips—but he hoped there would be time for that later. For now, he merely held Lara until her sobs subsided. God, how he had hurt her!

Slowly he propped his weight onto an elbow, then turned her face toward him with a tender hand. His mouth moved down onto hers and tasted the salt of her tears. Carefully he probed her lips open and searched the sweetness of her mouth with his tongue. She sighed, moved her lips against his, and brought a hand to the back of his head.

Branch began to unfasten the tiny buttons of her dressing gown until the front was open. He freed her breasts from the confining nightgown, marveling at their heaviness, swollen from pregnancy. The pink peaks responded to his touch and he kissed each one in turn, drawing their stiffness into his mouth, tasting the glory of her flesh.

His hand moved downward, lingering on the swell of her stomach—the child of his that grew within her womb. He raised her gown then, helping her out of the soft material until her naked body was his to wonder and marvel over: the fullness of her bosom, the slightly rounded belly, the smooth thighs that lay waiting to be parted.

He brought his hand down over the dark mound of her womanhood and explored her with gentle fingers. Lara moved against his hand while his lips sought a pert nipple.

Leaving her for a moment, Branch pulled off his clothes, then rejoined her on the bed. He parted her thighs with his knees and sought the moist entrance. Taking great care not to harm her, he probed her body with his shaft slowly, holding back the urge to fill her with his desire. He moved within her carefully, penetrating her, then withdrawing, then filling her again.

Lara responded to his gentleness with a passion of her own, holding him close to her, murmuring words of love and need until her frame shook beneath his weight and a cry was torn from her lips. Branch held her tightly, felt the sweet throb of her inner flesh, reveled in her until he, too, found release in the softness of her woman's body.

Still locked in embrace, Branch knew a desire for this woman greater than he had ever dreamed possible. Jewel had been a passionate woman, but only at the very beginning and then, if and when he felt a need for her, she had lain beneath him merely performing her duty.

He had stopped seeking her out altogether even before she had taken up with that drifter.

No, he realized now, there was no comparison between the two women—Lara was too much like the land surrounding them: wild, proud, beautiful.

They stayed together in her room, rediscovering the glory of their passion, until dawn broke over the land in a tide of pink-pearl waves. Branch knew he could never have enough of this woman; she had bewitched him thoroughly.

And now she carried his child.

"Lara?" He propped himself up on the bed with her pillow behind his back.

"Ummm . . ." She opened sleepy eyes.

"Marry me. Today."

A heavy silence fell over the room. Branch waited, feeling the dull thud of his heart.

"Can I speak honestly?" whispered Lara, and he felt his heart pound more heavily.

"Go ahead, Lara. I need your honesty."

"I do want to marry you, Branch. Perhaps more than anything else in the world. I only want to be with you, to raise our child together." Then Lara also propped herself up against the brass headboard. "You know, I couldn't even have imagined talking to you like this only a short time ago. I don't know what's changed exactly, but something has, hasn't it?"

She searched his face with wide green eyes. He could have drowned in them. Instead, he answered her, gravely, with the attention her comment deserved. "You've grown up, Lara. You're judging the situation with your own sensibilities instead of your father's. I reckon it's a big step for anyone to take, and one of the hardest. Some people, you know"—he pushed a lock of raven hair behind one of her shell-pink ears—"never can take that step."

"Oh, Branch," she sighed, stroking his arm, feeling the curling blond hairs under her fingers. "Why? Why has this been going on so long? What *was* there between Joe and Frank that started it all? Couldn't they have talked it over?"

"No," he mused, unable to be totally frank, "I guess not. These things happen. Look at Romeo and Juliet." He leaned back against the headboard, smiling. "Their fathers never could get together, could they?"

"No. But that was only a story . . ."

"They say that truth's stranger than fiction sometimes," he mused, leaning forward to brush her shoulder with his lips.

She was quiet for a long time. Then: "Branch?" Her voice was a mere whisper. He could only see her profile, her downcast eyes, the sweet way her black lashes lay on her smooth cheek.

"Yes?" His hand trailed on the covers over her thigh.

"I do want to be with you. I can't imagine anything else. It's just that . . . well, it's always the same story. In my heart I can't imagine you doing anything wrong, especially to me. But then in my mind I can't help but remember all the . . . incidents. The poisoned water holes, the cut fences . . . and our barn, Branch."

"You still think I . . . or my family, let's say . . . had a part in that?"

"I can't think anything else."

"How can I ever hope to make you believe me, Lara?" His hand took her chin, turned her head toward his. "Can't you just trust me? I swear, we *never* did have anything to do with those incidents. Lara, we've had cut fences, stolen cattle before, too. I don't pretend to know who did those things or even why. I just know that you've got it all wrong."

They were both quiet for a long moment. Finally, Lara said, "There's something else, too. Do you remember the day I arrived back in Rifle from St. Louis?"

"How could I forget it, Lara?"

"You were staring at me . . . in the dining room at the Winchester."

He laughed lightly. "I remember. Couldn't keep my eyes off you. Little Lara Clayton, all grown up."

"Why did you stare so?"

"Why do you think?" Again he chuckled.

"Because I saw you in the hall or I thought I saw you . . . in front of that poor man's door, the one who was shot." Her words were met with stony silence. "I also heard part of the argument." She went on hastily now, as if she had to get it all out or she would burst. "I heard the name Taggart."

Branch swung his legs over the side of the bed and reached for his pants. "So all this time you thought I was a murderer, too," he stated flatly.

"No . . . I really didn't know what to think, and it was only after you'd been staring at me in the dining room and then I saw you in your Stetson. It was exactly like the one the man in the hall had been wearing. I was so ready to believe the worst of you then."

He began pulling on his shirt. "And what do you think now?"

"I don't think you're a killer. But there are the other things, too. I just don't know what to think." Lara watched him with wide eyes, fearful.

"As for my killin' the man in that room, that's very simple. Ask your friend Noah. We were just cutting into our sirloins in the dining room when that happened." His voice was tinged with bitterness. "Or don't you like the idea of asking Noah about me? Goddamn it, Lara, I can't spend the rest of my life justifyin' myself to you!"

"I'm sorry," came her voice, small and lost. "It's just that . . ."

"So you're sayin' no to marrying me? Is that it?" His mounting anger played in his voice now. Was there no way to prove his innocence to this girl?

"I didn't say that," came her soft words. "I just would like a little time to think."

He strode to the shattered bedroom door, turned, faced Lara once again. "If there was any way I could prove to you how wrong you are, I would, Lara. But I think you've just got to search your own conscience and decide then. At least give me a fair trial."

"Branch?" Her voice touched him softly. "There's something else. There's something that's still bothering me." She paused, her eyes reached across the room to him. "I'm not sure you want to hear this, but you said you wanted me to be honest . . ."

"Go on."

"It's about that man, Colt Farnsworth. I don't believe your story about him working for the Cattlemen's Association."

Branch's mouth turned down at the corners into a frown. He'd have to tell her the truth now if there were to be trust. "What do you want to know?"

"I saw you in the lobby of the Hotel Glenwood." She hesitated at his sharp, indrawn breath, the curse muttered under his breath. "That was months ago. Then I saw him the morning Brownie threw me at your ranch. What on earth were you doing in the company of a man like that if it wasn't . . . well, if he didn't have something to do with . . . the fire?"

"The fire?" Branch growled harshly, his body tensing. "You think we hired him to set the fire, don't you? Makes perfect sense. Go on—tell me that's what you believe."

"Yes," came her quiet but firm reply.

"Well, you're dead wrong. How many times do I have to say it?" Branch ground out.

"Then prove it to me," she implored, unafraid of his sudden anger.

"All right then." He took a deep breath, tried to control his temper. "I was just as baffled by the fire. Then there was the cut fence I saw that day up on the range. Something about it stuck in my craw. So I did some checking around. Talked to some of the drifters around here, some of the ranch hands too, but everyone knows me, and if they knew anything at all about the accidents at Bitter Creek, they sure weren't talkin' to me." He stopped, reluctant to go on. He hadn't wanted Lara to know. She was too proud to accept what she would call "charity." He looked across the distance separating them; comprehension was playing across her features. "That's right, Lara. I hired Farnsworth to find out what was going on around here."

"You . . . you went behind my back and hired *that* man to . . . to spy on us!" she half-cried.

"Not spy on you, Lara. For Christ's sake, calm down and think! *If* someone was stirrin' up trouble at Bitter Creek, it only made sense to hire an outsider to look into it. Farnsworth is a detective."

"He's an awful man!"

"Maybe. But he knows his business."

"Oh!" she moaned, frustrated. Then she sat silently

glaring at Branch, swallowing the bitter taste of her pride. Finally, still quite angry, she asked, "And did he find out anything, this, this *detective?*"

"No . . . I'm sorry to say he came up empty-handed."

"So you wasted your money. And what did it prove?"

"It proved, Lara," he said roughly, "that the Taggarts had nothing to do with the fire or anything else for that matter."

"How? How do I know that's *really* why you hired him? You lied to me before about him."

"I'm not lying this time, Lara. Sometime you're just goin' to have to trust someone. I hope it's me."

"God, Branch!" she wept abruptly. "I do want to believe you! I really do. Please . . . just let me have a little more time, to think. Please?"

"Take some time if you want," he said honestly. "But don't expect my patience to last forever, Lara. I'm only human and I can only take so much . . ."

Branch had the entire ride home to dwell on the absurdity of the situation. He was frustrated beyond normal limits; anger lay seething under his hard surface.

That girl! He'd put up with a darn sight more foolishness from her than anyone in his life. And still, despite her tantrums, her unjust accusations, her pure stubbornness, still, there was that undefinable something about her that he loved with a passion that shook him.

It amazed him that he was able to be so patient with her, so sure of her eventual capitulation now. After Jewel . . . there had been those years of dark bitterness, distrust of woman, fear of getting involved with one only to repeat the tragedy.

But with Lara he was more sure than ever, now that he'd seen her again, that it would be different—she thrived on the life of the West, disdaining clothes and balls and city life. She loved the land with a strength that matched his own. The fear was gone that she would ever want to leave the rangeland she defended so stubbornly.

A smile twisted his mouth at the thought of her obstinacy. It wasn't easy to love Lara Clayton, he reckoned, but it would be real interesting.

Chapter Seventeen

IT WAS QUITE NIPPY ON THE OCTOBER MORNING LARA BUN-
dled up in her wool cloak and climbed up on the
buckboard with Shad to make the trip into Rifle; Jennifer
and Harriet were arriving home at last. The horses'
breath plumed on the sharp air and the sky was as
brilliant as sapphires. Lara gave an involuntary shiver as
Shad clucked and slapped the reins on the pair's backs.

It would be quite exciting to have company for a
change; admittedly, she'd grown lonely on the ranch all
by herself and was looking foward to seeing her sister and
mother again. It was only for roundup, she knew, but she
desperately needed to talk to somebody about Branch—
and the decision that ached unceasingly in her brain.

He couldn't be put off much longer, she knew. His
visits lately had been necessarily brief because of the
busy season, but she found herself living for those few
stolen moments. It was obvious that she could not bear to

exist without Branch. And yet . . . and yet . . . there *had* to be trust in a marriage. That was vital, basic. Lara was not love blind to the point where all logical considerations were thrown aside—she'd learned to analyze a situation objectively from her father and she'd had plenty of leisure in which to think lately. There had to be trust and there had to be forgiveness.

She needed to talk to Jennifer about it. Jennifer had surprisingly astute judgment about those things. Her sister had seen Branch's love for her before she had and had told her to marry him. Maybe she was right.

The train lumbered into Rifle on schedule, disgorging passengers, loading luggage. Jennifer stepped onto the platform first, dressed in a cunning suit of royal blue with fox fur trim and a matching hat and muff of fur. Harriet followed, looking lovely in a dusty rose dress and matching short cape. Lara felt a bit shabby in her long green cloak, but she'd grown out of the habits of Denver City—rapidly and gladly.

They hugged, asking a dozen questions each, all at once. Then Harriet held Lara at arm's length and looked at her carefully. "Are you well?"

Lara knew exactly what she meant. "Yes, Mama," she replied brightly. "Perfectly well."

The ride out to Bitter Creek was filled with questions, answers, gossip. Jennifer's news came first.

"I'm engaged!" she cried ecstatically, pulling off her glove and flashing a large square-cut diamond set in gold filagree. "Alfie finally asked me. We're to be married in the spring!"

"I'm glad for you, Jenn, really glad. I hope you'll be happy." Lara felt vaguely wistful, wishing she were as exuberantly sure as Jennifer.

"I will be! Oh, we're going to live in a mansion that his

father is giving him and he's going to work in his father's office and someday he'll be president of the company and I'll have lots of parties and lots of children and a coach and four. No! I'll have one of those new horseless carriages and wear a long duster and goggles!"

"He is an excellent match for your sister," said Harriet. "I'm so pleased. Frank would be pleased too, I'm sure." Then Harriet chuckled. "I hope we have a good roundup this year. We're going to need some of the profits to put on Jennifer's wedding properly."

"I think we will. Shad's been getting an idea and says it looks good even with the cut fences and all. And guess what! Branch Taggart caught the Appaloosa and brought him over one day. He's ours now."

"Branch?" asked Jennifer, raising an eyebrow, looking hard at Lara until she felt her cheeks redden.

"Yes, it was neighborly of him," she said firmly.

"Yes, it sure was neighborly," murmured Jennifer, suddenly turning very quiet.

"That nice Mr. Temple sends his regards and asks when you'll be returning from your visit," said Harriet.

"Never, I hope," laughed Lara.

"He was a sweet young man, though," sighed Harriet. "Poor fellow."

"Mama, I think *you* liked him a whole lot better than *I* did," teased Lara.

"Oh, hush now, you silly girl. And how's Noah been? Now there's another nice young man."

"He's fine. He's been very encouraged lately. He's gotten a letter from his fiancée, Katie, and she's considering coming out here. She may already be on her way, for all I know. 'A trial run' Noah called it."

"Are you sad to have to leave Alfie for a few weeks, Jenn?" asked Lara then, turning to her sister.

"Gracious no. You know what they say—'Absence makes the heart grow fonder.' He'll shower me with attention when I get back. A little distance between us won't hurt. But, oh! All that cooking and washing on the roundup will ruin my hands!"

"Now I told you not to fret," said Harriet. "We have cocoa butter and lavender water and cotton gloves for your hands. They'll be fine."

"I guess so. I'd hate to miss the roundup anyway. All those sad old songs around the campfire and camping out and all. If only it doesn't snow," mused Jennifer. "And then there's the Harvest Gala. I wouldn't miss that for the world."

Harriet was patting Lara's hand. "I hope you've been all right by yourself, dear. I worried so about you."

"I've been fine. Very busy. Much happier than in Denver City. *Very* happy, in fact. Shad's kept a close eye on me. He's worse than Daddy would have been."

"You can't stay alone on the ranch all winter, Lara, you know. And now I have to be in Denver, getting ready for the wedding. There's so much to do . . ."

"Mama, don't worry. Something will work out." Her words were supremely confident.

"Lara, what've you got up your sleeve? You sound entirely too self-assured and cheerful at the possibility of coming back to Denver with us. I know you." Harriet cocked her head questioningly.

"Nothing, Mama. Don't fret over me. I'm fine, I'm happy."

After Shad had carried all their bags in to the house and excused himself to the more accustomed surroundings of the barn, the three women sat at the old kitchen table Frank had made and discussed their plans for the roundup over a pot of strong coffee. Harriet checked and rechecked the lists of supplies for the chuck wagon: the pots and pans and basins and water barrels, the bandages and splints, bedrolls, kegs of molasses, beans, coffee, flour, and on and on endlessly. She had done it every year since she could remember. They needed each hand on the roundup and the women freed just that many pairs of men's hands for the roping and branding.

Most cowboys considered the cook second in importance to no one on the roundup. Besides fixing meals and keeping a pot of coffee available at all times, the cook acted as doctor, dentist, banker, and barber, if needed. It had always been Harriet's firm belief that fine food did more to get a good day's work out of a man than harsh words or even money. And Frank had agreed with her.

The roundup was almost a festive occasion. It was a break from routine for the men, a time to show off their real cowboy skills, to share and reminisce and meet old friends from other spreads when they exchanged strays. And Harriet's good cooking was a welcome change from bunkhouse grub.

They set out early the next morning when the frost still lay glittering on the grass, hitching up to the chuck wagon the pair of bays that usually pulled the buckboard. Normally Lara would have ridden out ahead with the men, but it wasn't possible this year because of her condition. So she sat wistfully on the jolting wagon as they followed the cowboys miles out toward the northwest to the base of the high country, where their cattle had strayed to the limits of their fences.

Shad sent one party out into the hills to round up any mavericks that were roaming beyond the fences. These were the near-wild stock, the ones that would rather fight and forage than be cared for by man. Still, they were worth something to gather.

The rest of the men set off to round up the cattle closer in, to drive them into rough corrals, where they stood trembling with fear while they were branded if they had been missed in the spring, and separated into breeding stock, steers ready for market, yearlings to be let loose and fattened another year, or cattle with strange brands who had wandered onto their range.

The day warmed rapidly. The dust billowed and the acrid scorching smell of branded cowhide hung on the air while the three women readied a lunch fit for hungry and thirsty men: smoked ham, beans, biscuits, and always the traditional chipped enamel pot of strong, pitch-black brew.

The women worked hard and willingly, knowing how important their job was, swapping remarks with the hands that stopped by for a cup of coffee. By the time they'd cleaned up after lunch it was time to start supper and the whole routine began all over.

Finally the eastern sky darkened and only in the west did a warm glow remain, silhouetting the humpback hills. The cowboys had each picked a spot for their bedroll and lay dozing in front of the campfire, or smoked a last cigarette, or warmed their hands on a last cup of coffee. The evening grew chill and breathtakingly clear as it does in the autumn. A lone star winked on the western horizon, then two, then a myriad. There was only the sound of the stream they were camped by and the soft lowing of the cattle bunched in the corrals.

Lara sat on her bedroll, wearing a warm jacket over her skirt and blouse, and hugged her knees to her chest. "I always forget how beautiful it is out here. When I'm here I wish I could stay forever, right out under the sky."

"Until it rains or snows," remarked Jennifer drily. "I know what you mean, though. It gets to you."

"Will you miss it when you're married and all?"

"Oh, sometimes maybe, but I'll be too busy, and then I can always come home and visit. It's not so far with the train. Not like it used to be. And then I'll probably miss the city when I'm here. It's kind of nice to have something to miss, though," Jennifer mused. "Then you always have something to look forward to, you know?"

"You girls coming to bed?" called Harriet from the wagon.

"Soon, Mama."

One of the hands had gotten out his guitar and was crooning an old ballad in a husky, surprisingly pleasant voice. Shad joined in. The cowboys knew it did the cattle good to hear the old songs: calmed them, kept them from stampeding or from agitating themselves into losing flesh. The plaintive notes hung together on the air like suspended teardrops, exquisitely sad.

"Jennifer, I have to talk to you about something," began Lara. "I've been waiting and waiting." She was a little nervous about discussing Branch; she hoped her sister wouldn't laugh at her after all the things she'd said about him. Her cheeks felt hot against the crisp night air.

"I had a feeling this might be coming," said Jennifer in a level voice.

"He wants to marry me. We're in love with each other . . ."

"Are you sure?" broke in Jennifer. "You hated him not so long ago, or so you said."

"I'm sure I love him. It's just that, you know, the barn—all those things that have gone on. The feud. Dad must have had a darn good reason for hating the Taggarts so much. I don't want to marry Branch and then . . . find out that all along . . . well, you know what I mean." Her face rose to Jennifer's, the flickering firelight touching it with gold and rose and black velvet shadows. "I want it to be *right*."

Jennifer sat staring into the fire for a long time, it seemed to her sister. Unconsciously, she hitched her heavy shawl up around her shoulders. She spoke, still staring into the flames as if mesmerized. "I have to tell you something, too, especially now. It explains so much." Jennifer's tone was uncharacteristically somber, her straight brows drawn together in a frown. "Daddy *did* have a darn good reason for hating the Taggarts. And I know what it was." She paused, as if gathering her thoughts. "A few days ago in Denver Mama let me borrow her sapphire earrings. It was for an engagement party. Oh—that doesn't matter. Anyway, I went to her room to find them. I couldn't at first. They weren't in her jewelry box." She must have felt Lara's questioning glance. "Now let me go on in my own way. I want you to know how it happened. I started looking in the drawers of her dressing table. That wasn't wrong of me, was it? In one drawer, under her handkerchiefs, I found it. A letter." Jennifer suddenly looked straight at Lara, her face a pale oval in the darkness, her expression oddly pained.

"It was a letter from Joe Taggart sent to Mama only a few weeks ago. I read it. You understand? I couldn't help it. I was curious and I thought it would be something harmless. I wish to God I hadn't." She took a deep breath. "The letter was a love letter. I swear, Lara, there was no mistaking it. It was the way it was written—a blind person could tell. They'd been lovers once."

"Mama and Joe Taggart?" whispered Lara in a shocked voice.

"Once I knew that, everything else was easy to understand, to figure out. The feud."

"I don't believe it. Not Mama." Lara shook her head, felt the sharp, cold air seep through her jacket.

"It's true. Obviously I can't show you the letter. Anyway, that wasn't all. I'll try to remember what the letter said. Something like, 'You should have told me about the child right away. I would have claimed it. I would have done something. Why has it taken all these years for the truth to come out, Harriet?'"

"The *child?*" gasped Lara, stunned. "You mean . . . one of us is . . . is . . . ?" She couldn't finish. Her words hung on the air; a cowboy's lament covered them with sweet notes.

"Yes. One of us is Joe Taggart's child. And Daddy knew. Somehow he knew. Poor Daddy. Poor Mama."

"Which one?" asked Lara suddenly. "Did the letter say which one of us?"

"No. Only what I told you."

"Why didn't Joe do something?" whispered Lara. "What kind of a man is he?"

"He was a married man, remember? His wife died after that. Her name was Tanya. We never knew her."

"I can't believe it. All these years. We never knew." Lara shook her head, disbelieving, trying to wrap her mind around the knowledge, trying to assimilate it. Suddenly her face drained of all color. "Jennifer . . ."

"I know," came her soft reply. "I knew you'd come around to that soon enough."

Unbidden Lara glanced down at the soft swell of her stomach, then at her sister. Her eyes were panic-stricken. "No," she whispered. "It can't be!"

"That Branch is your half-brother? Probably not. You look too much like Daddy. It's much more likely me or Craig. Probably Craig." Jennifer's tone was matter-of-fact.

"But you're not sure." Lara's tone was dripping with disgust, with horror. "It could be any one of us. Remember Mama always told us her parents were dark haired. Remember? It could be me, too. Oh, my God."

"Now calm down. It's not likely you. Branch probably already knows about it anyway."

"I can't marry him then. It's too horrible!" She shuddered, hugged herself with her arms, stared into the fire. "I don't ever want to see him again. If he touched me, I'd die." She began to cry silently, big, glistening tears sliding down her cheeks. "How could this happen?"

"It happens. Look at you. What you've done is not so very different, is it? Don't condemn Mama. It probably happened before she even knew Daddy. It was just her bad luck Joe was married."

"She should have told us," whispered Lara fiercely.

"It's hardly the sort of thing one discusses with one's children. Lara, look at me. It's pretty obvious who's the father of your baby. Mama didn't even bother asking. Don't you think she'd have demanded an answer?"

"Maybe. Maybe not. Maybe she couldn't bear to tell me after it was done—it would have been too horrible. I don't know. I don't know anything anymore. Everything's different. I feel different. I don't even know who I am anymore."

"You're the same as you were. That letter doesn't change you."

"That's where you're wrong, Jenn. It changes everything—absolutely *everything*. I reckon my mind's made up for me now." She gave a short, harsh laugh. "That was easy, wasn't it? And here I'd been wrestling with my difficult decision." Her words were scornful, bitter. "I should have known it was too good to be true."

"I should never have told you," reflected Jennifer softly.

"It's a damn good thing you did!" hissed Lara.

"Marry Branch. Just go ahead and marry him. Try to grab a little happiness for yourself . . . and the baby."

"I couldn't! Just the possibility. It's too horrible." Her voice was broken now, ragged with emotion. For an instant she thought to go to her mother, but she couldn't contemplate asking her. She couldn't even bear to think about it.

Hours later, long after Jennifer had gone to bed in the wagon, Lara's small figure huddled in front of the dying fire, alone under the vast western sky, alone with the thoughts that writhed like venomous serpents in her mind, endlessly circling, endlessly tormenting.

"I love you so much, Branch," she whispered to the dying embers, "but I can't have you." Her tear-stained face turned upward, the moonlight shining bone white on its artful sculpturing. "Oh, God, what am I going to do? What am I going to tell him?" Only the mournful howl of a coyote deigned to answer her.

It turned gray the next day; a dry wind kicked up dust devils across the range and scattered the tumbleweed. It suited Lara's mood exactly. She pulled her hair back roughly and pinned it in an unbecoming bun at the nape of her neck just to keep it out of the way, put on an old gingham skirt, a man's shirt with a heavy gray sweater to keep warm while she worked, and an apron over the whole outfit. She knew she looked drab and bulky but she didn't care. Who was there to see her? The men were too busy to care and so, for that matter, were the women.

It was while Lara was scraping the breakfast dishes, trying to ignore Jennifer's pensive glances, that they heard the pounding of horses' hooves and the bellowing of cattle. Jennifer looked around the corner of the wagon to see who it was.

"Must be a bunch of our strays some other ranch found. Wonder who they are?" mused Jennifer.

"Who is it?" asked Lara, suddenly anxious.

"Can't see. There's too much dust."

Lara bent back over the soapy water and washed dishes furiously. She was panicked. If Branch was bringing back a herd of their strays . . . He knew she was here. She'd told him, hoping she'd be able to see him during the roundup, give him her final answer. Oh, God, she couldn't face him now—not yet, not with her mind so unsettled, so dazed with this new, awful knowledge. She squeezed her eyes shut, leaned over the basin of dishes, and prayed it wasn't Branch with the strays.

But her prayer was denied.

When she looked up he was striding across the ground toward her, tall and lean and utterly self-confident, his white teeth showing in a cocky grin, his blue eyes squinting under the brim of his hat. She noticed, incongruously, that his spurs made precise clinking sounds as he walked and the curling ends of his crisp fair hair rested on the collar of his sheepskin coat.

She stepped back from the dishes, hearing her blood like a hollow drumming of wings in her head. Nervously, her hands rose to smooth her hair back, then she realized how wet and soapy they were and lowered them, twisting them in her apron to dry them. She felt paralyzed as he approached, so happy, so sure of himself . . . and of her. Part of her wanted to run to him, fling herself into his arms, tell him the whole thing, let *him* solve the dilemma —if it had a solution. The other part of her held back, repulsed by the breaking of the oldest taboo of mankind.

Her heart felt like it would tear itself apart. She knew she looked pale and drawn and . . . upset. He would see that something was wrong; she wouldn't even have to tell him.

Jennifer had conveniently disappeared. There was no one but her and Branch, facing each other across a basin of soapy water, across a chasm as immense as despair. Her hands were still hidden in her water-spotted apron. "Hello, Branch." Her voice was calmer than she'd expected.

"Lara. You don't look well." Sudden concern darkened his eyes, brought a frown to his brows. "Are you sick? Maybe you should be home."

"I'm all right. Just tired."

Relief lightened the stern angles of his face. "You better take good care of yourself. Maybe this work's too hard for you . . . now."

She turned on him, suddenly irritated by his useless solicitude. It was all a waste of time now. "Don't be silly. I'm fine."

"Come here, then, girl, and give me a kiss. I missed you."

"Branch."

"No one's around. They were smart enough to ske-daddle when they saw me comin' over here. Good thing, too. It's been too long, Lara." He grinned at her, charming, strong, capable.

She was silent, unable to take her eyes from him, trying to impress his image upon her mind like a photograph, so she could recall it at will.

Then his expression sobered. "You're shivering, Lara. Here, take my coat."

"I'm fine, really," she said, even while she knew her body shook with involuntary tremors.

But he was already taking off his thick sheepskin jacket and draping it over her shoulders. She stood there in his too-big coat, wishing she were somewhere else, anywhere else, afraid to meet his eyes. The wind suddenly pulled a strand of her hair loose, whipping it across her eyes, and she felt his hand brush the dark lock back. To cover her confusion she tried to shrug the coat off her shoulders, but his strong hand stopped her.

"What's wrong?" he asked softly, tilting her chin up. "Come on, tell me."

"I can't marry you, Branch," she blurted out, keeping her eyes averted, glad that the words were said, yet endlessly sorry too.

He was silent a long moment. She knew he was searching her face, but she couldn't bring herself to meet his gaze. Finally, agonizingly, her eyes came up to meet his; she saw a puzzled frown on his face, a trace of anger.

"Why not, Lara?" he asked, keeping his tone level, keeping himself under tight control.

"I just can't. It won't work. I don't feel like discussing it." There was nothing else she could say; her mind whirled in black futility.

"What about our child? You're not bein' fair to him or to me . . . or to yourself." His words washed over her without her really comprehending them. She tried to keep her mind on her main object—to make Branch leave her alone so she could face things and rethink her life. His presence was so distracting, so powerful.

"I'll manage," she murmured.

"Did your mother say something—is that it?" he asked.

"No, no. It's not that. Please Branch, just go. It's over." She looked down at her hands, still clenched in the apron. Would he torment her until she wept and plead-

281

ed? She tried to hold on to her last vestige of control. Let him think her hard and unfeeling—that, at least, gave him a reason to stay away from her.

"You've said that before and I didn't believe it then. I refuse to believe it now. You'll come around," growled Branch.

Her green eyes flew up to meet his. Lord! Did he think she was being coy? He *had* to believe her. "This time I mean it. I can't ever see you again. I don't want to . . ." Her last words were so faint he had to bend close to hear them.

"Lara, you crazy fool." His tone was caressing, gentle. "You have too much pride. It'll be your downfall. Listen to me. We love each other. I want you to be my wife. I'm not doing you a favor. I *want* you and my child. Do you believe me?"

"Yes," she whispered.

"Then why . . . ?"

"I just can't! I can't! Leave me alone! Don't you see?" Her words were choked off by a sob. She spun away from him, her shoulders shaking.

He stood by, helplessly watching her cry. What was wrong? Why had she changed from a sweet, loving woman to this sad child? Had he done something? Was it just . . . being in the family way? He'd heard women sometimes had funny moods when they were expecting. He couldn't bear seeing her suffer so.

"Lara." He put a hand on her arm and slowly pulled her back around toward him. She came, unresisting, like a dead thing. Her head hung and wisps of black hair strayed over the collar of his jacket. He longed to crush her to him, comfort her, but somehow he was hesitant. She seemed so vulnerable now, so fragile. It wasn't fair of him to use his strength and size to elicit a response from her. She had to come to him on her own.

"All right, I'll leave now," he said calmly. "You're upset. You'll feel better soon. Just remember, you're my woman no matter what. Nothing can keep us apart now. Take care of yourself." And he bent to touch her forehead with his lips, a touch as light as an errant breeze.

Then he was striding away, his spurs clinking, and she realized he'd left his coat still draped over her shoulders. She wanted to give it back to him, but she hadn't the strength; she couldn't face him again. She stood watching his horse carry him away from her, the wind molding her skirt to her legs and bringing tears to her eyes. Involuntarily, unknowingly, she was clutching his jacket with white fingers, holding on to it as if it were a life preserver and she were drowning in a high sea.

Jennifer knew she couldn't let things go on this way. She didn't know exactly what had occurred between Branch and Lara, but she assumed the worst from the way Lara moped around, red eyed and miserable. And it was all her fault. She'd been stupid to say anything; now she had to remedy the situation. As much as it would cost her to confess to Harriet the whole sordid mess, she knew she'd have to do just that.

She found the opportunity after lunch, when Lara pleaded exhaustion and disappeared into the chuck wagon to rest.

"Mama," she began, "I have something to confess." Her head hung in embarrassment. This wasn't going to be easy.

"Yes, dear?" Harriet was busy measuring flour for the dinner biscuits.

"I . . . I saw that letter from Joe Taggart in your dressing table. Mama," she confessed quickly, "really I didn't mean to. I wasn't prying. I was looking for those earrings . . ." Jennifer's words crowded together like cattle in the stockyards.

Harriet's hands froze, hung over the batter for an eye blink of time, then she slowly turned to her daughter, tiredly wiping the flour off her hands with her apron.

"So you know . . ." Her green eyes looked defeated. "All those years I tried to keep it from you children. I thought it was better that way . . ."

"Mama, believe me, I don't think any the worse of you. It happened so long ago. You've been a good mother and a good wife to Daddy . . ." She paused.

"And now you wonder if Frank was your real father," broke in Harriet. "I don't blame you. You've every right in the world to wonder."

"It's not me," faltered Jennifer. "It doesn't make a whit of difference to me. It's Lara."

"She knows?"

"Yes, I told her. And I'm sorry now. Oh, God, I wish I'd bit my tongue out before I'd told her! She thinks she's carrying her half-brother's child. You know how Lara is . . ."

Harriet stared off into the distance for a long time. It was obvious now why Lara had been so pale and silent all day. It was Harriet's own fault, too. She'd tormented her husband with her sins and now her precious daughter. "I'm thankful you told me, Jennifer. I'll take care of it."

"Oh, Mama, you're not mad at me? I caused so much trouble . . ."

"No, dear—it was bound to come out eventually. I'm just glad you trust me enough to confide in me. It's all my fault, you know. And only I can undo the harm that's been done."

"Then Lara's not . . . ?" The question hung on the air, unfinished.

"It is not Lara or you who is Joe Taggart's child."

"It's Craig then," breathed Jennifer. "I thought so."

"Yes," whispered Harriet. "My poor son . . ." And then she set her face toward the chuck wagon, determination etched clearly on her features, and prepared herself for one of the hardest chores of a mother's life—admitting a past mistake that had hurt her children. And yet, she knew, by doing so she would be making her daughter's life happy and complete and so it was all worth it.

And she and Joe *would* share something after all—their blood would mingle in a new generation; they would, in a sense, have fulfilled their youthful passion.

Chapter Eighteen

"MRS. TAGGART ... MRS. BRANCH TAGGART ... LARA Taggart," whispered Lara to herself, trying out the strange variety of names on her tongue. A smile uptilted her lips, her eyes glistened with a newfound contentment as she sat at her dresser, braiding her dark hair.

She had made up her mind; she would hold back no longer. Branch deserved that from her. She loved him so much, she'd told herself time and time again, that he could never, never have done those things she'd accused him of. She believed him when he denied having anything to do with burning their barn—she *had* to believe him. When he touched her, when he was close, she had utter faith in him. It was still true that when he was not with her faint, nagging questions surfaced to mar her belief in him. But hard practicality had decided her: she couldn't even stand to contemplate a life empty of him. She'd put aside her reservations—everyone, after all, must have *some* reservations when they married.

And then, too, her marriage to Branch would solve so many other problems: Harriet could live in Denver without a worry in the world because Branch and Lara would manage Bitter Creek. Harriet could come and visit her grandchild whenever she wanted. It would all be perfect now. She had only to tell Branch.

Tonight was the Rifle Harvest Gala—the annual round-up celebration that brought farmers and ranchers together from miles around. Lara was already preparing herself for the gala event; it was a regular Western hoe-down—a rodeo, a square dance in the evening, and mountains of food and drink. It was everyone's favorite day in Rifle, for the harvest was over and roundup was done and it was a time to relax and celebrate. There were no complaints of lost crops or missing cattle, no hard feelings between ranches—only good times. Lara knew it was the perfect evening to tell Branch of her decision. The unspoken rules of the Harvest Gala would forbid him to be too upset with her after their last painful confrontation, and even if he were, Branch would know better than to dwell on it tonight. This was the perfect chance to approach him.

Besides, thought Lara, once he knew the reason for her behavior at roundup, he'd understand. And she'd decided she had to tell him everything so they started out with the truth.

Lara was dressed in a crisp green and white gingham print with a black velvet choker around her neck. She pulled her thick braids up to the top of her head and secured them—Jenn would help her weave in a few autumn flowers just before they arrived at the McDuffy's barn, where the festivity was to be held this year.

She reached for her bottle of French perfume—a gift from Mrs. Bryant to all her students when they left St. Louis—and dabbed just a touch behind each ear and a little on her throat. She felt ridiculously feminine and saucy and thought for a moment to borrow some of Jennifer's rouge—which her sister kept hidden—but then decided that Branch might notice and think her silly or too bold.

"Well, don't you just look beautiful!" said Jennifer, whirling into the room.

"I feel pretty, Jenn. I really do!"

"You're just in love, ninny. It makes everyone feel simply wonderful."

Jennifer wore a lavender cotton dress with a high neckline and also had woven her long honey-blond hair into braids. She looked quite the down-home country girl, that is, except for her large diamond ring, which was in prominent display on her white hand.

"No more low-cut necklines?" observed Lara.

"No, I'm getting married soon, you forget. I don't need them anymore."

They laughed, then heard Harriet's voice from below. "Are you two coming or should I leave without you?"

Shad drove the buckboard, his own horse tied behind it, and kept them amused by saying things like, "Ya-hoo! Watch out for that thar muddy rut over yonder. 'Fore you know it, yer dresses'll be gettin' all splattered up with mud and ya won't be lookin' so darn purdy no more!" Everyone felt lighthearted tonight—they had earned their right to celebrate.

The McDuffys' was two miles east of Rifle, nestled on a gentle bend of the Colorado River; it was a lovely spot graced with tall, willowy cottonwoods. There were several buggies ahead of them on the road and more behind them. The bonfire at the McDuffys' could be seen from a mile away and heartbeats quickened in anticipation. Harriet and the girls had baked six peach pies and carried along a large wooden tub of whipped cream flavored with vanilla and honey to top the pies.

Shad delivered the ladies to the circle near the bonfire, then drove the buckboard back out the narrow drive to find a spot among the many vehicles already parked there.

The women moved through the growing crowd toward the long tables set up outside the barn, where they safely deposited their pies. Lara craned her neck for a sight of Branch but was unable to spot him anywhere. The Taggart ranch was farther out from Rifle; perhaps they weren't here yet. Probably they had ridden in the rodeo and been late returning to Wolf Butte to bathe and change. That must be it. And then she wondered how she would tell him, and where she would tell him. While square dancing perhaps, or over a plate of food? Maybe she should lead him out behind the barn and tell him there? Her stomach fluttered thrillingly at the notion.

She spoke to several acquaintances of the Claytons. No one ventured to ask about her sad marriage to Mr. Parks or mentioned anything about the baby. She was sure at least a few of the women noticed her condition, but most of the crowd didn't since the full skirt she wore hid her shape adequately.

And besides, Lara thought, nothing could dampen her spirits tonight!

She was glancing around for sight of Branch when Noah Ackroyd found her. "Lara? I thought that was you." He strolled up through the throng.

"Oh, hello, Noah," replied Lara, smiling, then noticed that he was not alone.

"Lara Clayton . . . excuse me, that is, Lara Parks." The girl stood next to him now; he took her hand in his. "This is Miss Katie Strafford of New York City." He smiled down at the pretty dark-haired girl. "Katie, this is Lara."

"How do you do?" inquired Katie easily.

For an instant Lara was slightly taken aback. And then she realized—this was the fiancée from New York, the one who had finally decided to come west. She was actually here. "So nice to meet you, Katie," replied Lara warmly. "And how do you like Rifle?"

Katie smiled genuinely. "I *really* do like it here. It's not at all like I imagined. Not one bit."

"You mean painted savages and all that?" asked Lara while returning the girl's smile. And then she wondered if Katie Strafford weren't curious about her. Had Noah ever mentioned Lara, in a letter perhaps, or maybe since Katie's arrival? "How long have you been here in Rifle?" asked Lara.

"A week today. And I should like to say what a wonderful town you have." And then Katie looked up at Noah, who seemed quite at ease with himself. "I must tell you," she said, gazing back at Lara, "that Noah's glowing description of you was an understatement."

Lara felt a flush reach her cheeks. What exactly had Noah said to her? "Thank you," she murmured.

And then Katie giggled. "That was terrible of me! I should tell you, if we're to be friends, that before your sad marriage Noah wrote to me of you and had the audacity to threaten me. He wrote that if I didn't come to Rifle, he was going to pursue Lara Clayton along with all the other available men of Rifle!"

"Oh, Noah!" gasped Lara, utterly mortified. "How could you?"

Finally, he looked a trifle shamefaced. "I do have a way with words, don't I?" he laughed tightly. "It was the only way I could think of to persuade Katie to come."

And Lara understood it all then. Noah had not really told his Katie *everything*—just enough truth to make the girl jealous. Suddenly Lara laughed. She looked again at Katie. "He's quite obviously a cad. If I were you, Katie, I'd make him pay dearly for such a fabrication, for as you can see"—Lara patted her stomach—"I am *hardly* available to steal away your man!"

Caught off guard, Noah coughed. When he found his voice, it emerged softly. "You see, Katie," he began, "Lara was married for a brief while and then . . ."

"That's history," interrupted Lara. "And, if you promise not to say a word to anyone . . . at least not yet . . . I'll let you both in on a secret."

"What is it?" asked Noah curiously. Then: "I promise I won't breathe a word."

"Branch Taggart has asked me to marry him and I'm going to accept tonight!"

Noah was visibly shaken. It was some time before he recovered enough to ask, "Are you *sure?*"

Lara noticed Katie giving Noah a questioning, sidelong glance. He never noticed it, but watched Lara intensely.

"Yes. I've never been more certain of anything in my life."

"Then I'm happy for you. Lara. Really I am. Congratulations."

"Thank you. And the same to you both."

They talked for several more minutes about Noah's and Katie's wedding plans and Lara found herself liking the girl very much; Katie was open with her feelings and genuinely keen to learn all she could about Rifle and the West. She even invited herself out to Bitter Creek, saying,

"Noah tells me what a wonderful ranch you have and I must see it if I may be so presumptuous as to invite myself."

"Of course, you must come," Lara insisted, then took a glass of punch from Noah, who had fetched them the refreshment.

"Where is Branch?" asked Noah as they moved toward the barn where the square dancing had begun.

On tiptoes, Lara glanced around the crowd. "I don't know. It seems as if the whole valley is here. Perhaps I just can't see him."

"He'll be along," said Noah, "Don't worry. He won the cattle roping at the rodeo today. Did you know? And he'll have to accept his prize and all the acclaim." And then he excused himself and led Katie out into the throng of dancers.

It was the largest barn in the valley, lit tonight with kerosene lamps and the glow from the bonfire outside. It was noisy, too, Lara noticed, what with the fiddles and banjos and the caller. Inside the barn smelled of hay and leather and perfumed women, while odors of barbecued ribs, steaming corn on the cob, and freshly baked breads wafted in from outdoors. An occasional "whoop" and "holler" echoed from the brightly dressed dancers as they whirled by, onlookers stomped feet and clapped hands, occasionally calling out encouragement to one of the dancers.

Lara looked on the scene with affection: She had been coming to the annual gala since she was a child. Soon she would have one of her own out there on the floor trying the first steps of dancing with tiny, uncertain feet.

She looked around once more for Branch—why wasn't he here yet? He wouldn't stay away tonight to avoid her after their scene out on the range, would he?

She couldn't wait to tell him that everything was all right now. She moved through the crowd to find her mother or Jennifer, someone with whom she would feel comfortable while waiting for Branch to appear.

Neither Harriet nor Jenn was inside the barn, so Lara walked out into the glowing orange light of the bonfire and began searching for them. She had just spotted her sister, nibbling on a piece of chocolate cake, when abruptly a strong hand touched her arm lightly from behind.

Startled, she whirled to face him.

"I wasn't sure you'd be here." His tone was cool, noncommittal, as if he were protecting himself.

She let out her breath. The flickering light from the fire lit his hair to a golden shade, caught in his eyes and turned them to a deep blue. His face was carefully expressionless.

"You shouldn't scare me that way!" she scolded breathlessly, suddenly at a loss for words.

He was dressed handsomely in a white shirt and a brown leather jacket and smelled faintly of shaving soap—Lara would never have imagined Branch using a scented shaving soap, but she found herself liking it. Perhaps when they were married she would persuade him to take her dining and dancing once in a while.

"And I was beginning to think you wouldn't be here tonight," she replied hesitantly.

For an endless moment they studied each other in silence. Lara wanted desperately to tell him how sorry she was, how upset she had been that last day she'd seen him. Somehow the words wouldn't come. Being here with him, feeling the power of his presence—that was all she wanted. No more harsh words, no more accusing glances, or tormented thoughts.

"I'm sorry . . . about . . ." she began uneasily.

But Branch cut her off. "Don't, Lara," he said tightly, a look of pain touching his eyes for a fleeting moment. "We're here together. That's all that matters now, isn't it?" He smiled suddenly and Lara's heart melted.

"Yes," she whispered with all her being.

He took her hand then and she felt that familiar shock surge through her body. She sensed that there was an unspoken understanding between them; there was no past, only tonight. Branch, she was positive, knew this too.

"I didn't mean to frighten you," he said, "but who were you expecting? Don't tell me," he teased her lightly. "All your men sneak up from behind."

"Oh, Branch. You know better than that. I don't have any other men." And then she realized that he was treating her somehow differently, somehow more intimately that he ever had before. Did he suspect that she had changed her mind?

Robert and Guy came up to them then, interrupting the perfect moment.

"Branch, somebody's gotta go get Dad. He's gonna have a conniption if you don't get back soon," said stolid Robert. Then, tipping his hat; "Evenin', Miss Lara." Then his face turned beet red, his mouth opened, nothing came out. "I mean, Mrs. . . . Parks."

"Oh, Robert, don't be upset. Just call me Lara." Then she glanced questioningly at Branch.

"Our wheel broke just a mile or so back. Dad refused to leave it, so I promised I'd go back and get him. He's probably rooting around in the mud himself trying to fix it. To tell you the truth, I think it needs the blacksmith, but you know old Dad—stubborn to a fault."

"Oh, but I wanted to talk to you . . ." Her disappointment was only too obvious in the tone of her voice.

Branch gave her a keen glance; the deep lines that ran from his nose to the corners of his mouth seemed to become less evident, and his expression became youthful. He smiled at her. How could she ever have thought his mouth was cruel-looking?

"Send Robert or Guy," she said then, unashamed at revealing how much she wanted him.

He grinned ruefully at her. "Too late. They're gone. I always have to do everything and they know it."

Sure enough, they had slipped into the crowd somewhere, impossible to find in the noisy crush.

"It'd take longer to find them and convince them to go than it would to go myself. I'll try my best to get right back," he said gently. "Will you wait?"

"Well, Mother and Jenn may not want to stay too long. You know how things get here later . . . the drinking and all . . ."

"I know." He thought for a minute. "I'll tell you what. If it takes me too long, let them go on home. I'll see you back safely one way or another. You can wait inside the McDuffys' house for me. No one will bother you there."

He stopped again before leading her to Jennifer and took Lara's small hands into his. "Please, Lara, wait for me."

His touch, as always, sent a shiver racing up her limbs. "Yes, I'll be here."

And then, right in front of everyone, he leaned down and kissed her full on the lips. When he moved his head away, Lara was breathless. "I'm going to do that every time I catch you in public," he laughed, "and pretty soon you'll be such a scandal, you'll have to marry me."

"Branch?" said Lara with downcast eyes. She was afraid she'd never get the chance to talk to him. The evening wasn't going at all the way she planned.

"Yes?"

"Oh, never mind. We'll talk about it when you get back." She smiled then, wishing he didn't have to go but telling herself that they would have all the time in the world together after tonight. It was just that she was getting so impatient to tell him just how she loved him, how happy she was . . .

Branch deposited her safely in Jennifer's company, spoke to Harriet briefly, then disappeared down the drive. When he was gone from her sight, she experienced an odd sort of loss, odd but not unpleasant. It was a nice warm feeling to want someone, to want to be with them every minute, day and night. Still, Lara wished he was here to claim her for a dance—she might not be the best partner on the elegant ballroom floors of St. Louis or Denver City but here, whirling to a foot-stomping square dance, she could hold her own with anyone!

It was Jennifer, as it turned out, who nearly shoved a dance partner into Lara's arms. She had just finished dinner when Jennifer appeared, tugging Walter Krepps behind her.

"Lara!" called Jennifer. "Remember Walter? Sure you do. His father runs the barber shop on Main Street."

"Oh, yes, Walter. Hello." Lara took his warm hand in hers. He seemed so terribly young and yet Lara knew he must be at least twenty-one, maybe older. He was quite tall with dark, straight hair, a thin face with huge, brown puppy-dog eyes, and he was, she recalled, extremely shy. Jennifer shouldn't be so cruel, thought Lara.

"Walter is just *dying* to dance," said Jennifer. "Aren't you? And I'm much too tired."

Lara felt sorry for the young man but was left with no choice whatsoever when he stammered out an invitation to join him in a Virginia reel.

He took her hand, smiled boyishly, then walked her onto the dance floor. Walter turned out to be far less shy on the floor and quite at home with the steps. Lara, too, felt at ease and was soon moving to the snappy music while trying to remember her condition. Dancing this way really must be overstepping proprieties—she'd be the source of gossip for many days to come. Still, as the circle of dancers moved in and out in unison, Lara saw Mrs. Littleton across from her, at least seven months along, swinging her hefty frame quite easily. Lara supposed that in Denver City pregnant women behaved with far more reserve and added another item to the list of things she disliked about city life.

The music changed and Walter placed a hand around Lara's waist, then twirled her across the floor. His straight hair fell into his eyes and sweat popped out on his brow. Lara, too, felt the heat in the barn, but was having so much fun that she didn't care.

At one point she caught her mother's eye and Harriet smiled—so dancing couldn't be all that disreputable or Harriet would have been scowling.

Walter leaned down close to her ear. "You look real pretty tonight, Miss Lara," he muttered, then daringly gave her waist a small squeeze.

Can't he tell? she wondered. Her condition was obvious enough by now. Or maybe he just thought she was rather more substantially built than she really was. She returned his smile. The music stopped and Walter went to get them both a punch. Lara noticed that his cup came from a different punch bowl. So that was where his nerve was coming from—whiskey-laced punch! He wanted to dance again but Lara declined, confessing that the heat was finally getting to her.

"Thank you, Walter," she breathed while fanning her face with a hand, "but I really can't. Why don't you find another partner?" Lara nodded toward the far wall, where several young ladies watched the dancers with wistful eyes.

"I'll do that, Miss Lara," said Walter. "And I want to thank you for a mighty fine dance. I never thought I'd be so lucky!" His cheeks were flushed red and his eyes glowed from drink. "And I'm awful sorry about Mr. Parks, Miss Lara, I mean, Mrs. Parks."

"Yes." She lowered her eyes. "It was terrible." Lord how she hated that lie! But it would be over soon. She'd be Lara Taggart and there would be no more deception.

Jennifer was nowhere in sight and Harriet was deeply engrossed in conversation with her friends. Lara glanced around the barn—she wished Branch would return. She was bursting with things to say to him.

Feeling the heat more than she realized, she walked to a far corner of the barn and leaned against the wall for support. Perhaps the dancing was a mistake after all! She felt her brow with a hand; she was perspiring, damp tendrils of hair escaped from her braids and stuck wetly to her neck. She was beginning to feel dizzy, too.

While she leaned against the wall, thinking she had to collect herself and get out into the fresh air, she wasn't aware that her eyes were fixed blankly, unseeing, on a group of cowboys standing across from her against the far wall. The ranch hands, she registered, unconsciously, were drinking heavily, passing a whiskey bottle between them. Lara found herself growing faintly interested, her mind registering that most of the women here would probably have a fit if they knew that these men had brought their own liquor. Then it occurred to her that the group looked like a painting she'd seen in a book at Mrs. Bryant's—by a painter named Hieronymous Bosch—of a dark, seething, diabolical scene filled with misshapen and grotesque people against a smoky, dim background. What an odd notion! she thought, wondering what hidden corner of her mind it had come out of. It must be the heat and her dizziness.

Slowly she began to feel a little better, less lightheaded, while her eyes still fixed on the group of drunk men. Thoughts of Branch began to crowd in on her in spite of herself, thoughts of his touch, his charm. If only he would return so she could tell him.

One of the cowboys was growing drunker than the others and Lara watched him through the murky light as he flung his arms, apparently relating a story to his comrades. There was something familiar about him; she couldn't actually see his face because he was turned away from her. He staggered then a little and she was afforded a glimpse of his profile.

Why, she realized, it looked like the Taggart foreman, Sam Fuller. Probably she hadn't recognized him at first because he was quite duded up for the occasion. Why, the silver and turquoise jewelry he wore must have cost him a year's wages, she thought fleetingly.

Silver and turquoise jewelry.

Her back stiffened. Goose bumps pricked her flesh coldly.

Carefully, Lara tried to focus her eyes through the obscurity, taking in Sam's hatband—small turquoise stones laid in a silver band. And then her eyes traveled downward.

She wasn't actually sure when she realized Sam had turned toward her and had seen her staring so openly at him. But it didn't matter either, for her whole being was consumed with what she saw. She blinked several times. Automatically, she took a few hesitant steps toward him until she could be certain she saw him clearly, in stark detail.

Suddenly her breath snatched in her throat. Surely, she thought wildly, she was imagining the whole thing!

She took another step forward, mindless of the fact that Sam was frozen in his stance, weaving a little, watching her every move.

"Yes," she whispered, "yes." There *was* a large stone missing from his elaborate, turquoise-studded belt buckle. There was!

She drew in a deep, quavering breath.

If Lara had been more conscious of her obvious behavior, she would have turned and run away into the milling crowd.

But she didn't. Instead, she moved slowly toward him as if in a mindless trance.

And then Sam, too, moved slowly in her direction. It was as if the two of them were frozen in a void of their own, performing some sort of a weird dance. The noise, the flickering lights, even the heat seemed to dissipate, and they faced each other in a tunnel of endless time.

Then Sam stood before her, so close she could see the weathered lines in his brown, tough skin and the broken veins in his cheeks.

"I thought about not wearing it," he said, slurring the words. "Guess I should have given it more thought, right, miss? I *knew* I lost that damn stone at your place."

"It was *you*," she whispered. "All along I thought it was the Taggarts. They paid *you* to do it, didn't they?"

"Guess it don't matter now," he said, the revolting odor of his liquor-laden breath assailing her. "But you're

300

all wrong about one thing, little Miss Clayton. Nobody *paid* me to do it. I did it on my own—all on my own."

His words flew at her like stones, hitting her one by one in the face. "You . . . alone?" she half cried. "It wasn't Branch! Oh, thank God, it wasn't Branch!" She was sobbing with relief. "I should have known. You gave me Brownie to ride. It was you, wasn't it?"

And the years of bitterness drifted away like so many autumn leaves falling to the earth until the truth was laid at her feet—it had been Sam Fuller all along! Then, through the haze, she realized another terrible thing he must have done. "It was you in the hall wearing that Stetson . . . you killed that poor man at the Winchester Hotel, didn't you? But why?"

"He was a no-good drifter," slurred Sam. "Saw me cut a fence one day . . . tried to blackmail me."

"Oh, God," moaned Lara, "and all this time I thought it was Branch . . . all this time."

Sam kept talking in a low, groggy voice—to an onlooker nothing would have appeared abnormal. "Think you're pretty damn smart, don't you, findin' that stone? Where is it? Did y' tell the sheriff, Miss Smarty Pants?" He went on speaking and Lara became aware of his hand on her arm, leading her toward a door at the back of the barn.

She froze. "No," she whispered. But it was too late. Sam already had the door open and was pulling her out into the cool night.

"Come on," he said, "don't make a fuss . . . No one can hear you back here anyhow."

Lara opened her mouth to scream but the door grated shut behind her and he was half dragging her across the open field toward the isolated drive and the empty wagons.

"Let me go!" she cried fiercely, feeling his large knuckled hand bite into the flesh of her upper arm. "You'll never get away with this!"

Suddenly he stopped and gripped her shoulders, causing fierce pain to shoot through her. "You know why I did it?" his voice thundered at her.

Lara mutely shook her head, cowed by his fury.

"I made you pay 'cause that filthy brother of yours killed my little girl!"

"No!" Lara wept. "You're wrong. Craig loved her so much!"

Sam shook her roughly then. "You're lying. He left her all alone to take care of those damn cattle of his. If he'd been home, she'd never got sick! She'd a never died alone like that!"

"It wasn't his fault. The doctor couldn't even do anything! Oh, surely you see that!" Hot tears streamed down Lara's cheeks while the cold air slashed at her skirt, whipping it around her thighs in the night air and causing her to tremble even more fiercely.

"He's the one who deserved to die!" hollered Sam. And then his grip loosened slightly. "He deserved to die," he muttered in a hushed, terrible voice. "Not my little girl, not her."

"Please," Lara wept, "please let me go. Everyone will know. People saw you take me out here!"

But Sam seemed not to hear. He began leading her again and Lara started to struggle in earnest. It was no use. In spite of his drunkenness, he was far stronger than she, and soon he had her shoved up against the cold side of a buggy.

With great effort, she forced herself to think more rationally. It was simple; she'd humor him. That's what she had to do—keep him talking. The man was obviously out of his mind. If he didn't feel threatened by her, if he felt she understood, sympathized, then maybe she could talk him out of it, or at least put off whatever he was planning to do until she could escape or someone came after her. Surely someone would begin to worry soon— someone would come looking for her! If she remained calm, in control—if she didn't panic—she'd be able to talk to Sam. She fought down the terror that threatened to overwhelm her. Oh, if only Branch had stayed with her!

"Sam," she said as softly, reasonably as she could. "I know how you feel, really I do, I understand, but this won't help matters any. Listen to me, Sam."

She must have gotten to him momentarily because he loosened his hold for a split second. It was enough time for her to kick at his shins, and then amazingly she felt herself freed. In sudden new panic she scurried away from him, her heels catching on the loose ground. If only she hadn't worn high-heeled slippers!

She felt herself stumbling, falling. She fought desperately for balance, but it was no use. She hit the ground hard, pain shooting into her knee. Her hands, too, were skinned, but she barely noticed them as she tried frantically to scramble up.

And then his hands were on her again, dragging her to her feet. Terror ripped through her and she couldn't even find her breath to scream again.

He was shoving her against the side of a buggy. Panic and fear were swallowing her, when Lara thought—or did she dream it?—that a voice was shouting something from a great distance. Perhaps it was Sam, or her own voice. She didn't know.

Then, while Sam's hands were still on her, she felt him being pulled away, dragging her with him. Suddenly she felt herself free and she was falling again, up against the front wheel, where she landed, sprawled, her body limp and painful.

Through blurred vision she saw two men struggling; their feet were very near, shuffling up against her legs once. She cowered back against the hard-rimmed wheel.

Then one of them—Sam, she saw—fell, knocked to the ground only inches from her feet. Her eyes flew upward into the darkness and she thought, Yes, it had to be Branch—there was no mistaking his tall, broad-shouldered form even in the dimness.

"Lara . . ." He reached down for her and automatically she placed her own trembling hands into his strong, warm ones.

Breathless, still unable to stem the flow of her tears, she let him help her to her feet then drape his leather jacket around her shoulders. She felt nauseated from the ordeal and she was shaking so badly she felt herself sag weakly up against him.

"It's all right. It's over," he whispered, drawing her tightly up against him, sharing his warmth and strength with her.

"Do you feel all right, Lara? I mean . . ."

"Yes," she managed to reply. "I bruised my leg, that's all. The baby feels fine."

He let his breath out in a low whistle. Lara moved closer to his warmth, brushed against his hand. Branch groaned.

Quickly she looked down at his arm hanging limply at his side. His hand was bleeding. "You're hurt!" she gasped, forgetting abruptly her own fright.

"It's nothing."

"But . . ."

Branch smiled, then tilted her face up to his with his

good hand and gently wiped at her tears. "I reckon," he said quietly, "you better tell me what this is all about. After all," he laughed tightly, "I think I just broke my foreman's jaw, not to mention my hand."

"Oh, Branch," she sighed, "it was Sam who set the fire. I recognized his belt . . . the missing stone . . ."

"Hold it there . . . back up a little. You've lost me." He stroked her hair tenderly, trying to calm her.

She took a deep breath and began again. "A while back I found a turquoise stone," she said, "at the burned barn. I guessed it belonged to the arsonist. Oh, Branch, I thought it might even be yours." She cast her green eyes down, away from his suddenly taut face. "Sam admitted everything to me. He even said he did it on his own. He bragged about it!"

"I'm so sorry, Lara."

"It wasn't your fault! Oh, Branch, don't you see? It was worth it just for me to find out . . . to *know.*"

His hand turned her face up to his again. "How did you know it was Sam? What happened in there tonight?"

"It was after I danced . . . I was a little dizzy . . ." She could barely stand to meet his pensive gaze but forced herself to. "Then I guess I was just staring into nowhere when I noticed his belt buckle and the missing stone. I could hardly believe my eyes."

"Sam must have been a fool to wear it. You know, *I've* even noticed that he's been turnin' into a crazy old coot lately." Branch began to lead her away from the buggy, his arm still around her shoulders. "We've gotta get Ned Lawson out here." He looked back over his shoulder. "But I guess there's no big rush." Branch laughed tightly. "Looks like old Sam is passed out cold."

"How did you know I was out here?" asked Lara, still letting herself press closely against him for warmth.

"Very simple," he replied. "I saw you go out the back door. I'd just walked in, lookin' for you. I thought I saw you talkin' to Sam. Knowing the Claytons aren't his favorite people, I got sort of concerned when I saw you leave with him. After all"—Branch grinned—"he's not really your type."

"Branch Taggart"—she giggled in spite of herself—"that's not funny."

She glanced up and saw the rear door of the barn; somehow she didn't want to go in yet, but they had to find Ned Lawson and tell him before Sam woke up and got away. She snuggled closer to Branch's side. "Can you ever forgive me?"

"I guess so, but you'll have to try real hard," he laughed, then bent his head and kissed her cheek tenderly.

They found Ned Lawson and drew him aside; there was no point in upsetting everyone there. Lara told the deputy everything that had transpired that night and the things to which Sam had confessed. "He did it all because of Craig," she finished, tears glistening once again in her eyes. "He blamed my brother for his daughter's death. All these years it was Sam's hatred."

Ned Lawson left the barn then, promising to get in touch with Branch the following day.

"What's going to happen to Sam?" asked Lara.

Branch's brows drew together in thought. "He'll have to stand trial."

"But what will they do to him?" she implored. "He's not sane."

"If that's the case, Lara, they'll put him where he belongs, where he can't hurt anyone again." He tipped her chin up. "Don't forget that he was about to harm you. Don't waste your tears on him."

Lara nodded weakly, then abruptly remembered. "Your hand! Is it really broken?"

"It's nothing. Let me worry about that later."

Drying her tears with a fist, Lara said, "Oh, no you don't! Doc Tichenor is here and I'm going to find him." And with that determined speech Lara moved back into the crowd, glancing over her shoulder with a reassuring smile to where Branch stood helplessly waiting.

By the time Branch's hand was set and bandaged, half the town knew what had taken place and was busy telling the other half that didn't know yet. Harriet and Jennifer waited with Branch inside the McDuffys' house while Noah fetched the buckboard and told the rest of the Taggart men to go on home without Branch.

Amidst much ado and many explanations, and much to Branch's mortification, Lara drove the buckboard away from the McDuffys' toward Bitter Creek.

"Will you let me drive now, Lara?" growled Branch. "My hand's fine."

"No. You sit still. You heard the doctor."

"Well, I'll be damned if I'm goin' to let a woman drive . . ."

"Hush up, Branch," came Harriet's firm voice from the rear seat. "Lara is a capable driver."

"Dear Lord! Is this what I have to look forward to?" He sank back against the leather, pulled his Stetson down over his eyes with his good hand, and groaned. "I'm already henpecked!"

By the time they reached Bitter Creek it was well after two in the morning. It had been decided to put Branch up for the night in Lara's room while Lara would bunk in with Jennifer. Branch had eyed Lara irritably, then glanced at Harriet and subsided. "That's fine," he agreed hastily.

Harriet and Jennifer retired, exhausted, while Lara fussed around her room, helping Branch out of his boots and clucking over him like a mother hen.

"You're not going to sleep with Jennifer," he remarked offhandedly.

"I most certainly am." She fluffed the pillows behind his head, then pressed him down onto the mattress.

"My God, Lara," he muttered.

She walked to the dresser, ignoring his temper. She drew the hairpins from her braids, dropping them with deliberate pings onto the glass top. "There's something I have to tell you, Branch."

"What," he growled.

"I don't think the wedding should be too large." She flattened her dress against the swell of her stomach, then caught his eyes in the mirror. A slow smile gathered at the corners of her mouth.

"You mean . . . ?"

"I waited all night to tell you."

"All night? Even before Sam?" He watched her in the mirror warily.

"Yes, Branch." Lara turned around to face his squarely. "You see, I decided that no matter what you or your family may have done, it didn't matter. I love you." And then she decided to make a clean sweep of everything right then—sweep under the carpet all the ghosts that had stood between them. "There's something you probably already know, Branch," she began. "It's about Craig." She waited, studying his face—yes, he knew.

"Go on, Lara. It's all right." His blue eyes held hers steadily, unflinchingly.

"I only found out recently about Mama and . . . and Joe. It was awful, Branch." She remembered the pain in her heart, the horrible fear that it *could* have been her.

"For a time, until I talked to my mother, I thought it might be me . . ."

"During roundup," he stated flatly.

"Yes." Lara tried to smile. "Can you understand how I felt . . . thinking that . . ."

"It's over. You know the truth. I only wish you'd confided in me, Lara. I've known about it for a long time now." His blue eyes swept her frame. "Come here."

Slowly, loving him more than she dreamed possible, Lara walked to the bedside.

With great care Branch took her hand and pulled her down onto the bed until she was sitting next to him. "Do you know when I first started loving you?" he asked thoughtfully.

"No." She felt her heart throb wildly.

"It was years ago. You were still a scrawny kid and I used to see you at the dry goods store with your father. You were so serious, so determined to be like a son to him."

"Yes . . . I suppose I was," she whispered in reflection.

"And then when I saw you that night at the Winchester Hotel and you'd blossomed into the most beautiful woman I thought I'd ever seen—I knew then I was going to have you."

"And I was so mad I could have slapped your face," Lara laughed mildly.

"I know. And then, upstairs in the hotel hallway, I was about to kiss you. It was crazy. I'd never even thought about doing something like that before. You'd already bewitched me." Branch laughed. "You know, this is a devil of a way to join our two ranches." And then he placed his good hand behind her head and drew her down to meet his lips. Lara met his passion with one as deep as his.

309

Finally, breathlessly, she pulled away. "I keep the fences on Bitter Creek range, Branch."

"You have the next fifty years to convince me of the merits of fenced-in ranching," he chuckled. "This valley is big enough for the both of us. It'll support us and all our children and grandchildren for a hundred years, Lara. There'll always be riches here for us Taggarts. Now come here. Enough talkin'."

"But my mother . . ."

"Guess she'll just have to get used to nighttime disturbances."

"Branch!"

"Come here, you black-haired witch. I want to show you how much I love you."

"Oh, Branch." But this time the tone of her voice was quite different.

POCKET BOOKS PROUDLY INTRODUCES TAPESTRY ROMANCES

Breathtaking new tales of love and adventure set against history's most exciting times and places. Featuring two novels by the finest authors in the field of romantic fiction — <u>every month</u>.

TAPESTRY ROMANCES

pledges itself to the highest standards of quality while bringing the reader never-before-published novels of rich imagination and storytelling power.

ON SALE NOW

MARIELLE
by Ena Halliday

DEFIANT LOVE
by Maura Seger

THE BLACK EARL
by Sharon Stephens

FLAMES OF PASSION
by Sheryl Flournoy

442

Enjoy your own special time with Silhouette Romances

Take 4 books FREE!

Silhouette Romances take you into a special world of thrilling drama, tender passion, and romantic love. These are enthralling stories from your favorite romance authors—tales of fascinating men and women, set in exotic locations.

We think you'll want to receive Silhouette Romances regularly. We'll send you six new romances every month to look over for 15 days. If not delighted, return only five and owe nothing. **One book is always yours free.** There's never a charge for postage or handling, and no obligation to buy anything at any time. **Start with your free books.** Mail the coupon today.

Silhouette Romances